PRAISE FOR
RON FAUST

"Faust is one of our heavyweights. You can't read a book by Ron Faust without the phrase 'Major Motion Picture' coming to mind."

—Dean Ing

"Faust has it all: lyrical prose, complex characters, and provocative plots . . . a superb read."

—*Kirkus Reviews* (starred review)

"Confirming Faust as a novelist to be reckoned with, this intricate omnium-gatherum, told in chiseled prose, seduces the reader with both wit and passion."

—*Publishers Weekly*

"Wonderfully evocative of time and place."

—*Buffalo News*

"Faust is a Homeric storyteller with an eye for the odd character and a fine gift for Spartan dialogue."

—*Library Journal*

"Faust is a real talent with great storytelling ability and characters both real and strong."

—*Affaire de Coeur*

LORD OF THE

DARK LAKE

RON FAUST

TURNER

Turner Publishing Company
424 Church Street • Suite 2240 • Nashville, Tennessee 37219
445 Park Avenue • 9th Floor • New York, New York 10022

www.turnerpublishing.com

LORD OF THE DARK LAKE

Cover design: Glen Edelstein
Book design: Glen Edelstein

Library of Congress Catalog-in-Publishing Data

Faust, Ron.
  Lord of the dark lake / Ron Faust.
    pages cm
  ISBN 978-1-62045-442-8 (pbk.)
  I. Title.
  PS3556.A98L67 2014
  813'.54--dc23
                                            2013025162

Printed in the United States of America
14 15 16 17 18 19 0 9 8 7 6 5 4 3 2 1

To Grace Ladd,
and the memory of John W. Ladd

LORD OF THE DARK LAKE

PART ONE

The Family

1

Now it seemed that a kind of psychic force field remained near the lip of the precipice where Stavros had vanished. It attracted and it repelled. Those few yards dominated us. Stavros's absence exerted far more power than his presence ever had. He had grown in death. Death had conferred on Stavros Kamis a stature that nature had denied him. What impressed us most, what awed us, was that he had not cried out; he had fallen the ninety feet to the rocks below without uttering a sound. Those few seconds of silence had ennobled him in our minds.

On weekends I worked alone at the little temple. Saturday I unearthed a battered bronze incense burner that after more than two thousand years still held a solidified residue of olive oil in the cup. Its flame had burned in honor of the god Poseidon. Gods die, and usually their temples are—like this one—vandalized by partisans of a rival god.

I stopped working at seven o'clock and went into the cabin tent and stripped off my soiled khaki shorts and T-shirt, underwear, sandals. The sweat-stained Stetson was sailed onto a cot. My face and neck were hot and taut from sunburn. There were gritty salt crystals on my cheeks. I filled a bucket from the last jerrican of water and washed as well as I could. Every evening for weeks I had picked my way down the steep zigzag cliff path to bathe in the cool sea, but not lately, not since the accident. Now I resolved to descend for a swim tomorrow morning. The path was dangerous, but so was unmastered fear.

I pulled on Levi's, an old polo shirt, and sneakers, poured two ounces of whiskey into a tin cup, and went outside to sit in one of the canvas deck chairs.

The light had changed during the time I'd been inside the tent. Now the sea was a darker blue, cobalt, with a violet sheen in the shallows, and the surf crashing over the reef was tinted pink by the setting sun. Far off other shadowy islands rose steeply out of the sea, the larger ones ringed by surf and crowned by spiraling vapor.

I sipped my whiskey and tried to imagine this evening, this view, two and a half thousand years ago. No doubt the air was clearer then. And surely the sea was cleaner, pure and rich with life. But the sea and sky and the rocky islands had not changed so much that I could not visualize a pair of triremes half a mile offshore. The wind was blowing hard, but the sailors were coming into harbor now, and so they had lowered their sails and were rowing the boats. I could picture the rhythmic flutter of the oars and hear the work chant of the sailors. The vessels skimmed over the big swells, escorted by gulls and porpoises, protected by Poseidon. The men were traders, warriors, pirates.

Twenty-five hundred years ago the little temple would have been intact. Now it lay in ruins less than ten feet from the edge of the cliff, a scatter of half-buried rubble, marble columnar drums, slabs of fascia and frieze, floor and altar, marble chips that would have to be fitted together like a jigsaw puzzle. But I could visualize it as it was then and how it would look when completely restored. Small and white and graceful. Poised on the rim of sea and sky. Open to the fresh winds and the limitless blue. Those old Greeks did not confine their gods. They provided a site of beauty, a patch of cool shade, and offerings of food and wine.

When I got up for another drink I saw a dust cloud moving down from the high end of Krisos. The island was a little more than seven miles long, and the cloud was already more than halfway to my camp. Alexander on his motorcycle, driving too fast down the rutted dirt road. The plateau was desertic and could barely support the small herds of goats, but even at this distance I could see the green smear—the oasis—that surrounded his villa at the summit. The rest of us rationed water; Alexander Krisos squandered it on orange and lemon and apricot trees, palms and figs and dates, flower gardens, pools, and fountains. But it was his water; his island.

I went into the tent, poured two ounces of whiskey in my cup and twice as much into another.

One hundred yards away the motorcycle emerged out of its dust cloud. Krisos coasted in and stopped next to the Land Rover. He was powdered with the chalky dust and grinning; his grin looked like an ordinary man's furious grimace.

He dismounted the motorcycle and stalked toward me as if advancing into combat. He wore baggy shorts and sandals. Alexander was an ugly man, face and body, with short, bowed legs, short, thick arms, a great barrel chest, and a disproportionately large head. Whorls of black hair grew on his shoulders and back as well as his chest. He was often compared to powerful animals, described as "bearlike" or "bullish" or "apelike." People were deferential to his wealth while scornful of his person. They could not believe that this ugly, frequently coarse peasant, this "ape," was acutely sensitive and highly intelligent.

He accepted the cup of whiskey. His eyes were dark, nearly black, and the pupils made minute adjustments to the light (or maybe his thoughts), expanding slightly and then dilating.

"I heard," he said. "Stavros, eh? The fool." His voice, a rich tenor, always surprised; one expected a hoarse growl, a rasp.

"Over there," I said. "He backed up half a step too many."

"Son of a bitch," Krisos said. "Well, let's drink to the fool."

We drank. Krisos's eyes studied me over his cup's rim. He lowered the cup and ran the fingers of his free hand through his stiff, wild hair. His body hair was still black, but the hair of his beard and scalp had during the past year become threaded with white.

"I just got back a few hours ago," he said.

"I heard the helicopter."

"I was in West Africa. Do you know what it's like for a poor Greek in Africa?"

"But you aren't a poor Greek."

"I was for five weeks."

"Why do you do those things, Alexander? There's no need."

"I don't want to forget. I don't want to get soft, ever. Every time I feel that I'm forgetting, I go away."

Great sums of money, he'd once told me, made men soft. Softness is the natural consequence of wealth. Softness and a weakness of the will and an intellectual impotence. "I am still the hungry goatherd," he would say. "I am still the poor fisherman. Kill me when I begin acting like a rich man." But he acted like a rich man nearly all the time. He went off on his adventures a rich man and returned a rich man.

His cup was empty. I went into the tent for the bottle, and when I returned he was standing on the lip of the precipice. I circled the temple ruins and joined him there. The cliff face was not quite vertical; it slanted very steeply down to the rock-strewn sea. There were ledges and fractured slabs and dark cave mouths between here and the rocks. We looked down as the surf periodically buried the jagged rocks and then, family withdrawing, exposed them again. The sounds lofted up were like slow breathing, sibilant inhalations and exhalations. The sea and sky were darker now, and I could see pinpoint lights glowing against the shadowy form of the nearest island.

"This is where he went over?"

"Yes."

"What happened?"

"He was careless. We all became accustomed to working close to the edge. We stopped being fully aware of the danger. Stavros just made a mistake."

"Like that."

"We saw him. He made a sound. He was trying to

regain his balance. He nearly succeeded. He was in a sort of squat at the edge, his arms stretched out toward us. You could see that he was trying to shift his center of gravity forward. None of us said anything. We could do nothing but watch. When he knew he was going to fall he looked at us. I won't forget his eyes. He looked directly at me. That's what I thought, anyway, but there were five of us and we all thought the same thing, that Stavros was appealing to each of us with his eyes."

"Spyro said that he fell silently."

"Without a murmur. When he saw that he was going to fall, that he couldn't avert it, he kicked out hard, pushed off backward. I suppose he thought he might clear the cliff face and the rocks."

"Yes."

"He was buried Friday."

"Yes. Well, I shall settle a pension on his family. The widow and the four children. Dim-witted children, like their dim-witted father. Stavros was stupid, demented, but you know, Chandler, I liked him. He was a fool, but sometimes there is a wisdom in fools. Their very simplicity prevents them from making the big errors. They are anchored in the here and now, today; they are confined to the particular. The compulsion to generalize causes most of humanity's problems."

I said, "That's a broad generalization by a complex man."

He smiled.

It was dusk now and we could see a hectic white fluttering at an offshore reef as birds returned to their rookery. And at the same time, as if coordinated, thousands of bats rose like smoke from a cave on the promontory to our right. Even at this distance we could hear the harsh cawing of the birds and, faintly, the high-frequency twittering of the bats.

"You know," Krisos said, "with luck, with the right sequence of events, Stavros might have made it. You said that at the last instant he kicked away from the cliff. Suppose that it was a flood tide. Suppose that the surf was as heavy as it is tonight. Suppose that a large wave entered the defile at the right moment. He might have survived."

"I don't think so."

"No?"

"I don't think the water down there deepens enough, even with a high tide and heavy surf."

"I disagree. Should we try jumping later, when the tide comes in?"

"No, we shouldn't. Are you hungry?"

"I could eat."

I built a fire and prepared a meal from the last of my supplies: cheese and butter and bread, olives, peppers, onions, grilled sardines, and a bottle of wine.

For three days a hot, dry wind had been blowing out of Africa. It was another unusually clear night: the dense sparkle of the Milky Way was reflected on the sea and diagonally bisected by a frosty trail of moonlight. Other tiny constellations glowed on the silhouetted islands. Zigzagging bats hunted insects in the air above us; some came so close that we could see them in the fireglow and hear the crepitant patter of their wingbeats. And we heard the remote barking of a fox. Krisos was a hunter and had brought foxes to the island. Foxes, grouse, partridge, and pheasant.

He was subdued tonight, almost gentle. He had temporarily lost his rage. Perhaps it was only that he was exhausted. Fatigue made him seem ordinary. Tonight he did not generate that electrical tension that made everyone, even members of his family, anxious about his swift changes of mood. In the shuddery orange light of the campfire you could see what Krisos would look like in fifteen years, when his enormous vitality was depleted and his power ceased being personal and became only a matter of money.

He told me about his voyage to Africa. He had shipped out on a tramp freighter and for five weeks had worked like a mule while the ship—a rust bucket of Liberian registry—had gone from port to port along Africa's west coast: Dakar, Freetown, Monrovia, Lagos, Luanda . . . There had been trouble with thieves in Freetown, and two men had been killed. Piracy still thrived in some waters, some ports. It was hot day and night, that humid West African heat, and he had slaved as stevedore (and repeller of pirates) as well as deckhand. He had, he told me with pride, worked harder and longer than men half his age, and he'd fought the thieves who had swarmed aboard during his night watch. He believed that he had killed one of them, but he could not be sure—the action was chaotic; one merely shot at a shadow and hoped that it was a thief and not a fellow crew member who screamed. Violence is never orderly. . . .

"It doesn't make sense," I said. "Why do you do it?"

He did it to test himself; to ensure that wealth had not totally insulated him from a man's world, the hard world out there; and to reaffirm that he was still strong, still a man of uncommon courage and strength.

"All right," I said. "But you're still rich and powerful, Alexander, even while you're chipping rust off a freighter's deck plates or shooting at thieves. You aren't like the other men. They have nothing, nowhere to go, no retreat. That is their life. But you have your houses and your yachts and your special place in a special world."

He told me that I did not understand. While he was aboard that ship he was no richer than the fellow next to him. They ate the same food and worked beneath the same blistering sun and shared the same risks.

"My money won't stop bullets or turn a knife blade or save me from being crushed by a thousand-pound crate that's broken loose, or save me from a storm at sea or a bacterium in port. For five weeks, Jay, I was no richer than the other men. For five weeks I was only as strong as my body and as hard as my will."

It was the sort of thing that Krisos did every two or three years: turn his business affairs over to subordinates and ship out on a tramp freighter that had been abandoned by its rats, one that carried scrap iron or salt fish or contraband; or he worked on the docks in Anatolia, alongside Turks who despised Greeks; or he labored in a German factory; or he cooked in a Greek restaurant in Detroit. He vanished into anonymity and returned five or six weeks later restored, so he said, reinvigorated.

But I could see that this last voyage had tired him, perhaps damaged his health. He was fifty-three years old. He was proud of his capacity to work like an ox, but it was not his body that made Krisos extraordinary—the world is not short of muscle. Krisos was Krisos because of the quality and subtlety of his mind.

I walked into the darkness to urinate, and when I returned Krisos was standing at the edge of the cliff.

"Jay," he called. "Come here."

He stood with his toes curled over the rocky lip of the precipice. His stance was a deliberate challenge. Stavros had fallen from that point. I joined Krisos there. I did not hang back. The night dropped away below us, ninety feet of air down to the rocks and spume and boiling sea. Farther out the fractured waves reflected the moonlight in many oddly cut facets. We stood shoulder to shoulder. I realized that I did not wholly trust my old friend. I wondered if he trusted me.

The blowhole was active now. Surf rushed into a network of shallow caves and was compressed into an area too small for the volume of water, and so it then erupted with a thunderous crack out of a stone channel no bigger than a cannon barrel. The blowhole's exit was about a third of the way up the cliff's face. We watched as a powerful geyser of water exploded outward, arched, and dissolved into mist. I could feel the rising mist on my cheeks. The air around us became hazy for a moment. It possessed the tart salt and iodine odors of the sea.

"Watch, Jay," Krisos said.

A surge of water, foaming along its crest, was entering the little cove. It made a sound like the angry humming of bees. It rushed inward, sizzling, rose higher and turned concave, and then collapsed into an avalanche that covered the rocks and crashed into the cliff. The water continued to deepen for a moment, rising; then there was a pause, a stillness, before it began swirling back toward the open sea.

"It deepens quite a lot," Krisos said.

"Not enough."

"Are you nervous standing here, Jay?"

"No, are you?"

He smiled. "Yes. It would be easy to lose one's balance."

"That's true."

Still smiling, he said, "Some of the swells are much bigger than the average. You have a series of small waves and then a big one. It's not necessarily the seventh wave—but if you watch carefully you can pick out the big ones, the doubled waves, quite far out. It's not only their size; it's also the particular way they curve and foam along the crests."

"Very interesting," I said.

He pointed seaward. "There, do you see that one? A monster wave."

"Not monster enough, Alexander."

"Are you afraid?"

"No, because I'm not going to jump."

"You're afraid."

"No. I'd be afraid if I thought you could talk me into this."

"I may jump," he said.

"Well, okay. Geronimo."

"You don't think I will?"

"You might."

"But you really don't think so."

"No, I don't."

He was silent for a time. "You are fairly certain that I'm bluffing."

"Yes." I realized that I had said the wrong thing.

You should not dare this man to risk his life. "Well, sure," I said, "you'll jump if you choose to jump. But I wish you wouldn't."

"We'll both jump," he said.

"Not me. No."

"I'll go first. You follow."

"No."

"Jay?"

"No."

"It can be done," he said. "It's not as dangerous as it looks. You time the wave correctly, wait until it has expended all of its force, and then take a run and leap. A short, hard run will take you out far enough to clear the rocks at the base of the cliff. Beyond the rocks is a patch of sandy bottom."

"What can I tell you? It's a stupid idea."

"Would you do it for, say—fifty thousand dollars?"

I looked at him.

"You can't doubt that I would pay you."

"I don't like this."

"One hundred thousand dollars, Jay."

"I've done a few crazy things," I said. "This—I *might* try jumping if I were in the right mood, on the right night, for the sheer hell of it. Maybe. But it isn't something I'd do for money. You understand that, don't you, Alexander?"

"I do."

"So let's forget this bullshit."

"I'm going to jump."

"I can't dissuade you?"

"Of course not."

"Then give me time to make my way down the cliff

path. I'll be in a position to help you or recover the body, whichever."

"If I require help, I'll expect you to descend rapidly, through the air. This isn't the kind of thing that can be delayed."

"All right. Go, then."

We stood silently for perhaps sixty seconds, watching the series of waves advance, and then Krisos slowly backed up, counting his steps, and then, breathing deeply, he stopped.

"Give me the signal."

"I'd rather not participate in this."

"Please do as I ask, Jay."

I looked seaward. His "monster wave" was rapidly approaching. It was third in the long line of swells rushing silently across the dark expanse of sea. Krisos's chosen wave did not now appear any bigger than the ones before and behind it. They all rolled swiftly inward. The first of the three entered the cove and crashed foaming against the base of the cliff, and a moment later a great stream of spume exploded out of the blowhole and gradually dispersed, fogging the air.

"This is the moment," Alexander said. "Always. Isn't it, Jay? When you've bet it all."

I turned to look at him. His stance was casual and he met my gaze with a quick smile that acknowledged our complicity. I had no reservations now. I was his accomplice in this foolish stunt. Let him leap; let him fall; let him live or die. Everything was so dreary, so boring, until Krisos arrived, and then one's interior vision was altered, sleeping emotions were aroused, and life repossessed its clarity and peril and fun.

The wave, his wave, had entered the cove. I now saw that it really was bigger than the others, a seething graybeard that remained concave as it rolled on another fifty yards and then cracked like a whip as it collapsed, cracked again when its surge met the rock wall (I dropped my arm and shouted, "Go!"), and cracked once more as, violently compressed, it exploded out of the blowhole. Alexander was falling then, windmilling his arms for balance, and he fell slowly (it seemed) through the spume and mistfog and entered the water straight and clean a yard beyond the half-ring of sharp rocks. The splash lifted thirty feet into the air. A boiling mushroom of water appeared at his entry point. I stood on the edge of the cliff and watched it seethe.

The wave had exhausted its force and was now retreating back to the sea. I waited. I waited and then I saw Krisos surface in the middle of the cove. He waved. I thought I saw him wave. He rested, letting the rip take him out another twenty yards, and then he began swimming in with the next wave, riding it all the way in past the rocks. He vanished briefly in the spray and mist, and when he reappeared he had reached a safe spot. He rested again and then began climbing.

The first third of the cliff wall was easy; the last two-thirds were not hard by mountaineering standards but were nearly vertical, and the rock was slippery wet, and it was dark. I poured the last of the whiskey into his tin cup.

He accepted the cup but was unable to drink immediately. His breathing was fast and deep, with a tearing sound, and I saw that he favored his left leg as we walked toward the fire.

"Are you all right, Alexander?"

He nodded.

"Did you hurt your leg? Your back?"

"My back, a little."

"It was a fine leap," I said. "A superb leap."

"Yes, it was, wasn't it?"

He drank the whiskey in a single swallow, handed me the empty cup, and walked stiffly to his motorcycle. I followed him.

"Come to dinner tomorrow night," he said. "I want you to meet my fiancée."

It sounded strange to hear a man of Krisos's age refer to his "fiancée."

"I don't own a tux," I said.

"You don't? Well, wear the best that you do own."

"All right."

"There will be only a few people."

"What time?"

"Eight, for cocktails."

"Are you hurt, Alexander?"

"Be there. Please."

Krisos rarely used the word *please*.

He mounted the motorcycle, started the engine, and switched on the lights.

"Well, that's done," he said.

"Did you hurt yourself?"

"Good night, Jay."

I watched as he drove the winding ruts north toward his villa at the summit. I could see lights shining up there, window lights and floodlights and the red flash of the aircraft warning beacon. Eventually the lights of Krisos's motorcycle separated from the darkness and entered the bright milky aura of his island home, his summer palace.

2

I drove east across the plateau and then began descending the switchbacks that tacked down to the village. The road had been blasted out of rock. There was stone rubble on the surface, and on the third switchback I heard the hissing crackle of sand and pebbles falling on the car's roof. Last year a landslide had swept a vehicle over into the sea.

The road cut back again, and I could see the village below, an ancient fantasy in the moonlight, a symmetrical stack of white cubes and rectangles (except for the Oriental dome of the church) arranged compactly along the hilly streets, wall abutting wall, rooftop looking across to rooftop. The harbor, a horseshoe of smooth water three-quarters closed by a stone breakwater, lay below the town. The night lights of the moored boats were scattered here and there, white, red, and green planets among the haze of reflected stars. Fishing boats had been hauled up on the beach or tied along the stone quay.

It was only a little after ten, but the town was dark. Evidently the generator had failed again. I parked in the small central plaza and filled the jerricans with water from a spigot. It took a while; the cistern was nearly dry. A half-starved mutt lay snoring beneath one of the iron benches.

One of the villa's vehicles was parked outside the Café Socrates. The café had not closed. Tables and chairs had been stacked on the sidewalk terrace and covered, but the double front doors were open and lights glowed dimly within.

There were half a dozen men sitting at the tables inside. Theo, the owner, greeted me. I saw Stavros Kamis's brother in the dimness, and said hello to two of the temple workers. They nodded, courteous but not friendly—this was their territory, I was an intruder. I was associated with the Krisos family. They were, Kon liked to say, "the lord's vassals."

Konstantin was sitting at a table in the rear of the room. I approached. There was a bottle of Metaxa on the table, a glass, a pitcher of ice and one of water, an ashtray, and five candles that sputtered and smoked like dud fireworks.

I pulled out a chair and sat down across from him. "When did you arrive?"

"Today."

"With your father?"

"No."

"Is Maria here?"

"She has a recital in Lyons tonight. She'll be here tomorrow."

"And Nico?"

"Tomorrow."

You had to know Konstantin well to tell when he

was drunk. His eyelids descended a fraction, his speech and movements were slower and more precise, and that was all. If you knew him very well, as I did, you became aware that he was gradually being seized by anger. His father seemed angry even when he was not; Kon always appeared calm until the moment when he hit you.

"I'm going to meet your father's fiancee tomorrow."

"Lucky you."

"Have you met her?"

"Unlucky me. They're also arriving in the morning."

"They?"

"Her father is coming, too. Maybe as chaperon for the sacrificial virgin, maybe to determine the suitability of the match, maybe to inventory the silverware. Do you know that she's only twenty-five? Younger than Maria. I don't know why he doesn't marry one of his round-heeled movie actresses or international tarts."

"Maybe he's in love with her."

Kon laughed.

"Why not?"

"He's in love with her pedigree. You'll find most of her ancestors listed in the *Almanach de Gotha* or *Debrett's Peerage*. Noble blood flows through her veins. She's a reservoir of recessive genes."

"Will they be staying for the party?"

"Of course."

"Will you?"

"Fools require an audience."

Theo came over with another glass and a clean ashtray. Kon waved him off when he started to wipe the table.

Earlier tonight I had looked at Alexander Krisos and seen how he would look when very old; and now

Konstantin, softly immersed in shadow and candleglow, seemed very young, a boy. Kon and I were the same age, but while I looked my thirty-seven years he appeared no more than twenty-five even in a hard outdoor light. The dissipation did not show, the alcohol and the drugs and the irregular hours—the playboy's life. He was still boyishly slender and still good-looking in a film actor's way, with carved features and expressive eyes. Neither he nor his sister much resembled their father (although Nicolas was like a clone of the old man, a faithful replica).

"Kon," I said, "do you want to be alone?"

"Drink," he said.

"You're in one of your moods."

"Just pour yourself a fucking drink, will you?"

"One drink," I said. "Because you're going to get mean in about twenty minutes."

"Not so."

I poured brandy over ice and lit one of Kon's cigarettes.

"Your father jumped off the cliff tonight," I said.

He was interested now. He looked up at me and smiled. "The cliff by the temple?"

"Yes."

"Did he want you to jump?"

I nodded.

"Well, and did you jump?"

"No."

"You refused?"

"Of course."

"That surprises me."

"That I didn't jump? Why?"

"Because that was a good opportunity to please him."

"That was an opportunity to crack my spine."

"My father is mad," he said. "He's always been mad. And each day he gets madder. And I'm the only one who will say it. He's a mad king and there are hordes of people who will jump off a cliff if he commands it."

"I didn't jump," I said.

"When I was a boy, fourteen . . . fifteen, I think, he took me down to the cliff. It was a night like this—a full moon, a heavy swell running down from Africa. A big tide. The thought of jumping off that cliff in daylight is terrifying. But at night! Well, he was mad then and he's mad now. I sometimes think that night on the cliff screwed me up forever."

"You didn't jump?"

"What? Oh, no. I jumped. The mad king told me to jump, and so I jumped. Did I have a choice back then? I'm still jumping."

"But you're not fifteen now."

"So you declined my father's invitation to leap off the cliff. He may respect you for that. Of course, he may despise you, too. It's hard to tell with mad kings."

"One thing bothers me," I said.

"Yes. There is always at least one thing."

"He offered me money."

"To jump?"

"Fifty thousand dollars at first, then one hundred thousand."

"Ah. Were you tempted?"

"For a moment."

"Sure. One hundred thousand dollars for a few seconds' dangerous work. That's generous. Don't you think that's generous, Jay?"

"Offering money to me was not an act of generosity."

"There are millions, billions, who would gladly jump into hell for that kind of money. It was brave of you to refuse. Or maybe it was cunning."

I let the "cunning" remark pass. "Your father never did that before. Used money, I mean, as a bribe or a tool of manipulation."

"You just lost your cherry."

"I've been your friend, a friend of the family, for many years. Isn't that so, Kon? Money was never mentioned, not ever. A family friend, almost a family member. And then tonight. It was an act of contempt. I believed your father respected me. The offer of money to jump off a cliff makes me think that he doesn't."

"But you're taking his money now."

"That isn't the same thing and you know it. That's a job. Fair wages, no more."

"I don't know that my father understands that kind of punctilio. You're an employee now, Jay. We all are."

"It's late," I said. "Come on; I'll drive you up to the villa."

"I have a car. I can drive myself."

"Theo wants to close the café."

"Then Theo can tell me so himself. We don't require you to act as intermediary."

"Kon, you're in no shape tonight to drive these cliff roads."

"Piss off," he said. "Okay?"

"Okay." I stood up.

"Good night, *quate*."

Theo looked at me and raised his eyebrows as I went past him and outside to the Land Rover. It had been a long time since Kon had called me *quate*. It was a Spanish word that literally meant "twin" but colloquially could be defined as "good friend, brother," "mate" in the British sense.

Konstantin and I had been good friends for many years, since college. We were *quates*. But lately he had begun regarding me as—if not an enemy—a neutral in a conflict that disallowed neutrality. He believed that I was being co-opted by his father, seduced by Krisos's charm and money and power. Kon now saw me as a probable traitor.

I did not understand the covert war between Kon and his father. The grievance was obscure, the tactics devious, and the prize of victory more symbolic than real. But there it was, and there I was, deeply involved because years ago I had been more or less absorbed into the family. We had mutually adopted each other, and now the intricate skein of relationships was beginning to unravel.

The camp seemed vacated, abandoned like the temple ruin. It was no longer my place. I did not inhabit it as before. Alexander arrived with his vitality, and when he went away you were left depleted and in a sort of emotional vacuum.

I had been living in Guatemala when the terse invitation—summons, rather—arrived from Krisos: "Expecting you soonest to commence restoration Temple of Poseidon. Telephone immediately with your travel arrangements. Regards, A."

There were scores of Greek archaeologists far better qualified than I to excavate the temple ruin; the job offer was a contrivance, a way of enabling me to spend a summer with the family. I accepted gladly.

The camp required light, heat, voices. I fed sticks of wood into the still-hot embers and then added some charcoal. When the fire revived I went into the tent and got my portable radio and dialed an Athens station. Two men and a woman, all three with rich, melodious radio voices, were discussing the political situation vis-à-vis Macedonia. My Greek was not sufficient to grasp the details, but the situation appeared volatile. Or maybe it had ceased being volatile and was now merely uncertain.

I sat in a deck chair by the fire and drank what remained of the wine. The moon was well to the west now, and the sea shined as black and hard as obsidian. The tide was out, the blowhole silent, the wind continued to blow out of the southwest.

Konstantin and I met during our freshman years at Stanford. Even then I intended to become an archaeologist; the past had always appealed to me more than the present or future. Kon planned to enter the business school. We immediately became friends. Our contrary personality traits meshed in a way that made us stronger as a pair—*quates*—than individually. He was lighthearted, careless, often irresponsible; I was very serious then and conscientious to a fault. He lightened my moods; I discouraged his wilder excesses. Our odd-fellow friendship even helped us athletically: neither of us was good enough at tennis singles to play at the collegiate level, but we succeeded in making the Stanford squad as a doubles team.

I did not know until my junior year that he was the son of the "eccentric" Greek billionaire Alexander Krisos. At that time Kon went under the name of Konstantin Kouris.

In 1977, when I was twenty, my parents were murdered—slaughtered—in their bed by a pair of intruders. I was devastated, of course. I went a little crazy. Alexander Krisos flew in his private jet from Athens to Palo Alto to see if he might in some way assist his son's best friend. I soon regarded Alexander as my friend, too, and later Nicolas, and the young Maria. The family absorbed me. I skied with them in the Swiss Alps in winter and cruised the Mediterranean in their yacht during the summers. I never felt like a guest. I was one of them. Another son for Alexander, another brother to Kon and Nicolas and Maria.

The police were certain that they knew who had murdered my parents, but they could not gather enough evidence to bring the case to trial. "We'll get them eventually," they told me. But less than a year afterward, on the basis of an anonymous tip, the police found two mutilated corpses in a remote canyon. Some time later I abruptly realized that Alexander had probably arranged the torture and murder of the two men who had killed my mother and father. But I never asked him about it, and he never referred to the original crime or the subsequent reprisal. The subject was closed.

I fell asleep in the deck chair and awakened stiff and cold near dawn. In my dreams I had been vaguely aware of the increased noise of the surf and the spaced detonations from the blowhole. An especially loud crack awakened me. A fine, cool mist descended upon my cheeks. The tide was high again. The air was suffused with mist and the feeble light of false dawn, a luminous gray that softened all contours and betrayed one's perceptions. My left leg was numb; it tingled and then burned as circulation returned. I was stiff and cold and hungover and in a sour mood. My dreams had been senseless and with no apparent reference to my life—like the intercepted dreams of a far different man.

I kindled a small fire, brewed some coffee, and carried a cup to the precipice. The endless rows of swells were uniformly large. You could smell desert herbs in the wind. The rising sun spread an expanding fan of color over the sea and sky.

I threw the coffee cup aside, removed my shirt and Levi's and sandals. The timing was not a problem: you heard the surf hit the base of the cliff and then sprinted for the edge. I preferred to dive rather than jump; my horizontal push would be greater, the arc of descent wider, and I could more easily control the angle of entry.

And so I sprinted the few yards and pushed off hard, stretching out toward the horizon, hurling my weight out into dream time, dream space. Below me was the sea, blue and green and creaming white around the sharp rocks. The blowhole had exploded just prior to my dive, and I descended swiftly through mistfog and spray that was like heavy rain. I cleared the rocks easily and entered the sea at the precise—the perfect—angle. I hit the sand bottom, but not hard, opened my eyes, and saw that I was encapsulated in a globe of fizzing silver bubbles. I rose with the bubbles toward the bright distorting lens of the surface.

3

Late in the morning the wind died, and within a few hours the sea was nearly flat. At six I descended the cliff face and bathed and shaved in a shallow tide pool. Tiny fish were intoxicated by the soap and delicately nibbled at my legs.

Lizards, sunning on the ledges, scuttled into crevices as I climbed the stone wall. Cool, damp exhalations issued from the cave mouths. One of the workers had told me that these caves extended all the way to the heart of the island, that the island was honeycombed with tunnels and cathedral-like caverns, and—of course—that there were fantastic treasures secreted away in the labyrinth.

Back in the tent, I sorted through my duffels and found a clean pair of khaki pants, a clean but wrinkled shirt, a pair of scuffed loafers, and my old Harris tweed jacket. It was a very good jacket, though a little worn now and smelling faintly of mothballs.

At quarter to eight I got into the Land Rover and drove up the twisting, rutted road to the villa. The parched land produced mostly flinty stones and chalky dust. There were only a few stunted trees and shrubs, some cacti, and a sparse, dry yellow grass that somehow supported the herds of goats. Halfway to the summit, a bad-tempered ram, protecting his harem, blocked the road. I stopped the car and waited. He had charged the Land Rover a few weeks before and knocked himself out. Now he glared and feinted attacks until honor was satisfied, and then led his scruffy tribe into an arroyo.

Some distance to my left as I reached the upper plateau was a cubical white house with a slate roof and small, deepset windows barred by iron. Nearby was a goat pen, a henhouse, some dusty, withered olive trees, and a red-painted iron pump that lifted water from the cistern. Krisos's first wife, Sophia, lived there, the mother of Konstantin and Nicolas and Maria. When Krisos had, in the biblical phrase, put her aside, she might have claimed many millions of dollars in the settlement and lived anywhere, in any style; but instead she chose to live like a peasant in that house, on this bleak, rocky island. It was, perhaps, a kind of vengeance, a perpetual rebuke to her husband.

She was reclusive. I had never met her, though I had often seen her from a distance: a small figure dressed entirely in black.

On a ridge outside the villa's walls was a tall flagpole with two cross spars: seven flags flew in conformity with the complicated protocol; Greek, French, American, the Union Jack, one that I could not identify, and the elaborate heraldic standard of the Créneau family. I knew little about heraldry, but even so, I realized that was an impressive Achievement of Arms, the shield quartered and then quartered again, with each space emblazoned with additional coats of arms claimed by the Créneaus. It contained most of the colors of the armorial spectrum: argent, gules, azure, vert, purpure, sable, and was scattered with obscure symbols and stylized animals, eagles and falcons, dragons, lions both rampant and couchant, coronets and fleurs-de-lis, and crosses, the Maltese, the Crusader's, the Saint George, the crosses Patonce and Saltire. . . . It was, for those few who understood the encryption, an entire genealogy.

Krisos's personal flag also flew today: a trident, a leaping porpoise, and an ocherous Catherine wheel sun, all set on a sea blue background. The flag was one of Alexander's few affectations. His engagement to a remnant of the old French nobility was another. The French government and institutions did not recognize the nobility as such or their titles, but nearly everyone else did, and so did Alexander Krisos. He was a man who greatly appreciated talent and beauty, but a few months ago he had chosen to marry a bloodline.

He intended to start a second family. This, perhaps, was the source of Konstantin's furious brooding. Kon was like a prince who was being eliminated from his rightful succession to the throne.

Also outside the walls, west of the gate, was a semicircle of guest cottages. They were set in a grove of trees, and their facades were bright with flowering vines. Some distance away, on the plain, were the stables and kennels and garages; and located on a steep grassy hill behind the villa was an outdoor theater modeled on the ancient theater at Epidaurus. Some temporary structures had been erected on level ground below the hill: a bullring fence not yet painted, and a spiderweb of poles and wires and swings, the type of rig used in circus high-wire acts.

Alexander's parties were famous for the entertainments provided and notorious for the scandals produced. There were many rumors: a famous movie actress had attempted suicide after an all-night debauch; a Saudi princeling had sadistically maimed one of his servants; an American oilman had lost millions to Krisos at *chemin de fer,* a British politican had suffered heart failure while in the embrace of a servant girl . . .

I had never attended one of the parties, although I had been invited to most. I was not sure I cared to attend this one. It seemed to me that a temporary exile in Athens was preferable.

It was Sunday and I saw no workers either outside or inside the walls, though a pair of Krisos's security men were sitting at a patio table just beyond the gate. Heinrich and Gunther. There were others like them, psychic twins, all former members of an elite West German antiterrorist police. The kind who, maybe, would have been officers in the Waffen SS fifty years ago. All were truly hard men whose hardness was not vitiated by the correctness of their manners.

"Hello, Heinrich," I said. "Gunther. Any mad bombers around today?"

"Good evening, sir," Heinrich said with cold deference.

Gunther returned my greeting with a nod that was almost a bow.

"No mad bombers today, Mr. Chandler," Heinrich said. "Unless you are one, sir."

The Germans' loyalty to the Krisos family was absolute; it had been both purchased and earned.

The courtyard was a vast riot of color and noise,

visual and aural confusion that only gradually revealed an underlying symmetry and order. The whole was enclosed by three shady colonnades, and straight ahead was the house, a rambling three-story white stucco building with balconies and tower rooms and ornamental wrought-iron railings and steep ceramic-tile roofs. It was big, but not the "stupendous mansion" described in the tabloid press. The bell tower—an unnecessary architectural flourish—half-spoiled what was really a pleasing structure.

There were brilliant flower gardens. There were fountains and waterfalls and graceful masonry bridges that spanned the channeled "brook" that meandered through the courtyard. There was a big asymmetrical swimming pool with a mosaic tile bottom depicting events from the *Iliad*. The gardeners always saw to it that fresh flowers floated everywhere on the shimmering multihued water. It looked like a pond in an Impressionistic painting, a Renoir or Monet.

Elsewhere there were palms and great lacy ferns, nut and fruit trees, and flowering hibiscus and frangipani and bougainvillea, and other trees that I could not name. It was like a horticultural exhibit, and like an aviary, too, for everywhere there were bright, shrill, flitting birds, few of them native to Greece, few native to Europe, quarreling squadrons of exotic birds.

A servant admitted me and led me through the foyer and down a wide corridor to "the hall," a huge room that was furnished more like a gallery in a museum than a house. The ceiling was three stories above, vaulted and heavily beamed. A great many antiquities were displayed in cases that were temperature- and humidity-controlled. Alexander displayed objects here from the archaic, classical, and Hellenic periods of the Greek past, all of museum quality. It was possible that the value of objects assembled in this room exceeded that of the house.

Now Alexander, a drink in hand, was looking in one of the cases. He turned and stalked toward me. He wore a white linen dinner jacket, ruffled shirt, and black tie.

"Look at you. I told you to dress in the best you owned."

"This is the best I own," I said.

"You look like an American slob."

"I *am* an American slob, Alexander."

"You're meeting my fiancée. My fiancée's father."

"I'm sorry," I said. "I'll go."

"You shame me."

"Christ, I said I'll go."

He suddenly grinned. "When did you jump off the cliff?"

"What?"

"You heard me. Don't stall. There was another high tide this morning around dawn."

"I didn't jump."

"Don't lie to me. I can always tell when you are lying."

"I didn't jump; I *dived*."

"See? I know you. I knew you could not refuse my challenge."

"I didn't do it for the money."

"Certainly not. My offer of money was an insult. A goad. So how did it go?"

"Very well."

"I am in pain. I ache everywhere. My body is purple."

"It looked to me like you entered the water cleanly."

"I got bruised on the rocks while swimming in. My body ricocheted off every rock. So, Jay, you did not disappoint me. You jumped—you dived—off the cliff."

"I'm disappointed in myself."

"Why?"

"Because you were able to predict my behavior. I did what you expected me to do."

"Not what I willed?"

"No."

"Not what I compelled?"

"No, Alexander."

"Of course not. Get a drink. There's something I want to show you."

I asked the barman for a Kir, and then Krisos led me over to a long glass case filled with papyrus scrolls. It was his latest acquisition, he said; they'd been smuggled out of Egypt by a more or less honest dealer in contraband antiquities. Some of the scrolls appeared to be in good condition; others were ragged and sort of melted together in a pulpy mass.

"There's no telling what some of this stuff will turn out to be. But I know there's a fragment of a play by Meander and some of Aristotle's *Politics* and scraps of this and that. Some old Egyptian peasant found it in his fields. What do you think?"

"Looks interesting."

"Do you think they might be forgeries?"

"I couldn't guess."

"It wouldn't be easy to forge half-rotten papyrus scrolls."

"They can forge anything nowadays."

"I'm aware of that," he said dryly.

Krisos had been badly stung by forgeries in recent years.

"Simon Rye is here to evaluate them for me. Do you know of Rye?"

"No."

"Classics scholar. He was a don at Oxford some years ago when there was an ugly scandal, something about Rye and an eleven-year-old boy. He's a fatuous bastard, but he knows his stuff. Fatuous—by God, is there anyone anywhere more fatuous than a fatuous Englishman?"

"A fatuous Frenchman, maybe."

"Or American. And Rye's had the gall to bring into my house his lover of the moment, a Moroccan boy who can't be more than thirteen or fourteen, though Rye claims he's eighteen. Abdul something-something. A nice-enough lad, but Jesus! Rye calls him Ganymede. Can you beat that?"

"From myth, isn't it?"

"Ganymede was a beautiful boy who was carried up to Olympus by an eagle. He was the cupbearer of the gods."

I laughed.

"Ganymede. The son of a bitch."

4

Simon Rye was a tall (six feet four or five), gangling, awkward man in his seventies. His shoulders were round, his chest concave, his hair sparse and lank. He approached in a shambling gait, and each stride was like a blind step to an unknown elevation, a fall averted.

"Jay Chandler," he crooned to me.

He had white, bony hands with spatulate fingers and split yellowed nails. (Maria later said that he had fingernails like an old woman's toenails.) My hand—not small—vanished inside his damp, warm clasp.

"Jay Chandler," he repeated. "Yes, so p-p-pleased, really."

His moist eyes—blue with black pinpoint pupils—bulged, and when he spoke a fine spray of saliva hung in the air like dust motes. Rye was grotesque and evidently delighted to be so; his timidity and befuddlement seemed intentionally exaggerated, lampooned. He did not mind at all if he disgusted you.

"You must meet my p-p-protégé: Abdul. Come here, you naughty rascal. (An aside to Krisos: "He's a thief, Ganymede is; guard your t-t-treasures.")

The boy was slender and dark and shy, pretty in the androgynous way of some early adolescents, male or female. He had dark long-lashed eyes and arching eyebrows. A small scar slightly twisted his thin upper lip.

"So very pleased," he said in a thick accent. And he nodded and smiled shyly, stepped back.

He looked very young and absurd in his tuxedo, like an overdressed child entertainer or ventriloquist's dummy.

A man and a young woman entered the hall, and Alexander hastily left us. Rye and I strolled around the perimeter of the room, followed by the confused Ganymede. We paused briefly at each case. There were a great many pots, including some superb red-figure and black-figure vases; coins and seals; parchment and papyrus manuscripts; slabs of temple friezes; ancient weapons, corroded bronze swords and daggers, some with gold hilts; shields and armor; arrowheads and javelin tips and sling projectiles; helmets dating from the battle of Marathon and before; jewelry, gold and silver and ivory and onyx; and marble statuettes and busts—one piece attributed to Praxiteles.

"Mmm," Rye murmured, pausing to study a case full of Minoan objects. "Are *all* of these p-p-pieces Minoan, Jay Chandler?"

"They appear to be."

"You don't think, you don't imagine that that little cup and that bracelet just might, might be Mycenaean?"

"I don't know. Are they?"

"Oh, sorry. I thought you were an archaeologist."

I smiled. "I'm mostly interested in Mesoamerica."

"Meso-America. Ah, those b-b-bloody Aztecs and Mayans and such."

"And such."

"All those human sacrifices en masse. Delicious."

"Human sacrifice isn't all that rare," I said. "The early Greeks sacrificed people. So did the Sumerians and Babylonians and Hebrews and just about every other tribe."

"Yes, but they were discriminating. Moderate. Restrained. I love the Aztecs because they sacrificed many thousands in a single day, cut out their b-b-beating hearts. B-b-blood flowed in troughs. It must have been a glorious spectacle, don't you think? Unfortunately, that sort of thing is nowadays frowned upon by the . . . by the b-b-bleeding hearts." His laugh was a sort of stage whisper "heh-heh-heh."

Alexander rescued me by clasping my arm and leading me across the hall to meet the Créneaus: Marquis Jean Saint-Jean du Créneau and his daughter Francoise. They pretended not to notice my shabby clothes and ugly accent in French. Soon they switched to English. The marquis was a middle-sized, prematurely bald man with a thin, almost lipless mouth and half-hooded eyes. A deep line, like a saber scar, vertically creased each cheek.

His daughter had fine dark blond hair and good skin and hazel eyes.

As we chatted, it occurred to me that *créneau* meant "battlement" in French. Perhaps some remote ancestor had successfully resisted a long siege behind his battlements. John Battlement, Frances Battlement—the names were less impressive when Anglicized.

After a few minutes of small talk, I excused myself and wandered away. They remained in place while Krisos fetched Rye and Ganymede. Rye fawned over the Créneaus satirically; the boy smiled and nodded shyly in response to remarks in a language he did not comprehend.

Konstantin and Maria (releasing each other's hand) entered the room.

Kon's face was a mask of disdain as he met his future stepmother and her father. He ignored the marquis's offered hand. Créneau accepted the insult gracefully, but Krisos was quietly furious. Maria, unaware of the tension or indifferent to it, was ebullient. She seemed younger than her twenty-eight years, still girlish, still carelessly impulsive. She had always laughed easily, and now she laughed at something Créneau said.

Maria wore a white gown that was cut and pleated to resemble the ancient Grecian chiton. Her brown hair was up and bound by a white band. She wore sandals, and jewelry from the time of Periclean Athens. She might have been a beauty from twenty-five hundred years ago. And it was amusing: Maria and her brother, the children of peasants, looked as one imagined aristocrats would look, while the marquis and his daughter were quite ordinary in appearance and bearing.

Simon Rye appeared at my side. "Why is it," he inquired softly, "that so many rude b-b-buccaneers like our friend Alexander wish to marry into those godawful impoverished noble families? Centuries of incest have reduced their chins and their p-p-property and their intelligence and p-p-probably their genitalia. P-p-poor Alexander. I thought better of the old p-p-pirate."

I said nothing.

"Don't you love to observe billionaires who have come from nowhere and nothing?"

"I only know one billionaire," I said.

"They are poor, and suddenly they are rich, and they may indulge every whim. One can chart the interior landscape of such a man by what he b-b-buys and how he chooses to live. Alexander has p-p-purchased a history."

"Do you think it's proper to gossip about your host, Mr. Rye?"

"P-p-proper! Why, of course, dear boy. Otherwise what's the p-p-point of being a guest?"

"The Créneaus seem nice enough."

"Nice! That appalling Americanism, *nice!* They're p-p-perfectly dreadful and you know it. You dissemble. You are being . . . *nice!*"

Ganymede tugged at Rye's sleeve.

"What is it, dear boy? Do you have to p-p-pee?" To me Rye said, "Moslems have smaller bladders than Christians."

Maria, smiling, was coming toward me. I went to meet her, and as we embraced she lifted up on her toes and kissed the corner of my mouth.

She stepped back then and said, "Jay, you're so tan. You look like a Red Indian, except your hair is bleached and sun-frazzled."

"And you look like you just stepped out of an old play."

"A play by Sophocles? *Antigone,* maybe? Do you see me as Antigone, Jay?"

"No, she's a tragic heroine."

"I hope you're not going to say that I'm comic."

"You used to be comic."

"But now I'm a formidable woman and you'd better not take me lightly."

"I won't. How did the recital go?"

"Never mind that; I want to show you my lovely new horse. She's mine, but you may look at her as long as it's not a covetous look. Come with me."

"Do you think we should leave now?"

"Certainly we should, unless"—she lowered her voice—"unless you like being bored."

As we were leaving the room I heard Kon say to Simon Rye, "I've met pederasts before—you can't avoid them these days. And I must have encountered a catamite or two. But this is the first time I've met both old pederast and young catamite socially, bugger and buggered, over canapes."

We strolled through the courtyard and out the big gate (Heinrich was sitting alone at the patio table now) and up the sloping ground toward the stables. Maria took my arm.

"Those Germans," she said. "They're everywhere. They even invade my dreams."

"I suppose it's difficult."

"Difficult! It's unendurable. They lurk. They intimidate my friends. They lurk; they spy; they hover. I hate them."

"They've probably saved your life several times and you don't know it."

"Perhaps."

"And look at Nicolas."

"Yes, poor Nicolas. I suppose I shouldn't complain. But God, Jay, you don't know how lucky you are to be poor."

She was startled by the arrogance and absurdity of her remark and began laughing, and she was still laughing—spooking the horses—when we entered the stable.

She led me to a stall. "This one. There, look at her, Jay; isn't she gorgeous? Smell her. Yes, go on. See how sweet and wheaty she smells. I love her."

The horse was a white Arabian mare, and to my ignorant eye and nose she was not much different from the other horses that stamped and snuffled in their stalls.

"Kiss her, Jay. Kiss Athena. Yes, you must kiss her on the nose or she'll think you dislike her. I won't have that and neither will she."

I kissed the air a few inches in front of the horse's nose.

"Shall we go riding tomorrow?" Maria asked. "We'll ride down to your little temple and picnic and swim. All right?"

"If you can find me an old, tired horse and a Western saddle."

"And we'll stop and visit my mother. You've met her, haven't you? Of course you have."

"No."

"No? How is that possible? Well, you'll meet her tomorrow."

The sun was below the horizon now, but the sky was still a brilliant blue and the high clouds were incandesced by the invisible sun.

"You didn't actually kiss Athena," Maria said as we walked down toward the villa. "You cheated. You faked a kiss. Is that how you kiss girls, Jay?"

"If they're as ugly as your horse, yes."

She stopped. "Kiss me."

I kissed the air a few inches in front of her nose.

She laughed, and we went on down to the new bullring and leaned our arms on the fence. The ground had not yet been laid with the correct mixture of sand and clay. The *burladeros* hadn't been constructed, nor the *estribo,* but work had started on the corral behind the ring and the tunneled chute through which the bulls would enter.

"Father's bringing in some huge Spanish bulls and famous Spanish matadors," Maria said. "There will be a complete *corrida*. It was my idea, actually. I suggested it."

"Do you like the bullfights?"

"Yes, thanks to you."

"Why me?"

"Don't you remember all the lies you told me?"

"Vaguely, yes."

"Well, I think the bullfights are cruel, of course. Barbaric. But beautiful, too. Father says that fighting bulls are descended from the wild aurochs that roamed Europe thousands of years ago. Bulls have always been feared and worshiped. Remember the myth of Theseus and the Minotaur. So it is cruel, and I hate that part of it, but there's also something—I don't know—something really magnificent and . . . profound, too."

I saw Heinrich walk down the flagstone path to the theater, apparently intent on his cigarette and the view, but really watching us. Or, rather, watching over Maria.

She smiled and teasingly said, "Father says that we may persuade you to fight a bull."

"Your father doesn't have any difficulty in thinking up dangerous stunts for me to perform."

"Well, didn't you used to boast about fighting *toros* in Mexico?"

"Did I?"

"You certainly did."

"They weren't *toros*, Maria; they were *toritos*."

"You made them sound as big as elephants."

"That's how one talks to admiring adolescent girls."

"But admiring adolescent girls remember." And then, still teasing, she said, "Are you going to dedicate a bull to me, Jay? Fight and kill a terrifying brute? Present me with his ear?"

"No."

"Maybe Father will buy a *torito* for you to play with."

"Not even then."

"My childhood hero won't even try to live up to his boasts."

"Not by half."

"You are a disappointment."

There was an element of seriousness in her teasing.

"I'll tell you about it," I said.

"Please do."

"After getting out of college, I went on an archaeological dig in Mexico, near the town of Aguascalientes. They grow wine grapes in that region and raise fighting bulls. The town was boring, my colleagues were boring, I was boring, it was a boring excavation, and so I began to amuse myself by hanging around the town's bullring, where the young *noverillos* worked out every morning. I made friends with a few of the kids, and they invited me to practice with them. So I did. Later I was able to wangle invitations to some of the bull ranches during the testing. I played with some calves, got tossed around by some cows, learning a little but not enough. Not nearly enough."

Heinrich was now sitting halfway up in the amphi-theater. No doubt he could hear our words; the acoustics were very good, gathering in sound and amplifying it.

"One thing leads to another," I said. "Foolishness usually begins as innocence. I fought in three *novilladas* in three different Mexican cities. I did it only for the experience, the excitement. I had no intention of becoming a torero. It was a lark."

"El Larko," she said. "El Goofo."

"I fought six young bulls in all, cut one ear, and got a horn driven six inches into my upper thigh. It missed the femoral artery by a quarter of an inch. The wound developed gangrene and for a while it looked like they were going to amputate my leg. I retired after that. I cut the pigtail. And I'm not about to grow a new one."

"You never told me about your wound. Did it hurt terribly? Will you show me the scar?"

"It's in an awkward place."

"Being gored by the bull didn't . . . incapacitate you, did it?"

I laughed. "Was I emasculated? No."

"Whew!" Maria said. "I bet you're glad of that."

I said, "We may be delaying the serving of dinner."

"It was a pathetic and sordid story, Jay. And now you simply might fight and kill a bull. For revenge."

We walked slowly through the perfumed, twilight-hazed courtyard. The birds were settling in for the night. Later colored lights would come on and illuminate Krisos's magic garden. Music would issue from concealed speakers, summoning forth fauns and nymphs and randy goat-legged satyrs, and maybe the great god Pan himself, the original cause of panic.

5

We tethered our horses to a thorn tree outside the gate. A path lined with whitewashed stones tacked through the gardens to the front door. The door was painted dark blue; there were flower boxes outside each of the blue-framed windows, and flowering wisteria vines climbed the trellised walls to the steeply pitched roof. Swallows nested beneath the eaves.

Maria's mother admitted us into the house. There was a small foyer with a pair of low benches and wooden clothes pegs in the walls, and an arch led into the living room.

Sophia Krisos spoke broken, thickly accented English. She welcomed me, said she had often seen me, chided me for never having visited. "Why you no come see?" Then she and Maria went into the kitchen to gossip and brew coffee.

The furniture in the living room was old and solidly framed with dark woods. There were a pair of settees, some straight-backed chairs, tables, a china cabinet, a fireplace with a marble mantle, and many icons hung on the white plaster walls. The ceiling beams were black with age and smoke. A door led to the kitchen, another to a bedroom, and a steep stairway led up to the attic loft. The place was without electricity, and so kerosene lanterns and candles were scattered around the room. In the corner there was a sort of altar, a linen-covered table that contained candles, a Greek cross, and three icons. I saw only one book in the room, a worn leather-bound Bible, and one photograph, a picture of Kon, Maria, and Nicolas when they were children.

The cottage was tidy and simple, perfect in its way, an ideal peasant cottage rather than an actual one. Its austerity was partly negated by the dozens of valuable icons and silver candelabra.

Sophia Krisos and Maria returned with a tea cart. We had Turkish coffee, almond and honey cakes with thick sweet cream, and fruit. Our talk was less a conversation than an interrogation. Maria smiled at me while her mother asked questions. Her voice was low and husky. Where are you from? Who are your people? How do you earn your living? What are your politics? What is your religion? She must have known most of the answers; perhaps she wanted to verify what she had previously heard about me. And so she served her questions and I volleyed back my answers, often facetiously. Her directness, her rudeness, was at least partly due to her difficulty with English.

I had expected her to be a shy woman, timid and probably sullen, certainly defeated. After all, she was a recluse. She had evidently turned her life into a silent expression of grievance and repudiation. She always dressed as if in mourning. And observed from a distance (black-clad, slow-moving, stooped as she worked in her garden), she appeared old and gnarled, twisted physically in conformance to an equal psychic twisting. But that Sophia Krisos was a construction all my own.

The actual Sophia possessed great energy and rough good humor and bright, alert, mischievous eyes. She was a handsome woman who must have been beautiful in her youth, as beautiful as Maria now was. She was slender and fine-boned, like Maria and Kon, with thick dark hair and greenish eyes and a wide mouth that smiled naturally as she talked.

After forty-five minutes Maria and I thanked her, said goodbye, and went outside and mounted our horses. She sat lightly, expertly, on her precious Athena; I wrestled with a stone-mouthed brute named Bully.

"Did you like my mother?" Maria asked.

"Yes," I said. "I didn't think she would be like that."

"Like 'that'? Like what, Jay?"

"Well, I'm sorry, but I guess I expected your mother to be a little crazy."

She laughed. "And you're disappointed?"

"The way she lives, sort of lost in time, and alone, and her extreme self-denial."

"But she doesn't deny herself anything she truly wants."

"Perhaps not."

"She has all she wants or needs. She has sacrificed nothing."

"It seems to me that she's sacrificed a great deal."

"You're wrong."

"Okay."

Maria laughed again. "Still, you're correct, my mother is a little crazy. But isn't everyone a little crazy?

At least part of the time. I know that I am. Aren't you a little crazy, too, Jay?"

"I think we have a linguistic problem. First we should establish our definition of crazy."

She laughed. "Yes, yes! God yes, but not today, please."

We rode down the high spine of the island, surrounded by sea and sky, immersed in blue. The morning was cool and shadowy. Small lizards, the same grayish color as the soil, sunned on flat rocks. You could not see them until they moved.

At the camp we tied the horses to a tree and removed the saddles. Maria said the temple ruin still looked like a pile of rubble; what had been accomplished in the months of work? I told her it was like assembling a twenty-ton jigsaw puzzle.

"And you think my mother is wasting *her* time."

Maria went into the tent to change into her swim suit. I stood on the rim of the cliff and looked down at the foaming surf, the rock fangs, the little patch of beach. Had I really dived off this cliff two days ago? What a fool.

She emerged from the tent barefoot and wearing a blue bikini that, for a moment, made her self-conscious. We carefully picked our way down the cliff face. I carried the backpack that contained our lunch. She was familiar with the route and unafraid of the height; she moved confidently from hold to hold, and jumped the last few feet to the beach.

The sea smelled sharp and clean, astringent. There were bird tracks in the sand, and small fish and squid had been trapped in the tidal pools. The surf cracked and hissed. Gulls sailed by, heads cocked, looking for a handout.

We swam out side by side and then floated in the deep, cool water beyond the surf line. I stayed close to Maria; she was not a strong swimmer, and there were tricky currents in the cove, sometimes dangerous rips. Her hair was darkly wet and sleek like a seal's fur, and her eyelashes were spiky. She laughed for no reason.

Back on the beach I rubbed her with suntan oil and we lay together on the blanket, drowsing in the sun, lulled by the sound of the surf and the mewing of gulls. I was aware of her body next to mine, her flesh still cool from the sea, the scent of her hair, and the odor of coconut oil.

I sensed that Maria was equally aware of me. She was waiting. If I moved just a few inches I might kiss the nape of her neck, her ear, her cheek. We would make love. It was what we both wanted. It was an act long anticipated and long delayed. This was the moment. But I held back; my relationship with her and her family was already too confused and contradictory. For years Maria and I had been like brother and sister. That had changed, but certain obligations remained. I was trusted by Alexander, Kon, all of them, and it seemed to me that it would be dishonorable, a betrayal, to radically disturb the family's balance (a precarious balance) by becoming Maria's lover. All of our complex relationships, each to each and each to all, would be changed irrevocably. The Krisos family was like a small paranoid state, and I was half a citizen, half a foreigner.

An hour later we swam again, then returned to the beach and ate the lunch Maria had prepared: cold chicken, bread and butter, cheese and fruit. We ate it with the bottle of white Bordeaux she had looted from her father's cellar.

I then slept for a time, and when I awakened Maria was gone. Her things remained on the blanket—sunglasses, suntan oil, wristwatch, a paperback novel. It was two o'clock and very warm now. She was not in the water, not swimming, nowhere out in the glittering sea, and nowhere along the curving shoreline or out on one of the promontories.

Perhaps she had gone up to the camp to see to the horses, give them water. I wanted a cigarette, but I couldn't find my butane lighter. Maybe she was angry at me and had returned to the villa.

I climbed the cliff face to the plateau. The horses stood placidly in the shade of the tree, their skin and tails twitching at flies. She was not in the tent, nowhere on the sun-blasted plateau.

I went to the edge of the precipice and stared out over the sea. No, she was not in the cove; she was not floating, alive or dead, in the deep blue water beyond. She had not swum out to one of the small, rocky islands to collect shells or bird feathers. She was gone, vanished. For an instant I thought I heard her cry for help, but it was only the mewing of a distant gull.

Where could she be? I closed my eyes and tried to think. Where? The caves. My missing cigarette lighter.

I got a flashlight from the tent and descended the cliff. The rock face was riddled with holes, only a few large enough to admit a person. I selected the largest and crawled inside. It ran straight for perhaps thirty feet and then hooked to the left. I could stand erect here. The walls were wet with condensation. There was a dank, sewery smell. The sound of the surf outside resonated through the chamber, hummed at a pitch that, while not loud, hurt my ears. Ahead a pair of tunnels forked deeper into the mass of limestone. They converged deep in the labyrinth: you could follow either one, but the left was bigger.

It slanted downward at a gentle angle, narrowed to an aperture so small that I had to squeeze through sideways, scraping the skin on my chest and back, widened again and forked off into two more tunnels. One entered a tortuous maze that went nowhere; the other eventually ended in a large chamber—but I could not now remember which was which.

The flashlight's beam was weakly reflected on the wet, faceted stone walls and appeared faint and yellowish, dying. Perhaps the batteries were failing.

I switched off the flashlight and the darkness compressed, rushed in as air rushes into a vacuum. Water dripped ticking from the walls and ceiling. The air around me hummed with an accumulation of exhausted echoes. In the general hum I could distinguish a dim ringing, the remote vibration of the ocean surf, my breathing, the echoes of echoes. The darkness was absolute. I felt calm, far from panic, but my thoughts skittered irrationally. This darkness seemed much more than the mere absence of light; it had a weight, a density, a mind. It was a thing. There was a horror here. Or rather, I was in a neutral enclosed space that I perceived as horrible.

"Maria!" I shouted, and the voices of a dozen strangers repeated her name.

I thought of the myth of Narcissus and Echo. Echo

was condemned to live forever in a cave and forbidden to speak except to repeat the words of others.

I switched on the flashlight and shone it down the right-hand tunnel. "Maria, can you see the light?" I thought I heard her voice, faintly, far-off, among the multitude of voices.

She was sitting on the stone floor in the center of a large stone room. Stone walls, floor and roof, a cavern of stone. Her legs were drawn up and encircled by her arms. She winced and turned away from the flashlight's beam. Flesh, the color and texture and warmth of flesh, seemed a kind of miracle here in this stone tomb.

"Maria Krisos, I presume," I said.

"Don't be funny," she said. "Just get me out of here."

I helped her up.

"What took you so long, Jay?"

The sunlight hurt Maria's eyes, half-blinded her, and so I helped her down to the little beach. She collapsed on the blanket.

"Idiot," I said. "Why didn't you—" and then I saw that her right hand was scorched and blistered. "What happened?"

"The cigarette lighter exploded. I let it burn too long."

"We'd better get you to the house."

"No, not yet. Let me rest. I feel very weak."

She had the vague and distracted air of a crime victim or the survivor of an automobile accident.

"I didn't panic," she said. "I didn't weep or shout or pray. I just sat down and waited for you to find me."

"That was the right thing to do."

"It took you such a long time."

"No, that's just how it seemed."

"I felt myself becoming smaller and smaller, dwindling. You go along believing that you're a distinct person, unique. I am Maria; you are Jay; he is he and she is she. But it really isn't like that. If you dig down to a certain level you'll find no one. I mean, I could feel myself dissolving, my personality, my self, Maria. Ten hours in that cave and I would have been no one, no thing."

"How do you feel? Can you make it up the cliff all right?"

When Maria felt stronger, we climbed the rock wall to the plateau and went into the tent, where I kept a first-aid kit. I gently cleaned her hand with alcohol and then loosely wrapped it with gauze. The skin was glossy and inflamed and there was a rash of blisters, but the skin had not been broken.

I saddled the horses and we mounted them and rode up toward the villa. Maria was quiet. Her burned hand hurt and she was still in mild shock from her experience in the cave.

6

I was working alone at the temple the next morning when von Rabenau, chief of the German security team, drove up in one of the villa's cars. He wore khaki shorts and a bush shirt, ankle-high suede boots, and a khaki military-style billed cap. He looked like a World War Two tank commander. Von Rabenau was very tan, and his hair had been bleached blond-white. His eyebrows and lashes had been bleached, too, and his eyes—the same luminous blue as a gas jet—seemed at times to possess the unfocused stare of a blind man.

"Good morning, Chandler," he said.

"Good morning."

He stood next to me and slowly glanced over the ruins. "You seem to be progressing. It really does seem as though you'll eventually stack all this rubble into a temple."

"I think so."

"Very good. Perhaps you'll permit me to help you from time to time. I know a little about archaeological work. I enjoy it. If you wouldn't mind . . . ?"

"I can use you," I said.

When speaking German, von Rabenau sounded like a man ordering vast reprisals, terrible retribution, but his English was mild in diction and almost deferential in tone.

"An important discovery was made near my home village when I was a boy. Neanderthal remains. Most of the cranium, some teeth, other bones. It was quite exciting. A forensic pathologist concluded that the Neanderthal man had been murdered some thirty thousand years before. I thought then that I would become an archaeologist."

"Why didn't you?"

He shrugged. "One is diverted."

"Would you like a cup of coffee, Walter?"

"No, thank you. I've come to ask if you have seen the Englishman, Simon Rye."

"No, not since the night before last, at dinner."

"He's vanished. Alexander is concerned."

"How long has he been missing?"

"Since last night. He left the villa on a bicycle at dusk and failed to return. His Moroccan boy doesn't know where he was going. Rye said nothing to Alexander. He just went off down the road toward the village and that is all."

"Well," I said, "it's a small island."

"Yes, very small, but surrounded by sea and honeycombed with caves. In my opinion, Simon Rye will never be found. He is gone. Searching for him is a waste of time."

"He may show up eventually," I said. "Like your murdered Neanderthal."

"Perhaps."

"The cliff roads are steep and dangerous. He might have lost control of his bicycle. That seems the most likely explanation."

"Does it?"

"You'll probably find him and his bicycle on the rocks."

"No. My men have looked everywhere."

"Was he seen in town?"

"No one admits to seeing him in the village."

"Well . . ."

"Do you know what I believe, Chandler?"

"Yes," I said. "I know."

"Then you are thinking the same thing."

"I'm afraid so, yes."

"The filthy pig."

At noon I washed, changed clothes, and started walking the dusty road toward town. On the cliff overlooking the harbor I saw that Krisos's yacht had returned from Piraeus. And the water boat was tied alongside the quay. It was a small converted freighter that twice a week provided the island with freshwater, pumping it into tank trucks that then filled the many cisterns in town and up at the villa.

Theo had saved my usual small table on the terrace of the Café Socrates.

"*They* are arriving," he said with quiet scorn. *They* were the strangers, the rude and peculiar outsiders who each summer invaded the island for a week. *They* were Alexander's guests, men and women from around the world, the rich and powerful, the famous, the beautiful, pop gods and goddesses. The islanders used an old Greek word to describe them—*barbaros*. *They* were regarded as barbarians by the locals, and their behavior often justified the appellation.

The waiter brought my luncheon salad and a glass of wine. I asked him if he by chance had seen an Englishman in the village last night or this morning, a tall, very thin, somewhat peculiar man named Simon Rye. The waiter's face, normally expressive, became cold, impassive. "No, we have not seen this man."

I ate slowly, practicing my comprehension of demotic Greek by eavesdropping on the conversation at a nearby table where three men were discussing the national soccer team.

"May I sit here?"

I looked up and saw a woman in a white linen sundress.

"All of the tables are filled, you see. You have an empty chair, and I thought . . ."

"Of course," I said. "Sit down, please."

She smiled briefly, sat down, and placed her purse on the table.

Inch-high silver initials, a *P* and an *M,* were pinned to the purse's flap.

"Is the menu in Greek?" she asked.

"Yes. I'll translate it for you if you wish."

"You know Greek, then."

"I know the menu. I've eaten here once or twice a day for months."

"Perhaps I'll have a salad like yours. And a glass of wine. It's not that awful retsina wine, is it?"

She spoke with the crisp "received" British accent:

every vowel was rounded, each consonant given true value. She was in her middle to late twenties, with the kind of beauty that stares out at you from the pages of fashion magazines: sculpted cheekbones and jawline, widely set blue eyes, and an exquisitely curved mouth. Her hair was thick and crow-feather black, gleaming with reflected blurs of light. Her skin was flawless. She was one of those rare creatures who, for a few years, happen to match the time's standards of beauty. She did not seem quite real.

"Will you order for me? The salad, but without the crumbled cheese. And a glass of the wine."

I called the waiter over, ordered her lunch, then said, "My name is Jay Chandler. And your name is . . . Penelope Bradshaw."

"Hardly that."

"Patricia Brown."

"Never. No, I could be neither a Patricia nor a Brown."

"Pamela Blake."

"You're getting warm."

"Petrushka Babushka."

"I am most recently Juliet. I am also Blanche DuBois. Tomorrow I might be Ismene."

"So you are an actress."

"Pamela. Not Pam or Pammy. Not ever. Pamela Bristol. And who are you, besides your name, and what do you do, and why are you captive on this ghastly island?"

I was about to reply when she said, "Oh, God, it's that fool Mel and his horrid little Miranda."

I looked up and saw a gray-haired man dragging a dummy the entire length of the terrace. He held it by the wrist, letting its feet drag along the stones. It was a female dummy, less than a yard long, with a blue ribbon in its straw-colored hair, a blue-and-white dress, white stockings, and black patent-leather shoes with buckle closures. Its china-blue eyes were fringed by absurdly long lashes, and there were dimples at the ends of its giddy, frozen grin.

"I hate this," Pamela Bristol said.

A four-top table had been vacated at the end of the terrace. The man reached it, lifted the dummy, and placed it in a chair. It sagged, head lolling, and gradually toppled facedown on the floor. The man picked it up, carefully returned it to the chair, and then disgustedly watched as it again spinelessly slumped, tilted, and fell. "Bitch," he said. Finally he sat in the chair, leaned over to pick up the dummy, and placed it on his knee. His right hand moved behind its back.

"It's so cheap," Pamela Bristol said.

The dummy suddenly became animated. She was alive now. She cocked her head, blinked slowly, and in a quacking voice said, "I'll have a double martini, Daddy." The man's lips barely moved.

"No, Miranda," he said in his own voice. "You'll have a glass of milk."

"Booze."

"No."

"Booze."

"No."

"Milk?"

"Yes."

"Booze."

Miranda's head moved jerkily as she looked around at the café's customers.

"Rabble," she said. "Swine."

"Miranda," the man said, "you shouldn't talk that way. These are nice people."

"Scum."

Miranda's eyes engaged mine and she said, "What are you looking at, Bunky?"

"A dummy," I said.

"Me, too," Miranda said, and a few of the customers laughed.

"Don't they freeze your blood?" Pamela Bristol asked.

I'd sensed that there was something wrong about the dummy from the beginning; now I realized that Miranda was a midget, a small, well-formed woman. She was a dwarf, but without the deformity present in most cases of dwarfism. Her makeup, her movements, her performance were very convincing, and so I (and many of the customers) had been deceived by her size—one did not often see yard-tall women pretending to be ventriloquists' dummies.

"Aren't they wretched?" Pamela Bristol said.

A waiter went to their table and was comically abused by Miranda. It was strange: an ordinary ventriloquist wants you to believe that his dummy is alive; this man tried to convince you that the little woman was wood and plastic, a dummy.

"I simply cannot bear them."

I heard a motorcycle engine and turned; Alexander Krisos, grimly staring straight ahead, was cruising slowly down the street. Von Rabenau followed him in a Jeep. They proceeded around the square and then angled off down a narrow lane between the church and the old hotel.

"Pamela, I've got to go. I hope to see you soon."

She smiled neutrally.

"Are you staying up at the villa?"

"No, we aren't guests. We're here to entertain the guests. They put us up at the hotel."

"How many are there in your group?"

"Ten."

"Including Miranda and her master?"

She made a face. "I'm afraid so."

"Good-bye for now."

"Yes, all right, good-bye, then."

I left the café and walked diagonally across the square, scattering pigeons. Two old men were playing dominoes at one of the tables. Several old women, dressed in black, their heads covered by black shawls, were slowly climbing the church steps.

The cobblestone street led down into a crowded residential section of the village. There were doors and windows set into the walls on either side, and small balconies above, and lanes too narrow to permit vehicular traffic angled off into shadowy courtyards. Somewhere off in the maze a baby was crying; a radio played; a woman laughed. The air was rich with the garlicky odors of cooking food.

The street hooked to the right and descended a hill to a cul-de-sac bounded on three sides by apartment complexes. There was a crowd gathered ahead and below, a semicircle of men and women and children, and others were looking down from balconies and rooftops. I saw one of the tank trucks, von Rabenau's Jeep, Alexander's motorcycle, and two of the blue cars used by the island police. I walked down the hill and made my way to the front of the crowd.

The corpse lay sprawled supine on the cobblestones. Simon Rye looked even taller in death, and leaner, and older. His clothes and hair were wet and stained with a greenish slime. His gelid, protuberant eyes were half-lidded; his jaw was slack, the mouth open to reveal a slab of grayish tongue. Rye had impressed me as an extremely vain man, and I thought, *If only you could see yourself now, Simon.*

Some deaths seem more emphatic than others. Illogically, a murdered man appears more truly dead, dead to a greater degree, than, say, a man who has died in his sleep.

He lay next to a cistern. The steel hatch had been removed, and the cylindrical stone pit below exhaled cool, dank air similar to the air in the seaside caves.

A few yards away Alexander was talking with the driver of the tank truck. Three policemen, looking confused and uneasy, stood nearby. They were members of the island police, Krisos's private cops, and not qualified for more than maintaining order; they could break up a fight, arrest a drunk, find and chastise a truant schoolboy, but they hadn't the training and experience to investigate a murder. I supposed that von Rabenau or one of his men would conduct the investigation.

Von Rabenau was sitting behind the wheel of his Jeep. Our gazes intersected; I nodded; he returned my nod with a faint smile and a shrug.

I walked over to the Jeep. "Well, Walter, Simon Rye reappeared thirty thousand years sooner than your murdered Neanderthal."

"Yes, unfortunately. Now there will be a scandal."

"I don't think I would care to drink the water in this neighborhood."

"No." And then: "How stupid of them to drop the body into this cistern, where it would certainly be found."

"Will you be able to find the killer?"

"Oh, yes. Easily, if Alexander permits it."

"Why shouldn't he?"

"Indeed, why not?"

"Why do you believe it will be easy to find the killer?"

"Half of the village knows who murdered this man. The other half will know by sunset. It's just a matter of locating the weak one, the one who will talk."

"Well, I don't wish you luck in finding him."

"Chandler, who was that woman with you in the café?"

"You noticed her, did you?"

"Who is she?"

"My fiancée."

"You lie."

"No, really, Walter, we're going to be married in the fall."

"Really?"

"Yes, really."

"My congratulations."

"Thank you, Walter."

I hurried back to the café, but Pamela Bristol was gone.

PART II

THE PARTY

7

Alexander had saved one of the bigger cottages for me.
It was two stories high, with the kitchen, dining, and living rooms downstairs. A spiral stairway led up to a big
bedroom with windows all around. Another steep flight
of stairs ended on a rooftop patio where there was an
umbrellaed table, a barbecue grill, and a pair of chaise
longues. A fancy wrought-iron railing had been set into
the low parapet. There were other cottages on either
side, half-concealed among the trees and shrubbery, and
to the east I could look over the grounds and villa wall
to the pool area and the upper levels of the big house.

I found clothes hanging in the bedroom closet: formal evening wear, two sets of black jackets and trousers,
a white dinner jacket, and several sport jackets with
slacks. And there were three pairs of new shoes in the
rack, two black and one brown. I tried on one of the
dinner jackets. It fit perfectly. Alexander had somehow
obtained my measurements and had these clothes made
by his Savile Row tailor. That was Alexander's style; at
once mysterious, generous, and arrogant.

In the dresser drawers were many pairs of socks,

underwear, handmade shirts, belts and suspenders, display handkerchiefs, ties—bow, foulard, and ascot—and even a box of cuff links. One set of cuff links had been fashioned from ancient gold coins; Alexander the Great's portrait had been minted on one side, a laurel wreath on the other.

Also in the closet I found a compact, powerful astronomical telescope and a box full of attachments: a tripod, timing and tracking devices, and a camera with which one could photograph the stars and solar system. Alexander did nothing without a reason; what was his purpose in leaving me this telescope?

I roamed around the downstairs. There was a fully stocked wet bar, of course, and a refrigerator filled with beer and champagne and food delicacies—a big tin of Beluga caviar, cheeses and fruits, pastries, a container of pâté de foie gras. There was more food in the cabinets, and a rack filled with French and German wines. Alexander's hospitality was oppressive.

Periodically I heard the clattering whir of a helicopter landing near the villa and then a few minutes later taking off again. It was ferrying Alexander's guests in from Athens. I wondered about the protocol: Did one board the helicopter according to one's accumulated wealth, richest foremost, or were there other criteria? Prestige? Celebrity? Accomplishment? Each of those men and women must have an exalted sense of his or her own importance. They were accustomed to being regarded with deference, servility even. Priority—primacy—would be crucial to self-esteem. Alexander, simply by his helicopter schedule, had established a pecking order, and I supposed that there would be many wounded egos at large during the next week.

On the telephone stand I found two sheets of parchment: one contained, in an elegant calligraphy, an alphabetical list of the guests and their telephone extension numbers; the other listed the schedule of events—theater, bullfight, etc.—and brief biographies of the performers.

I read the notes about Pamela Bristol. She was from Sussex; was a graduate of the Royal Academy of the Dramatic Arts; had been for three years a member of an important theater company; had made several television appearances, including the role of Katya in a BBC production of Turgenev's *Fathers and Sons*.

The guest list started with Aguilar, Antonio, and ended with Zastrow, Clayton. I recognized many of the names. Anyone would. Those names had come to possess a certain kind of magic through repetition and legend; they were like incantations, mantras.

My name (one that would not be recognized by the other guests) was listed: *Chandler, Jay. Ext. 9.*

I flinched when the phone rang. I picked up the receiver and heard Maria say, "Chandler, Jay."

"Krisos, Maria," I said.

"I'm bored."

"I'm bored, too, but I suspect that during the next week we'll look back fondly on our boredom."

"Oh, the party will be boring, too, in a different way. Big spectacles can be boring. Why am I so often bored, Jay?"

"I don't know. Maybe because you're rich."

"Maybe. But it must be even more tedious to be poor."

"Were you bored in the cave?"

"No, but one can't get lost in a cave every day. Aren't you going to offer me lunch?"

"I'll chill the wine."

I placed two bottles of Mumm's in ice buckets, made some toast and buttered it lightly, finely chopped an onion, quartered a lemon, opened the tin of caviar, and scooped it into a silver bowl that I set on a bed of ice. I arranged everything on a tray and was just opening the first bottle of wine when Maria came through the front door.

"Don't bother to knock," I said.

She was barefoot and wearing white shorts and a peppermint-striped blouse. Her burned hand had been professionally bandaged.

"I've been figuring," I said. "This particular caviar is worth more per troy ounce than gold."

"I don't like caviar."

"What do you like?"

"Peanut butter."

"You lie."

"Pickled pigs' feet."

"You lie."

"Spam."

"Oh, well, everyone likes Spam. Do you want to go up to the roof?"

"No."

I placed the serving tray and some plates and utensils on the counter that separated the kitchen from the living room, poured half an ounce of cognac in each of the flute glasses, and topped it with the champagne. We sat side by side on the counter stools.

"I thought you were going to Athens for the duration of the party," she said.

"I changed my mind. The party might be interesting. There are some people I'd like to meet."

"I've met most of the guests at one time or another, and I can tell you that they aren't terribly exciting."

"You *are* bored today."

"I think I'm lonely, Jay."

"Then you should see fewer people."

"God, I hate it when you speak epigrammatically. Say you'll stop."

"I'll stop. How can you be bored, Maria, when one of your father's guests was murdered and thrown into a cistern?"

"Simon Rye deserved it."

"Deserved to be murdered? Why?"

"Because, obviously, he went down to the village and molested one of the village children. And he was caught and punished. Who knows how many boys he seduced, molested, corrupted during his lifetime? Simon Rye got exactly what he deserved, except it should have happened thirty years ago, forty."

She took another square of toast, spread it thickly with caviar, squeezed lemon over it, and began eating.

"I'm sorry I don't have any peanut butter for you. What is going to be done about the Moroccan boy?"

"I suppose Father will give him some money and send him back to Morocco."

She took another piece of toast and smeared it with caviar.

"Maria, you said you knew most of the guests. Do you know Gypsy Marr?"

"I've met her."

"What is she like?"

"She's a whore."

"Well, that's her public image."

"She's a whore."

"Maybe you're confusing her show business persona with her actual self."

"She's a whore."

"Sex sells; she sells sex. She's sort of a parody of a whore, professionally."

"Jay, she's a whore."

I laughed, got up, and refilled our glasses with the brandy-and-champagne mixture.

"Who was the girl with you yesterday?"

"On the terrace of the Café Socrates? Her name is Pamela Bristol. She's an actress. She'll be performing up here."

"Someone told me that she's lovely."

"Von Rabenau told you. The café was full. She asked to share my table."

"Beautiful, von Rabenau said."

"Yes. But it's a fragile, brittle kind of beauty."

Maria gazed at me for a time and then burst out laughing. Her eyes narrowed to slits, and she tilted back her head and laughed at me.

I smiled.

She said, "The bullfighters have arrived. One is a stubby little fellow, but the other is very handsome. Aguilar. He's sort of the ideal Spanish matador, young and virile and beautiful in a masculine way. An Apollo. I imagined us making love, but then I thought, *No! No, he is too fragile. Too . . . brittle.*"

We laughed.

"Shall I open another bottle of wine?" I asked.

"No. I'm already a little drunk."

"I'll make more toast."

"I've had enough to eat." She paused, glanced sideways at me, and said, "Why didn't you make love to me on the beach? I was waiting. You knew that."

"Maria . . ."

"Of course, you don't owe me an explanation."

"It's very complicated."

"Ah."

"There are consequences."

"Ah," she said. "Consequences."

"You know that's true. What was it going to be? An afternoon beach—pardon me—beach fuck? A week of screwing and then you'd return to your life and I'd go back to mine? Love, marriage, children? What, exactly? We're much too close, Maria, to simply go off and enjoy a sporting fuck. And there would be reverberations that we can't even guess at."

"And this is what you were thinking about while I was lying next to you on the beach?"

"Yes."

"You couldn't just *act* and to hell with your bloody damned conscience and bloody damned scruples—your adding up and subtracting, your moral bookkeeping . . ."

"I don't think I was wrong."

"Fine."

"I was *nearly* overcome by passion," I said, smiling at her.

"Oh, well."

"I believed I was behaving responsibly."

"There are times, Jay, when behaving responsibly is an insult."

"I'm sorry."

"I don't know. Maybe you were right."

I said, "Life seems to proceed in alternating phases: sexual tension, and the lack of sexual tension."

"Is that an epigram?"

"I don't think so."

"Sexual tension or the lack of same. Yes."

"I think it was Euripides who, when he was in his nineties, was asked what it was like to finally be free of the sex drive. He said it was like escaping the control of a madman."

"Poor Euripides. Was he the one who was killed when an eagle dropped a turtle on his head?"

"No, I think that was Aeschylus. Or Sophocles. Or maybe Aristophanes—I can never get them straight."

She laughed. Maria was a little drunk and giddy, and she slumped against me, laughing.

I said, "Life is so comic that we require tragedy for relief."

"No more epigrams!" she cried. "You promised."

"Come on," I said. "I'll walk you home."

8

While walking Maria back to the villa, I noticed a commotion down by the new bullring. The winch on a flatbed truck was levering a big wooden crate toward the corral. The crate tilted, teetered precariously, and some workmen gesticulated and shouted instructions and curses at the winch operator. Nearby two men in suits watched calmly.

"Keep walking," I told Maria.

If the crate slipped free of the winch's chain and fell the ten or fifteen feet to the ground, the crate would likely break open and we would have a thousand-pound fighting bull free on the plateau. But the winch operator regained control, swung the crate out over the corral, and gently lowered it. The workmen cheered derisively.

"Another crisis averted," Maria said.

"Barely."

"Aren't you disappointed? It would have made a fine show."

I left Maria at the villa's door and went back outside. The truck and the workers were gone, but the two men in suits remained by the corral fence. They glanced at me as I approached, nodded, and turned back to resume study of the bulls. Both were young and well dressed in Italian-cut black suits. One was short and muscular, Maria's "stubby little fellow." The other was about five-foot-ten, slender and well built, with the rather bland good looks of his age—twenty-three or -four. Aguilar. He was a member of a famous bullfighter family.

The corral had been divided into a number of holding pens. A twenty-foot-long roofed chute had been constructed that led from the corral to the arena.

There were four bulls and two steers together in an open section of the corral. One of the steers had been badly gored in the flank, and blood pumped from the wound. The animals were extremely nervous. And they looked weary, dulled, frayed. All were smeared with greenish excrement; one had a bloody horn. It had been a rough few days for the bulls; they had been confined in individual wooden crates at the ranch in Andalusia, trucked to a Spanish port, and loaded aboard the ship that had taken them to this island and their imminent deaths.

"They're very big," I said in Spanish.

The men looked at me. "Very big," Aguilar said.

Each of the bulls weighed more than 550 kilos, maybe as much as 600 kilos. They were huge, massive in the shoulders and humps, and the horns were longer and wider than was usual nowadays. They were very serious bulls. Just looking at them, safe behind the corral fence, I felt a weakness in my legs, a kind of fearful lassitude. It was their power. The combination of their power and quickness and courage. The big cats, lions and tigers, were fast and strong and dangerous, and so

were sharks. Everyone dreaded venomous snakes. Man,
too, was an efficient killer, the most dangerous of all.
But the bulls, to me, possessed an almost-supernatural
strength and an almost-mystical significance. They were
living relics, anachronisms, and so were the rituals during which they fought and died.

"I'm not familiar with the brand," I said. "What
ranch are they from?"

"Cencerro," Aguilar said.

I hadn't heard of the ranch. "You don't see bulls like
this often," I said.

"Not even in my nightmares," the short man said.

"They're at least five years old," Aguilar said. "And,
at their best, dishonest. We've been tricked."

I introduced myself and we shook hands. The short
man's name was Alfonso Orozco.

"Do you follow the bulls?" Aguilar asked me.

"I used to."

"In Mexico?"

"How did you know?"

"Your accent." He asked me if I was an *aficionado
practicante*: one who fought bulls or *novillos* for the
sport.

"I was," I said.

"So. Then the *novillo* is yours."

"What *novillo*?"

"There are two more bulls down on the ship, and a
novillo."

Orozco laughed. "That *novillo* is bigger than most
Mexican bulls."

"No," I said. "I'm not going to fight anything."

Orozco laughed again. "Neither am I unless my

contract is renegotiated. I didn't agree to fight these Cencerro dragons. This is treachery. Fuck them. Fuck Señor Krisos."

He shook my hand again, laughed, and said, "Let Señor Krisos kill these buffaloes."

"Are the bulls as bad as he says?" I asked Aguilar.

"Probably. Cencerro bulls are rarely fought in plazas of the first category anymore. They have bad tendencies. The breed is no good for the modern bullfight. Look at them. The horns. And the size—Christ, these animals might be *six* years old."

"How do you fight them, then?"

"Pic them half to death, chop them down with the muleta, and then assassinate them. It isn't pretty."

"Do you have a surgeon with you?"

"A horn man will be here for the fight."

"Where are your cuadrillas?"

"At the hotel in the village."

I tried to imagine the hotel as it was now and would be all this week, packed from lobby to roof with actors and aerialists and toreros and flunkies of Alexander's guests and the staff of locals (and at least one midget).

"Do you know this Alexander Krisos?" Aguilar asked.

"Yes."

"Is he a serious man?"

"Most of the time."

"My English isn't good. Maybe he was joking with me."

"What did he say?"

"He said that I would be fighting one of the bulls in a cave."

"What?"

"The cave would be lighted, and there would be a safe place for the guests to watch, and I would enter and fight and kill the Minotaur. He called it that, Minotaur. He was joking, of course. Wasn't he?"

"Of course," I said, but I wasn't sure.

"I don't care how much money he offers me. I'm not crazy."

"Are you familiar with the myth?"

"Of the Minotaur, half-man and half-bull, who lived in the Labyrinth and devoured the youth of Athens? Yes. But that"—he pointed at one of the bulls—"is not the Minotaur, and I'm not Theseus."

"Alexander is obsessed by the Greek myths. He sometimes tries to make reality conform to them."

"Is that sane?"

"Alexander is one of the richest men in the world. The eighth richest, ninth, something like that. I don't think the superrich are constrained by the same sense of reality as you and me."

"I know this. That horn is real." He slapped his abdomen. "This is real." He cupped his genitals. "These are real."

I laughed. "You seem to have a fair understanding of essential reality."

Late in the afternoon I dressed in shorts, a T-shirt, and jogging shoes and went out into the heat and glare. The back door led into a vast jungly garden shared by all seven cottages. There were marble benches, trellised arbors, ponds that contained luminous orange carp and lily pads, and a network of flagstone paths that meandered here and there before ultimately converging at the rear gate.

I went through the gate and began jogging along a gravel path. The land abruptly became desertic, baked, and cracked—ashy soil and flinty stones and stunted, spiky shrubs. The air seemed sharper, drier, after leaving Alexander's oasis.

After a hundred yards the path circled back toward the cottages, but I continued jogging up the incline. Far above I could see the sharp dark line of the cliff edge silhouetted against the blue sky.

The gradient steepened. It was very hot. My legs felt deadened. The air had a scorched taste. And then at last I scrambled the last few yards to the rim, left the land behind, and stood alone in the sky. It was all blue and white here, sky and clouds, sea and surf.

I turned and looked back over the entire length of the island. The villa complex was miniaturized by distance. And there the semicircle of cottages (mine in the center) with the lush green gardens behind; and beyond, the sprawling red-roofed villa and its sky-reflecting pools; far to the right, the stables, garages, and kennels; to the left, the bullring and corrals, the aerialists' scaffold; and farther to the left, the fan-shaped stone theater rising up a hillside. I could see the flagstaff, like the mast of a great square-rigged sailing ship, today flying the flags of a dozen nations. I could see Sophia Krisos's cottage far out on the sere plain. I could see the speckled white glint of the little temple ruin at the far end of the island. I could see the rooftops of the village and the graceful curve of the harbor. It seemed to me that I could see Time, the geologic aeons.

*   *   *

A man was sitting in the gardens behind my cottage. He wore a big white cowboy hat and snakeskin boots. He removed a cigar from between his clenched teeth and said, "Staying healthy, Cousin?"

I stopped. Evidently he was a neighbor. "Trying to," I said.

"Don't go near my waaf."

"Pardon?"

"Stay away from my waaf."

"Okay," I said.

"She come down with some godawful Mediterranean disease; she's coughing green slime."

"Has she seen a doctor?"

"You satisfied with your accommodations?"

"The cottage? Sure, it's fine."

"I wouldn't put a syphilitic convict up in one of these shacks. We don't do things this way, home. But Greeks. Shit. Am I a guest or am I here to work in this Greek's olive groves? Is Poochy going to wait tables?"

He wore a Western-style suit that had been cut for a slimmer man; fat bulged in his thighs, above his wide leather belt, around his shirt collar. He had a jowly red face and sparse sandy hair.

"You're American."

I nodded.

"Well, course you are," he said as if I had denied it.

"My name is Jay Chandler."

He rose from the bench and clasped my hand. "Jack Clyde Black," he said. "Nearly everyone calls me Blackjack." His hand was chubby and short-fingered.

"Poochy—is that your wife?"

"Not my dog. What do you do, Jay Chandler?"

"I'm an archaeologist."

He had a drawling Texas accent and a movie cowboy's stance and squint. He was an exaggerated version of a historical type—the frontiersman, the cattleman, the sheriff. Most men were inferior copies of extinct archetypes; even so, this Jack Clyde Black impressed me as an absurd contrivance. I couldn't imagine why Alexander had invited him (and Poochy) to the party. There had to be an altogether different man concealed behind the born-in-the-saddle, dust-and-dung facade.

"I only knowed one Greek," he said. "Nicky. He owned a little restaurant."

9

Late in the afternoon I went upstairs and lay down on the bed. I meant only to rest for a time, but I fell asleep and when I awakened it was night. My dream quickly dissolved, though I managed to retrieve one image: the body of a huge bull, greater than the bulls in the corral, with the chest, arms, and horned head of a man.

In two trips I carried the telescope and its attachments up to the roof. It was a dry, clear night, dark except for the lights of the villa complex and the stars glittering in the black ocean of space. The moon would not rise for another hour or so.

I could see the lights of Sophia Krisos's cottage far out on the plateau, and see, across the stretch of grounds, the faint colored glow of the patio lights inside the villa's walls. Dim figures, like the images on film negatives, floated wraithlike through the rainbow of color, and voices and music penetrated the general hush.

I mounted the telescope on the parapet and focused it on one of the brighter constellations. The stars glowed brilliantly out of a powdery haze of distant galaxies. I hoped that Alexander had arranged to have some astronomy books placed on the shelves downstairs; during the coming nights I wanted to locate and study the planets and even, if the telescope was powerful enough and the night very clear, the moons and rings of planets, their auras. But I was soon bored by the stars; one looked pretty much like another to me, only a little brighter or dimmer, bigger or smaller.

The temptation was too great: I lowered the barrel of the telescope, made some minute adjustments of angle and focus, and gazed over the wall and into the villa's gardens. It was like being transported there. I was now among the people but invisible to them. Observing without being observed conferred a curious sense of power, a feeling of dominance.

I isolated Maria (she was dancing with Aguilar), Alexander, Nicolas (in a wheelchair), and Kon, who looked quietly drunk. The Texan, Jack Clyde Black, was standing near the little waterfall (which the telescope magnified into a Niagara), talking to a redheaded girl who did not look like a "Poochy." Slight movements of the telescope brought others into view, assured men and attractive women, many of them familiar from newspaper and magazine photographs, television and movies. In general, the men were older than the women, and they appeared grave and somewhat distracted, weary, perhaps. Most of the women, however, were gay and smiling and coquettish. The gems in their rings and necklaces and brooches glittered like the stars. One older woman wore a diamond tiara.

The telescope collected their images and projected them across the grounds, through the night, and up onto this rooftop. I felt that I could reach out and touch a hand, caress a cheek. One woman appeared to be staring directly into my eyes, seeing me and disapproving of my invasion, although I was not visible to her. It was intimate and yet remote. It was almost as if I had created all of them and could, like a god, will their behavior.

I did not recognize Gypsy Marr at first; she was not wearing her whore's makeup or one of her whore's costumes, and her whorish bleached blond hair was covered by an auburn wig. She looked ordinary in comparison to some of the other women, no more than pretty in the way of a suburban housewife. It was difficult now to picture her onstage fellating a dildo or leaning over to be "dry"-sodomized by one of the musicians or publishing a book of photographs of her crotch. Gypsy had brought pornography into the mainstream. Intentionally or not, she had proved that it is impossible to satirize or parody our sexual obsessions; there was no extreme in sex, no outrageously base or comical sexual act that would not be perceived as aphrodisiacal. Sooner or later she would publicly mate with a dog or pony and excite animal lovers everywhere. Gypsy was adored, worshiped like a Babylonian temple whore.

The Marquis du Creneau and his daughter were present at the reception but not participating; they stood together, aloof and isolated, contemptuous.

Shame forced me to step away from the telescope. This was dishonest. It was wrong of me to spy on people. I had discovered in myself a voyeurism not much different than the voyeurism that Gypsy Marr exploited, and which I despised.

I went downstairs and prepared a light meal, and when I returned the moon had risen well above the horizon. Its light fogged the air like mist and drew shadows out of the buildings and trees. A man was sitting in the top row of the little stone theater. He periodically lifted binoculars and looked down at the villa. One of the German security guards? He was dressed in black, and I only noticed him because of the pale glow of his face and hands in the moonlight.

I swiveled the telescope and looked at the moon for five or ten minutes, but that mass of dust and rubble could not compare in interest to Alexander's guests. I was about to again spy on them when I heard noises from the corral, clatters and bangs, splintering wood, the bawling of a steer. The bulls were a shifting black mass in the shadowy corral. Crescents of moonlight glowed along the length of their horns, glinted in their eyes. The mass heaved, divided, merged again. Another rail cracked with a sound like a rifle shot. Maybe a couple of the bulls were fighting. It was too dark, too far, for me to see clearly with the unaided eye, and the telescope's magnification was too great to provide a general view—it isolated a head, a flank, a blurred sequence of meaningless action.

I went down the stairs, out the front door, and began jogging across the grounds. The noises stopped when I was about halfway to the corral. I slowed to a walk. An aura of light glowed above the villa's gardens and illuminated the tops of the big trees outside the wall. The band was playing dance music now.

When I was fifty feet from the corral a figure emerged from the shadows and shone a light in my eyes.

"Who is it?"

"Chandler."

"What are you doing here?" It was one of the Germans. "Get that light out of my eyes."

He switched off the flashlight and walked toward me. I had been blinded by the light, and he was just a shadow emerging from other shadows.

"Heinrich?" I said.

"Von Rabenau. Why didn't you attend the reception, Chandler?"

"I didn't want to."

He stopped a few yards away. "Did you hear the noise?"

"From the corral? Yes. I was going over to see what it was about."

"I saw you running," he said. "It's not a good idea to be running around here at night. We might misunderstand."

My eyes had adjusted and I saw that he held a four-cell flashlight in his left hand and an automatic pistol in his right.

"Christ, Walter. Is death the penalty for running?"

"Sometimes."

"Alexander will skin you alive if you shoot one of his guests."

"I suppose that would depend on which guest," he said dryly. "Come along. We'll look at the animals."

"Put the gun away."

"I decide for myself when to take it out," he said, "and when to put it away."

We walked around the arena's outer fence to the corral. The bulls shuffled nervously when we appeared, all of them backing away and turning to face us in a defensive maneuver. They were very nervous. Their smell was strong but not unpleasant. The dominant bull tossed his horns threateningly. Von Rabenau turned on his flashlight, and we saw that the horns were red with fresh blood from the tips to the inward curve. We looked over the other animals but could not see that any had been gored.

"Vicious brutes."

"They aren't vicious," I said. "Give them an exit and they'll try to escape. Trap them, corner them . . ."

We slowly walked along the fence to the rear of the corral, where we found that two of the rails had been cracked.

"You'd better have repairs made tonight," I said.

We did not immediately see the body. The man was dressed in black: black shoes, trousers, and pullover jersey. Only his hands and face were uncovered, and they glowed with a kind of dim phosphorescence in the moonlight. He had been gored many times before the bull finally succeeded in tossing him out of the corral. There were wounds in both thighs, groin, belly, chest, and neck. His clothes were soaked with blood and there were smears of blood, like warpaint, on his pale cheeks. The bull had thrown the body some twenty feet beyond the fence.

"Do you know him?" Von Rabenau asked quietly.

"No, but I saw him earlier tonight."

"Where?"

"He was sitting in the top row of the theater."

Von Rabenau turned and looked up at the hillside.

"I thought he was one of your men. He had binoculars and was looking down into the villa courtyard."

"Did you see others?"

"No."

He gave me the flashlight, unclipped a compact two-way radio from his belt, switched it on, and spoke a few phrases of rapid German.

"Maybe he's one of the guests," I said.

"No."

"One of the performers, then."

"Chandler," he said impatiently, "do you believe that anyone is permitted on this island without first being thoroughly investigated? I have file cabinets filled with dossiers. Histories, documents, gossip, rumors, photographs. After this party we'll begin preparations for next year's party. This man does not belong here."

"Do you have a dossier on me?"

"Of course."

"I'd like to see it."

"It's not pleasant, reading one's dossier. Dossiers are never kind or sentimental."

I heard a noise and turned quickly; some men were running toward us from the grove of trees at the rear of the villa. I heard their feet beating on the earth and the click and jingle of metal and, when they were closer, their hard breathing. Each carried an automatic rifle and wore a backpack and pistol belt. They, like the dead man, were dressed in dark clothing, and their faces and hands had been smeared with charcoal. Even so, I recognized Heinrich and Gunther; the others were not familiar. Von Rabenau issued commands in his harsh movie-Nazi German, and the men immediately scattered. Two ran up the hill toward the theater, two more jogged around toward the front of the villa, and the last, Heinrich, remained with us.

"What's going on?" I asked. "Is this a palace coup, Walter?"

Heinrich grinned at me.

"Go to your cottage, Chandler," von Rabenau said. "Thank you. We can handle it now."

"Handle what?"

"Whatever it might be," Heinrich said.

"I'm going over to see Alexander."

"No," von Rabenau said. "We don't want to disturb the party unless we must. Those people are easily frightened. I'll discuss this with Alexander in a few minutes."

"Discuss *what?* Just what is going on?"

"Nothing is going on. Not now."

"Then it's over? Whatever it is?"

"It hasn't started. I'll walk you to your cottage."

"I don't need an escort."

"My men will be sweeping the grounds. Some of them don't know you. It will be simpler if I accompany you."

"All right."

When we were halfway to the cottage I said, "Really, Walter, I'm not a child—you can tell me what this is about."

"But I don't know what it is about. It's probably nothing."

"Nothing. The corpse of an intruder is found, and three minutes later a squad of commandos swarms out of the night. Nothing, you say."

"We can't know yet. So we must act as if it were a serious matter. You understand. Who is this man? What is he doing here? What are his intentions? Is he alone? My guess . . ."

We reached the cottage.

"Your guess?"

"I suspect that he is a tabloid journalist here to spy on the famous people, take long-range photographs, make his name and fortune. He wouldn't be the first who tried."

"Just the first to climb into a corral of fighting bulls."

"These paparazzi are not terribly intelligent."

I went up the steps and unlocked the door.

"Chandler?"

I turned.

"Perhaps you should stay off the roof for an hour or two. Until this business is cleared up. Our people might worry about you being up there."

"I was looking at the stars," I said.

"Of course you were."

We both laughed.

"Did your new people think I was a sniper?"

"They observed your stargazing."

"Too bad they didn't observe the dead man when he was alive and sitting in the theater."

"Stay awake," he said. "I want to talk to you later."

It was a little after eleven o'clock when von Rabenau returned. He dumped a large cardboard box in the center of the living room floor, removed his suit jacket and tossed it into a chair, and loosened his tie.

"Well?" I asked.

"Nothing much. The fellow was not carrying identification. He was not armed. We found his camera equipment and the binoculars. That's all, so far."

"Sit down, Walter."

"I would appreciate a drink."

"Help yourself."

He went to the bar and after a moment said, "Chandler, do you know that there is a bottle of fifty-year-old Armagnac here?"

"Open it."

After a pause, he said, "Ambrosia!"

"What's in the box, Walter?"

He returned with two balloon glasses nearly half-filled with brandy. He gave me one of the glasses and took the other to a chair near the bookcase.

"Walter, what's in the box?"

"Human heads and hearts."

"Come on."

"Many heads and hearts, speaking metaphorically."

"Go ahead, be cryptic."

"Dossiers."

"My dossier?"

"You said you wanted to see it."

"And you require a box that big to contain my dossier?"

"Your dossier, and the dossiers of all of Alexander's guests, all of the performers and entertainers—all of the people admitted to the island for the week's festivities."

"So."

"I want you to read them."

"No," I said. "Thanks anyway. Take the box with you when you go."

"It really is fascinating material, Chandler. Each dossier is like a novel in miniature. Each is a life up to a certain point—the present—but if you read carefully you'll see that the future is indicated as well. Character is fate. All of these people, the guests—never mind the others for now—all of them have more or less chosen their fates. You'll see that as you read. It's possible to predict the futures of most of them. They've gone beyond the point where they may choose an alternate life, a different fate. Success has limited them. I mean, failure usually forces a person to try another means, a different life. But success, especially the extravagant success these people have enjoyed, is extremely limiting. You understand. The rat finds a passage through the maze and is rewarded with a pellet of food. Success. Will the rat attempt to discover a new path through the maze next time? I don't think so. Why should he?"

"What's the point?"

"I want you to read the dossiers."

"I'm tempted—but no."

"Fine. Whatever you say. But I'm asking you to help me. That is, help me to help Alexander and his family."

"I'll take your dossiers and sell them to the highest bidder."

"You could not do that."

"Why not?"

"I've read *your* dossier. I know you from that. You aren't capable of that kind of treachery. At least not now. Maybe in ten years."

"Go to hell."

"May I have more of the Armagnac?"

"Bring the bottle."

When he returned he said, "You are an intelligent man. We shouldn't need the whole night to conclude an agreement."

He stood directly below the ceiling light, and I could now see the extent of his fatigue.

"I will proceed sequentially," he said. "Listen to me. I am responsible for the security of the Krisos family. They are rich and powerful and famous and therefore always in danger. I was hired by Alexander after his youngest son was nearly killed during a kidnap attempt. You know this. Nicolas is paralyzed for life. Well, of course the family obeyed me and my men for a long time. They were very anxious. But for years nothing has happened. There were no more violent incidents, hardly even the threat of one. And so they have come to see us as their oppressors. We are the only persons in their lives who dare to say no to them. We reduce their freedom; we violate their privacy; we remind them that they are weak, mortal. They have come to despise us."

"They don't despise you, Walter."

He shrugged. "In previous years Heinrich and I attended all of the party functions; we mingled with the guests; we were present in the event something occurred. But now," he said bitterly, "now we are excluded. We have less access to the family than the servants."

His bitterness was a surprise. Von Rabenau had always impressed me as a cool, ironic, enormously self-confident man. He was tough without being hard. I had admired his competence and appreciated his devotion to the Krisos family. He would, I was sure, die to save any one of them. That was his job. He was the perfect soldier; a very tough, intelligent man who also possessed an acute sense of honor. And it was his sense of honor, of justice, that had been offended; he felt that the Krisos family had violated a tacit understanding. And they had, in a way. He had always regarded himself as an equal, and now he saw (and he was right) that they had gradually come to regard him as a servant. A high-level servant, trusted and respected, but still a servant. And, too, I think that he was bitter because his men had been relegated to the same position. All had left the military, but they still regarded themselves as soldiers.

"Chandler, I need your help."

"In what way?"

"I want you to be my eyes and ears for the duration of the party. You must be my conduit."

"Your spy."

"Spy, then. All right." He smiled faintly. "You show an aptitude."

"Tell me about it."

"I don't trust the guests. I don't trust the entertainers. Why should I? I trust no one."

"You trust me, Walter."

"This is the seventh of Alexander's annual bacchanals. It's madness. Can there be a terrorist or ambitious criminal anywhere in the world who wouldn't like to crash this party?"

"Do you have information about some kind of raid or assault?"

"You have heard how birds and mammals can sense when an earthquake is coming. An earthquake, a hurricane, a flood. I don't know. There might be something to it. I feel an earthquake coming. Christ, man, I've felt the preliminary tremors for days."

"Get some sleep," I said. "You're exhausted."

"No, there are things I must do."

"Take the Armagnac with you."

"Thanks. I shall."

When he was gone I carried the big cardboard box

over to the kitchen counter and opened it. There were dozens of files inside, some thick, some thin, some old, and others more recently compiled. I closed my eyes and randomly selected a folder.

CONFIDENTIAL
Gypsy Marr
(Patricia Elena Martinez)

10

GYPSY MARR
(Patricia Elena Martinez)

Precis of file 191-USA
Authority: Von R.
Senior Compiler: Trans-Am 1
Access: Meridian

BORN: El Paso, Texas, August 19, 1962.

FAMILY: Father: Patricio de Vargas Martinez, a Mexican national from Morelia. Mother: Kathleen Mary Lynch, an American citizen of Irish and German ancestry. Sisters: Roberta Ann, born January 7, 1964; Lucille Maria, born April 29, 1966.

EDUCATION: Benito Juarez Elementary School, eight years; El Paso High School, four years; Bowie Junior College, two years. Average grades. Described by teachers as an intelligent but difficult student, often rebellious and challenging of authority. "Defensive." "A dreamer." "Troubled." Referred twice to school psychologist while a student in high school. (Those reports unavailable.) Patricia variously described by classmates as aloof, bossy, self-centered; energetic, imaginative, funny.

YOUTHFUL INTERESTS: High school and junior college theater productions, popular music, movies, and dance. (Her sisters have reported that Patricia would sometimes dance to recorded music for many hours, once to the point of collapse.) She had an extreme ("morbid") interest in the actress Marilyn Monroe, suggesting to her sisters and friends that she is Monroe reincarnate.

SIGNIFICANT EVENTS: (1) Patricia's father abandoned his family when she was nine, returning to his hometown in the state of Morelia, Mexico. He thereafter had no contact with the family. (Mrs. Martinez subsequently obtained a real-estate license and earned a modest living.) (2) In 1979, when Patricia was seventeen, she became pregnant (father unidentified), and in November of that year she had an abortion at a clinic in Guadalajara, Mexico. This has been denied by associates of Miss Marr. Her family refused to be interviewed. The clinic involved has suppressed the medical records; the owner and staff refused to discuss the matter. However, two former employees of the clinic, an OR nurse and a nurse's aid, report that because of medical complications a hysterectomy (complete removal of the uterus) was performed.

PSYCHOLOGICAL PROFILE: During 1992 and a part of 1993, Gypsy Marr consulted a New York clinical psychologist, Dr. Gregory Fassbinder. Dr. Fassbinder is board-certified, a member in good standing of the American Psychological Association, and the author of two popular books: *It's All in Your Mind* and *One, Two, Three, FREE.* Copies of transcribed sessions with Gypsy Marr, and Dr. Fassbinder's notes, have been obtained. Random excerpts here provided. Complete transcriptions are available in master file.

In 1982 Patricia left college and moved to Los Angeles to become a film actress. She resided at a number of locations in the Los Angeles area, sporadically employed as a waitress, sales clerk, aerobics instructor, and, she later claimed, prostitute. (The prostitution claim cannot be confirmed: she does not appear in police records; there has been no confirmation by her friends and acquaintances of the period, no reliable evidence. It is suspected that her confession of prostitution was issued for purposes of publicity.)

In 1965, after nearly three years of failure

in Los Angeles (Hollywood), Patricia Martinez (hereafter calling herself Gypsy Marr) moved to San Francisco. Within six months she was that city's most popular performer—a "cult figure." She formed a small group of backup singers and dancers, devised an act, and performed at homosexual venues in and around San Francisco. The primarily homosexual audience enthusiastically approved even the most amateurish aspects of Gypsy's dancing, singing, and acting. It has been suggested that if she had not been so amateurish, she would not have been so well received. The audience especially approved her blatant, exaggerated sexuality, which was viewed as a charming parody of the American "sex goddess myth."

"We adored her. She was fresh and decadent at the same time."

"Back then Gypsy reminded me of one of those inflatable female dolls, the kind they call the lonely man's companion. Her function was so obvious."

"She was so deathly pale and wriggly and squishy, and very sincere."

"Gypsy is so enormously, fabulously famous all over the world now, better known than Hitler, more loved than the pope. She has the most coveted pussy ever. Can you imagine—people take her seriously! And she started out as our own sly private joke."

"Gypsy was *your* (heterosexual) fantasy, not *ours*. She was sweet and comic and kind of sad, really."

"When I think about Gypsy, it scares me. She's a Dr. Frankenstein who created out of herself a Frankenstein monster."

After twenty-two months in San Francisco, Gypsy moved to New York. She hired a professional choreographer, musicians, and dancers and prepared a new act concerned with mother-son, father-daughter incest. Again she was enthusiastically received by the homosexual community, but she very quickly "broke out" and attracted a general audience that has since then grown and expanded throughout the world.

From Dr. Fassbinder's notes

To date Miss Marr has related three sharply conflicting versions of her childhood: they might be termed (1) Cinderella; (2) Street Gamine; (3) Normal Child. Each version of her early family life is a fantasy construct, and the details may change from session to session, or even within a session. She becomes irritable when contradictions are pointed out, saying that each version is true, and what is truth anyway but what one believes at a particular moment. At this point it is difficult to determine whether Miss Marr herself can clearly distinguish between the real and the fantasy elements in her life; that is, whether her various "legends" possess the affective resonance and motive force of actual experience. Conscious lies or ego-integrated fantasies? She also believes in every conceivable sort of "magic," i.e., the ability of the human "universal mind" to dissolve the boundaries of natural law and triumph over death, time and space, material reality. She may or may not be a victim of bipolar mood disorder, as I suspect, but she certainly fits the dictionary definition of solipsistic: (L. *solus,* alone, & *ipse,* self) the idea that the self is the only reality.

Today Miss Marr told me that her father and brothers had repeatedly raped her when she was a child. She had a very smug cat-licking-cream expression as she provided the licentious details. She had no brothers, of course, and her father vanished when she was nine. I believe she was trying out a new "legend" on me, perhaps the scenario for another video production or concert routine, and when I could not conceal my impatience she angrily walked out of the office. This is the third time she has broken off a session. She will return. I believe that she will keep coming back until, in her mind, she has defeated me—established an imagined dominance.

Miss Marr suffers from an insidious form of bipolar mood disorder with attendant paranoid ideation and delusional self-aggrandizement. She confesses to occasional hallucinations, terming them *visions* or *messages.* A definite *borderline psychotic.* In fact, it is likely that she periodically crosses the "line" and experiences psychotic episodes. These are not recognized by others (laymen) because of her great celebrity and her deliberately cultivated eccentric persona. The more aberrant (diseased) her behavior and theatrical performances, the more she is idolized, and thus the disease is reinforced. The world has difficulty in accepting that a person who is extraordinarily successful in his/her chosen field can be diseased or, further, that the disease itself may be responsible for the success. Fame, wealth, and adulation have deeply rooted Miss Marr's disease, driven her more deeply into the fortress of her self. Prognosis *very poor* at present. Only an extreme crisis of some sort, personal or professional, might cause her to become amenable to treatment. A prolonged psychotic episode, perhaps, during which she suffers greatly, might trigger a "conversion"; that is, a devastating disintegration of the personality might enable the therapist to commence the long and arduous process of "putting the pieces back together." She must then, paradoxically, become sicker before she can become well.

I have never treated a more stubborn or frustrating patient. No progress is being made. She is clearly determined to fight me every inch of the way, deceive me with false symptoms, contrived dreams, fake emotions, confused recollections, outright lies, insults, sexual provocations . . . She shares with the sociopathic personality the virtual inability to experience guilt, remorse, regret, self-anger—any consciously self-critical thought or emotion.

Today Miss Marr wasted an entire session telling me about her past life as the sister-wife of an Egyptian pharaoh, Rameses II as I recollect (my recorder malfunctioned). She told me, as if relating the most prosaic of memories, of an ancient court life, its leisures and intrigues, foods and games, religious and secular rites, and she described the personalities of priests and officials, including her "brother-husband" Rameses II. She paid no attention to my incredulity. Her version of ancient Egypt was childlike and filled with anachronistic nonsense. Toward the end of our session she told me, in lewd detail, about a wild palace orgy during which she copulated with nine men in succession. This, of course, is the plot of her most recent video. When I pointed that out, she said, "Of course. All of my artistic works are derived from my life." I have purchased and viewed all of her videos and movie tapes. Her life, if she is to be believed, consists mostly of palace orgies, lesbianism, incest, bestiality, necrophilia, pedophilia, and grotesqueries not yet named. It astonishes me that the public, her public anyway, not only accepts this sewage, but is positively enchanted by it. She has very shrewdly discovered the moral limits of a vast part of today's popular culture; that is, that there are no limits.

Today Miss Marr told me that last night she had participated in a satanic ritual during which a baby was dismembered and eaten. She watched me very closely to observe the expression of disgust on my face, and then she smiled slowly and with great pleasure.

Today Miss Marr attempted to seduce me. I have expected it. She has several times over recent weeks undergone a subtle transformation that makes one abruptly think of sex, and sex with her. It is a kind of softening and opening of the personality, with a strong hint of brazenness, a look, an expression around the eyes and mouth that signals availability. Probably most women project similarly when sexually stimulated, but Miss Marr is bolder than most, and highly seductive. Her intent could not have been clearer even if we had been apes and she, in estrus, had presented me her hindquarters. I calmly told her that I was happily married and that even if I had a desire to go astray, my professional ethics forbade it. She laughed at me. People are scandalized when a therapist has sexual relations with a patient. They do not know that, as often as not, it is the patient who is the active seducer. One must be strong.

What can I say in my defense? The flesh is weak; my intentions were good; I could not help myself? Afterward she was mocking and terminated the therapy.

Investigation continuing per instructions von R. Will attempt to confirm that subject tested HIV positive in March of this year.

All materials available in master file through standard access codes.

11

At sunrise I jogged across the grassy park and then up past the stables and garages and the tall aluminum mast—with its dozens of bright silky flags hanging limply in the stagant heat—and along the twisty rutted road toward the temple. At this hour the sky was nearly as dark a blue as the sea–cobalt—and filmed over with an opalescent vapor.

I jogged up one hill and down another, along a level stretch past Sophia Krisos's white cottage and its flower-speckled gardens, and down the long incline toward the east end of the island. Sun, heat, stones, spiny brush, sour-tasting air, dust dust dust. I tried to alleviate the boredom by pretending that I was Phidippides, the messenger who, some twenty-five hundred years ago, had run the twenty six—plus miles from the plains of Marathon to Athens. "The Persians have been defeated," he told the Athenians, and then he fell dead.

I ran helter-skelter down the long central ridge *(I have good news, Athens!)*, skidding in the dust, loosening rocks that rolled down the slope ahead of me. Athens—

the temple—was from this height just a scatter of mar-
ble-like tombstones. The sea beyond was luminous.

I reached level ground and sprinted the last hundred
yards to the cliffs edge. "Athens . . . ," I said. I was
thoroughly winded and a little dizzy, a little sick from
the heat and my exertions. A toothless hag clutched my
arm; a sick old man breathed his death into my lungs.
All of the able men and slaves had gone to fight at Marathon; only the old men, the infirm, the children, and
the females of all ages had remained behind. The crowd
anxiously pressed in around me. "Athens," I said. "We
have defeated the Persians." And then I staggered away
and died in the dark, cool shade of a tree.

Later, resurrected, I descended the cliff face and
swam for half an hour, and afterward began the long
walk back to the villa complex. It was all uphill. Within
a few minutes I was sweating again. The sun burned a
white hole in the smooth blue fabric of sky and glazed
the air with refracted light.

Sophia Krisos was working in her garden when I approached. She held a sprinkler can in one gloved hand
and beckoned me with the other. She wore a long black
dress and sandals, as usual, but today her hair was covered by a floppy wide-brimmed straw hat. The garden
was planted in alternate rows of vegetables and flowers:
squash, roses, carrots, marigolds, peas, tulips, onions,
violets, tomatoes . . . It seemed ten degrees cooler there
amid the bright splashes of color.

"Chay," she said. "Good morning." Her toes and
ankles were dusty.

"Good morning."

"You wet," she said. "You smell bad."

I smiled and nodded.

She lowered the sprinkling can to the ground and led me over to the stone cistern. There was a red-painted pump on top, and she began working the lever, saying, "This is a very thirsty day." After half a dozen pumps, clear water gushed out of the spout. I took the long-handled tin dipper, filled it and drank, filled it again and drank.

Then she led me to a little arbor of vine-covered slats of wood. I had to duck my head to pass through the arched doorway. The roof lattice was covered by vines, too, and inside there was a dim, aqueous light, a greeny bottom-of-the-sea feeling.

"Sit," Sophia said, and I obeyed and sat down on the white marble bench. "Wait," she said, and she went away.

I liked her. She was worth any number of Alexander's international tarts. It was hard to understand, though, why she remained here in this cottage, on this barren island, banished to a sort of self-imposed exile.

She returned with a platter containing two clumps of grapes, one red and the other green, a peach, and a glass of cool white wine. She watched me eat, sometimes making small motions with her lips and teeth, as if she were biting a grape, sipping the wine. Her eyes were a clear gray-green and, it seemed to me, expressive of considerable intelligence. One has a tendency to underestimate the intelligence of a person who is not fluent in his own language. But Sophia Krisos was very bright, like Alexander, Kon, Maria, like Nico.

I asked, "Do you mind if I smoke?"

"What?"

I held up a cigarette and the lighter.

"Yes, smoke. I like the man who smoke."

I lit the cigarette and blew smoke up toward the roof lattice.

"The party," she said. "It is good?"

"No."

"Bad party."

"I think so, yes."

"I think so, too. Bad people, bad things. Always every year."

"Will you come to the party?"

"Me? No, never."

"Well, it will be over in a week."

"How is the work?" she asked.

"Work? The temple? It's going very well."

She stared intently at me for a time and then turned away. "Someone must tell. The temple is new. Not old."

"No, it's quite old."

"I mean, temple is not old *here*. Moved here from other place."

She turned back to look at me and softly, sympathetically, said, "You understand?"

"I guess so. The entire temple ruin was moved here from another site. From where, Sophia?"

"This I don't know."

"When?"

"Three year."

"Why?"

"You know."

"Because Alexander and Kon and Maria wanted me to come here to live."

"Yes."

I felt as if I'd been kicked in the groin. No one, not von Rabenau, not one of the temple workers, not even the village drunk, had exposed the Krisos family secret. Secret, trick, joke.

"Thank you for telling me," I said.

"Is very bad?"

"I've wasted a lot of time and work."

"I am sorry."

I stood up. "Thank you for the fruit and the wine."

"Come to see," she said. "Bring Maria. Bring my sons."

When I reached the villa complex I saw that Aguilar and a plump, middle-aged Spaniard were working out in the bullring. I leaned against the outer fence and watched them. The "peon" ran the horns while Aguilar practiced with the *muleta*. Aguilar wore a T-shirt, sneakers, and a swimsuit not much bigger than a jockstrap that exposed the skin on his upper thighs—round, glossy, puckered wounds three and four inches in diameter. He had been seriously gored half a dozen times, a lot for so young a man. He was either foolishly brave or unlucky.

The paunchy Spaniard's clothes were soaked with sweat, and his breathing sounded like the panting of a dog. A few minutes after I arrived he wandered away, leaned over, and vomited onto the sand.

I climbed over the outer fence and then walked down the passageway between fences and out into the ring.

"Good morning," Aguilar said.

"Good morning."

"My man José drank too much last night."

"I thought that might be the case. Do you want me to run the horns for a while?"

"Will you? That will be fine. José, go and lie down in the shade." And then quietly he said, "José has received many serious wounds from the bottle over the years."

The *carretara* was like the frame of a wheelbarrow, with a bicycle tire, smoothly worn handles, and a set of bull's horns mounted in front. Aguilar experimented with a few passes, some good and others deliberately bad—potentially dangerous—to see if I would follow the cloth correctly. The idea was for me to behave as a good bull might.

"All right," Aguilar said, and I ran the horns for twenty minutes. Aguilar practiced first with his right hand, then his left, and finished with a series of *naturales en rondo*.

I was breathing hard and my lower back ached.

"You're a good little bull," he said.

"Then I deserve the *indulto*."

"Granted. You are spared."

"Where is Orozco?"

"He returned to Spain."

"Are you going to kill all six bulls, then?"

"I might. Unless you want to kill three of them."

"Sure," I said. "If I can call in air strikes."

He smiled and offered me the muleta and wooden sword. "Let me see you work."

"I'm a specialist with the cape. That's where my greatness is immediately apparent. I'm a poet with the cape."

"Well, *El Poeta*, let me see."

A cape was hanging over the *barrera* fence. I got it and shook it out while returning to the center of the ring. I had practiced hundreds of hours with the cape while living in Mexico; for me it had become an aesthetic exercise, a kind of ballet, separate from its application in the ring.

Amused, skeptical, Aguilar watched while I ran through my repertoire; *veronicas, media veronicas, serpentinas, chicuelinas, gaoneras,* the *mariposa.*

Aguilar applauded. "Very pretty," he said.

"I excel at *toreo de salon.*"

"A poet of the cape indeed." He laughed.

"As long as bulls are excluded from the salon."

"I think you are ready," he said. "Do you want to see your *novillo* now?"

"No," I said, but I followed him out of the ring and around to the corrals. The bulls gathered defensively and lifted their heads to watch us. Together in the corral, flank to flank, they seemed six separate components of a single entity—one beast. They were wild. They had been more or less domesticated for thousands of years, and yet they remained wild. These bulls possessed no more in common with beef cattle than wolves have with your golden retriever. Their instinctual integrity—their essence—had not been radically altered or diluted. They hadn't been bred for docility. They hadn't been bred for ease of handling or quantity of milk or tenderness of the loin. Instead, the fighting bull had been bred for the very qualities that should have ensured its extinction: power and speed and courage, a furious wildness.

The *novillo* was penned separately. He was a smaller version of the others, an adolescent among the adults.

Not small—small only in comparison with the others. I estimated his weight at about 400 kilos. He was heavy through the chest and shoulders. His tossing hump rose as we approached. His horns were perfectly symmetrical, thick and black at the base, curving outward from the head and then forward, tapering to the sharp ivory tips.

"How old is he?" I asked Aguilar.

"Three years. He's a real *novillo*."

"Does he appear honest to you?"

"He's young. The young are usually more honest. Are you tempted?"

"No."

"Are you sure?"

"I haven't trained for years. I haven't even looked at a fighting bull for years. No, it's impossible."

"We could blunt the horns."

"No."

"Well, maybe you'll train with me in the mornings. José isn't up to it."

"Sure."

"Tomorrow, seven o'clock."

"I'll be here."

He smiled and slapped me on the shoulder. "El Poeta," he said. "El Estético."

I remained behind to study the *novillo*. He was a superb animal, ideally conformed, and probably honest, as Aguilar had said. *Honesty* in this context meant "naive, stupid." Three-year-old bulls were less combat-wise than four-year-olds. The younger ones had weight, the deadly horns, they tried just as hard to kill you, but they were easier to fool. You could make a few mistakes with them and not end up in the infirmary. They were fast, eager, impulsive—"honest," you hoped. I had fought animals nearly as big in Mexico and done all right, with one exception. Still, the Spanish bulls were reputed to be more dangerous than the Mexican bulls; and I had not trained for years; and I wasn't a kid now, as "honest" as the *novillos*. The thrill, the crazy high, the adrenaline rush of fighting a big, extremely dangerous animal and then killing it—with a bit of deception and a sword thrust—no longer seemed worth the possible penalty.

Now, today, it was easy to imagine one of those horns entering my leg or belly or chest. The horn went into human flesh smoothly and deeply, like an ice pick into gelatin. You felt it go in. You knew the horn was in you although the pain was not immediate. It was a rather dreamy experience, revolving on a horn and then flying through the air, wondering if the bull would get in a few more thrusts before being distracted by your friends.

I walked to the cottage gloomily certain that somehow or other I would find myself in the ring with the *novillo* before this week ended. Unwillingly, reluctantly there, in the same way I had found myself diving off the cliff a few days ago.

12

Back in the cottage I showered, shaved, dressed, and went downstairs to the kitchen to scavenge a second breakfast. The only eggs in the refrigerator had been removed from the bellies of sturgeon. More fruit then, and toast and coffee.

"Yo."

Jack Clyde Black was standing on the other side of the rear screened door, a palm shading his eyes.

"You in there, son?"

"I am. Come on in, Mr. Black."

"Blackjack, call me Blackjack," he said, entering. He was wearing a cream-colored safari outfit, jacket and trousers, and beautiful soft, ankle-high boots that looked as though they wouldn't last half a day in rough country. His grizzled hair was parted near the center and greased flat.

"Care for a cup of coffee?" I asked him.

"That's what I come here about. We're having breakfast out back, me and Poochy and the fellow in the cottage on the other side. Come on out and sit with us. We ordered enough food for ten ravenous wetbacks."

"I'll just change out of these shorts and into trousers."

"Don't bother, unless you're concerned that your bare legs will unduly excite my Poochy."

"Poochy will just have to take her chances, then."

He smiled faintly, his face crinkling like dried mud.

"Who is staying in the cottage on your other side?" I asked.

"An Englishman. His name is Barley or Wheat or something like that. I don't know—he might be a lord. Lord Barley. He looks like a lord, and he walks like a lord, and he quacks like a lord . . ."

He squinted at me, then nodded, as if awarding me a point or two in some obscure contest, said, "Five minutes," and went outside.

I'd had time to skim Jack Clyde Black's dossier: oil money, natural gas money, real estate money, U.S. government contract money, money flowing in and out of Middle Eastern principalities and remote African nations. He had been indicted by several separate federal grand juries: for income tax evasion, violations of banking laws, fraud (a savings-and-loan company fiasco), and illegal arms sales. None of the cases had yet reached trial. He had, according to the report, lost nearly $200 million during the last ten years. He, like Alexander Krisos, had been born into poverty. He had started from scratch. But, unlike Alexander, he seemed rapidly en route back to scratch.

Poochy (Louise Lurleen Black, née Cory), twenty-six, was his third wife; they had been married less than a year. Her resume was standard for the trophy wife: cheerleader (at the University of Texas); winner of many beauty contests; model, dancer, singer, actress—bride. Her father had died when she was eight, and so she had been raised by her ambitious mother, who had worked very hard and sacrificed so that her daughter might someday qualify to marry a rich man.

Virtue may be its own reward, but beauty is frequently compensated in coin of the realm.

Two white-jacketed servants were preparing the table when I went outside. Jack Clyde Black and his wife were not present, nor had "Lord Barley" arrived.

The breakfast table was set deep into the gardens, shaded by a tree with leaves like an elephant's ears, and near a pond that contained dozens of the whiskered neon carp. I idly wondered why—since Orientals were supposed to possess such an exquisite aesthetic sense—why then, they elected to raise such blatantly ugly fish. One might as well fuss over toads or cultivate stink-weed.

The servants spread an immaculate white linen cloth over the table, laid down four place settings, and then arranged half a dozen chafing dishes around a central bouquet of pink and white roses. A door slammed, and I turned and watched the Blacks approach down the flagstone path. Louise Black was tall and slender, an inch or two taller than her husband, with hair that was a rare reddish gold, thick and wavy, gleaming. She was blond in the direct sunlight, a redhead in the shadows beneath the trees.

Jack Clyde was proud of her, his prize female: he presented her to me if she were a creature that he himself had devised and fabricated.

"Pleased to meet you, Jay Chandler," she said. "I've been wanting to greet my neighbor." Her slantwise gaze was quizzical, perhaps amused, as she measured my response to her physical presence.

I asked, "Do you mind if I don't call you Poochy?"

She smiled and drawled, "I'll mind if you do, sir."

We sat down at the table. The servants approached and quietly attended to our needs, pouring coffee and juice and water, and then discreetly withdrawing.

"And why are you here, Jay?" Louise asked me.

The question puzzled me for a moment, until I realized that she really meant: *Who are you? What have you done? What have you accomplished in your life? Who are you to be invited to this exclusive gathering?* She was demanding my credentials.

"I'm a friend of the family's," I said.

"*Are* you?" She helped herself to some of the food in the chafing dishes while evaluating this piece of intelligence, and then said, "Have you known them long?"

"Quite a while."

"You're a business associate?"

"I went to school with Konstantin, Alexander's son."

"Oh, yes." She tried not to show her exasperation. The question had not been answered. The problem remained: *Who are you? What do you do? What is your exact position in this delicately calibrated social machine?*

She ate slowly, in tiny nibbles, as if eating in public were a vaguely disgraceful procedure.

"But then," she said, "why aren't you staying in the house if you are a good friend of the family?"

"I prefer the cottage."

"I don't," Jack Clyde Black said. "Not one bit. It's an insult. I've been insulted before, but never by a Greek, goddamn it."

"The cottages are really much better," I said. "You have more space, better facilities, privacy."

"You don't get the point, son. It's a matter of proximity. Proximity to the throne. Here, I'm three hundred yards from the throne. I might as well be back home in Houston."

Blackjack had started explaining the necessity of being close to the throne—Krisos—when we saw a very tall, thin, round-shouldered man ambling toward us. Even at a distance he was disturbingly familiar. His uncoordinated walk and the movements of his head—like involuntary tics—suggested that he might be the victim of a neurological disorder. He skirted an ornamental sundial, ducked his head to pass below some low branches, lifted his long, bony face, and smiled at us. It was the kind of smile employed by actors playing Satan. He was a disturbing apparition.

He reached the table and bowed to Louise. "P-p-pardon my unforgivable t-t-tardiness," he said in a deep, fruity voice.

"Lord Barley," Blackjack said, "this is Jay Chandler. Jay, Lord Barley."

"So p-p-pleased, really," he said to me, inclining his head.

"Though I am neither a peer nor the particular grain named by our host. I am a Rye. Nigel Basil Rye."

He sat down between Jack and Louise and beamed at each of us in turn, as if to absorb our admiration as a reptile absorbs the warmth of the sun.

"I was acquainted with your twin brother," I said.

"Ah, poor Simon."

"I'm sorry about what happened."

"Your sorrow is noted, dear boy."

"Something happened to your brother?" Louise asked.

"Alas, he is no more."

"Oh, I am *so* sorry," she said. Blackjack nodded; he was sorry, too.

"I am here to attend to what is usually t-t-termed the arrangements. To dispose of, you know, the remains."

"Did he die here?" Louise asked. "On this island?"

"He was p-p-precipitated out," Nigel Rye said vaguely. He lifted the lid on a chafing dish, lowered it, lifted another, and peered inside. "He was my genetic r-r-replica. My biological ditto. I have been abruptly halved." He scooped a yellow mass of scrambled eggs onto his plate and began buttering a slice of toast. "Diminished incrementally, by age, and now this c-c-cruel stroke. I am, and yet I am not." He took a spoon and lavished raspberry preserves over the toast. "*Ab ovo, ad finem. Ad infinitum,* as well, for poor dear Simon."

"Where is your brother now?" Louise asked. "I mean . . ."

"Now? Oh my, now . . ." He lifted the lid of another chafing dish, stabbed a chain of pork sausages with his fork, and deposited them on his plate. "Well, he is in a meat freezer. So I was told. A meat freezer, can you imagine? P-p-poor, dear Simon."

"No," Louise said firmly. "Your brother is in heaven now, Mr. Barley."

He stared at her with rounded eyes, then sawed off a sausage link and said, "It's entirely possible that he now inhabits these lovely sausages. A s-s-secular form of t-ttransubstantiation, you know." And then he bit into the sausage with his incisors, spraying a mist of grease, and chewed while smiling happily around the table.

Louise Black's nostrils flexed; perhaps she had caught a whiff of sulphur in the air. There was something demonic about Nigel Basil Rye (and his late twin, Simon). She and her husband were clearly baffled by the man's lack of sentiment; he spoke cheerfully, with much eye crinkling and a mirthful display of yellowed teeth. And he devoured the fraternal pork sausages with a cannibalistic gusto.

I had known several pairs of identical twins, but none so uncannily alike as the Ryes, both physically and in personality. Nature and nurture had dealt them the same strange hand.

After a long silence, Louise Black asked, "And what do you do, Mr. Barley?"

"Rye. Do? My work? I am an antiquarian."

"Oh. An anti-aquarian."

"Madam?"

"You mean, you are against aquarians."

He stared at her, his lips stained by raspberry jam, and then he beamed and said, "Violently opposed."

"Is anti-aquarianism lucrative?"

"Indeed. Oh yes, indeed, boodles of lucre."

"Chandler here," Blackjack said, "is a friend of the family."

"Ah. Oh my, yes. A friend of *the* family. There is lucre in that, I'm c-c-certain."

Rye patted his lips with the napkin and then gravely studied the result. He seemed very pleased and, one by one, showed us the napkin, as if to say, "There! You see!" But what we were expected to see besides sausage grease and raspberry stains was not evident.

Blackjack shifted in his chair. "Why does food taste so good out of doors?"

Nigel Rye stared at him as if astounded by the originality and salience of the remark.

"Indeed!" he cried. "Why!"

13

Von Rabenau's office was tucked away among some trees on the east side of the villa complex. He was peering intently at a computer terminal when I entered. A massive computer softly ticked nearby, and there were terminals on the other desks, file cabinets, a fax machine, an elaborate radio transceiver, and in the rear a sofa upon which Karl Heinrich snored with a noise like a dog snarling.

Apparently, von Rabenau had not been to bed; his suit was wrinkled and stained, his eyes were puffy, and his cheeks glinted with blond beard stubble. The bottle of Armagnac, nearly empty now, sat on his desk next to a stack of paper cups and a paper plate littered with square crusts of bread. It was a strange way to eat a sandwich, from the inside out, leaving behind those peculiar tooth-indented relics.

He punched some keys and the printer commenced rattling. "So," he said. He linked his fingers behind his head and leaned back in the swivel chair.

I said, "I've just had breakfast with Lord Barley."

"Lord Barley."

"Nigel Rye, actually."

"Nigel Rye. Yes."

"Did you know he was on the island?"

"Of course."

"He's here to claim his brother's body."

"Yes."

"He said that it was being preserved in a meat freezer in the village."

Von Rabenau exhaled wearily, leaned forward to splash some brandy into two paper cups, and pushed one toward me.

"The corpse is no longer in the freezer. It was stolen late last night."

I looked at him.

"Vanished."

"That's great, Walter."

"Poof." He snapped his fingers and grinned. He seemed a little giddy from fatigue and brandy.

"So now there's a body snatcher on the island."

"Yes."

"What are you going to tell Nigel Rye?"

"More brandy?"

"I haven't touched this one."

"Actually, Chandler, I thought it might be best if you talked to Nigel Rye."

"No."

"Tell him . . . tell him that his brother's remains were inadvertently transferred to the mainland. And that we are confident that the corpus will soon be retrieved."

"Simon was misfiled."

"Something like that. We must stall him until after the party."

"This morning he made a joke about his brother being transubstantiated into the breakfast sausage."

"Really? What kind of man is he?"

"He's comical in a sinister way. Like his late twin. What about your investigation? Do you know who killed Simon?"

"There is no investigation."

"Why not?"

"Alexander doesn't want one."

"Why not?"

"Well, it's obvious, isn't it? He doesn't want me to find the killer."

"Does Alexander know who killed Simon Rye?"

"Certainly."

"And he wants to protect the man."

"Or men, yes."

"He doesn't want any publicity, turmoil, police looking into the affairs of his island. Is that it?"

Von Rabenau shrugged and poured the last of the brandy into his cup.

"Maybe Alexander killed him."

Von Rabenau nodded. "Eureka."

"No?"

"That might be true if this were a detective story."

"What is it?"

"A mess, a black farce."

The printer shut off and in the ensuing silence Heinrich snarled and then emitted a prolonged groan.

I said, "What about the man who was killed by the bulls last night? Was he stored in the meat freezer?"

"Yes."

"Was his corpse snatched?"

"No, unfortunately. We would not mind at all if he vanished into sausages."

"Have you identified him?"

"Not yet, but we will."

"Unless the corpse is spirted away."

"Even then."

Heinrich, writhing on the sofa, snarled and growled and woofed as if he were brawling with a pack of fellow canines.

"Karl has bad dreams," von Rabenau said.

"So must the island's cats. Walter, there is a file on Alexander among those you gave me."

He did not appear interested.

"Why was that file included?"

"It was not supposed to be included."

"Well, it was."

"Give it back."

"Does Alexander know such a file exists?"

"Of course. He authorized it."

"Why?"

"Guess."

"I can't imagine."

"Let us conjecture. It could be that he wished to learn how good his security apparatus is at finding out things. How thorough and efficient. How accurate. If we succeeded in compiling an exhaustive dossier on Alexander himself and his activities, it would mean that the other dossiers were reliable."

"I don't think so."

"I don't think so, either."

"Try again."

"Perhaps, if we compiled and coordinated all of the

information available about Alexander, dug it all up, then he would know pretty much what other persons and agencies could dig up about his life and family and friends and business enterprises and crimes. He would then know what could be dug up and what would continue to be buried."

"Do you think that might be it?"

"No," he said.

"Then why did he authorize you to investigate his life?"

"I've always wondered."

"It's obvious that you and your team didn't compile all of those dossiers. There's a tremendous amount of work involved. The subjects are from dozens of countries. It would be impossible for your team to do it all."

"We hire people."

"But then, Walter, the people you hire have access to all of the information—the dirt."

"They are discreet."

"I can't believe that. What keeps them discreet?"

"Fear. Money. Fear. Money."

"Maybe," I said.

"Have you read your own file, Chandler?"

"No."

He smiled cynically.

I stood up. "Walter, I respected you and your security team. But now . . ."

"You are giving me a headache." He pressed his index fingers against his temples.

"I saw you as a model of German thoroughness and efficiency. And then I came in here this morning and see that everything is disorder, confusion, chaos."

His fingertips pressed harder against his temples. He cocked his thumbs.

"And you eat sandwiches like a fucking idiot."

Von Rabenau closed his eyes and pulled the triggers.

14

There was not an attendant or mechanic on duty at the garages. I had intended to drive one of the utility vehicles down to the village until I noticed Alexander's motorcycle parked at the rear. The key was in the ignition. It was a big Harley-Davidson, a steel and chrome monster, a rogue machine. Only 180 miles had been clocked on the odometer. Alexander loved that bike. He felt about machines as Maria did about horses, and he would be very angry with me for taking it.

I wheeled it outside where the turning spokes flicked away lines of light and the layered crimson paint pulsed gently, like hot coals.

It was very hot now, well into the nineties. The dust smelled like burnt gunpowder. Much of the eastern Mediterranean was broiling in a stationary high-pressure system centered over the Libyan plateau.

But it was relatively cool on the motorcycle, with the speed-generated wind snapping my shirt and evaporating my sweat. My lower legs were invisible in the swirling dust. I drove swiftly down off the high ground and through the park in front of the villa (hoping that

Alexander was watching), turned right then, roaring between the hillside theater and the bullring, on through another grove of trees and past the security office and barracks and the squat building that housed the generators; and then I picked up the narrow, rutted road that meandered south, toward the sea.

This road, like the one near the temple, had been blasted out of cliffs. There were no rails, no reflectors, no signs warning of a dangerous curve or rockslide area. On my right was the cliff face; on my left, sky, air; two hundred feet below, the sea burst white and creamed over the reefs.

I left the motorcycle in a no-parking zone in front of the police station. The village was noisy and crowded with a mix of villagers and *barbaros*. Packs of strangers roamed the lanes, hustled by packs of impudent boys. Music played too loudly everywhere; dogs barked; the church's bells chimed the hour. Chairs and tables had overflowed the café terraces onto the sidewalks and streets. The carnival atmosphere would last all week. This impromptu party was a confused, vulgar analogue to the party at the villa complex. It was perhaps the better party, freer and gayer and more spontaneous. Anything might happen here. Little would occur up at the villa that Alexander had not willed.

I walked around the plaza several times and then sat on a bench in the park. A boy sold me a can of soda for twice the usual price. All around me the air hummed with a babel of languages: Greek, English, French, Spanish, Japanese, Arabic, and two tongues that I could not identify—one probably Slavonic, the other a glottal African dialect spoken by several black men in dark suits.

All wore wraparound sunglasses, and their faces were tense with pride and menace. They looked like gangsters. They probably were Biki Benematale's bodyguards, anxious now, furious at being separated from their master. Pamela Bristol was not in any of the cafés or bars, and the desk clerk told me that she was no longer registered at the hotel. I found her down at the harbor, sitting alone on a stone bench at the end of the quay. Gulls fluttered around her like moths around an electric light; she was surrounded by a flashing cloud of harshly demanding birds. They scattered when I approached, went off to perch on pier posts and bollards.

She turned and looked up at me. "Oh. Hello."

"Hello, Pamela. How did you charm the seagulls?"

"I charmed them with magic words and a bag full of bread pieces. But then they wouldn't go away. I started fearing them. You know, like Tippi Hedren in the Hitchcock film. I was afraid to move. I thought that in an hour or two I should be cemented inside a pile of bird mute."

She wore sandals, white shorts, and a blue-and-white-striped blouse.

"The desk clerk told me that you'd left the hotel."

"Did you come to the village to see me?"

"Yes."

"How nice. Yes, I left the hotel. I moved in with a sweet family whose name I cannot pronounce."

"Was the hotel too noisy?"

"There were drunken strangers pounding on my door all night long. Why is it that when some men get drunk they immediately run off to a female's hotel room and pound on the door and beg for entry? Do they actually believe that any woman would let them in? 'Oh yes, you strange drunken brute, how pleased I am that you stopped by to do me.'"

"Well," I said, "it's always worked for me."

She smiled.

"I'm excavating a little temple on the cliffs south of the village. Would you like to see it?"

"I don't know. Would I?"

"It's a beautiful spot. There might be a breeze. We could bring a picnic lunch, swim, relax."

"Well . . ."

"Yes, Pamela. The word is *yes*."

"Is it? All right then."

We walked up to the plaza and had a drink in the Café Socrates while the kitchen packed a picnic lunch; then walked to where I'd left the motorcycle. It was surrounded by a group of somber boys who appeared to be reverently praying over the bike as to some great new idol.

Pamela laughed. "What a fantastic machine! Is it yours?"

"No, Alexander's. Climb onto the seat behind me. Hold tight."

"Did you borrow it?" she asked, mounting the passenger seat.

"I stole it."

"Stole it. Well, Alexander won't be happy about that, will he?"

"That's the idea."

"You want to make him angry?"

"Yes."

"Why?"

"Because he makes me angry."

I turned the ignition key, and the shiny techno-god softly rumbled. "Ah!" the boys said. The engine was not loud at 8,000 RPMs, but implicit in the sound, waiting, were earthquakes, volcanic eruptions, thunderclaps and lightning, godly manifestations. "Ah!" the boys cried piously when we pulled away from the curb and cruised toward the cliff road.

Neither the temple nor my camp had been disturbed. The villagers wouldn't take anything, but I wasn't so sure about some of the *barbaros*.

Pamela was delighted with the temple ruin and the clifftop view of the cove, the expanse of sea and the hazy islands to the southeast. But she would not approach the edge of the cliff, saying that she suffered from vertigo. "I'm afraid I'll become dizzy and fall. Or impulsively hurl myself into space."

"I impulsively hurled myself into space here recently."

She gave me a slantwise skeptical look.

I told her about the night with Alexander, his challenge, and how I had later returned and dived from the precipice. "It isn't as dangerous as it looks, if there's a big tide and high surf."

"Are you boasting?" she asked.

"Yes," I said. "Of course."

"You're both quite mad."

"Would you like to swim now?"

"How do you get down to the water?"

"There's a cliff path down to a little beach."

"You *are* mad. No."

I got a blanket from the tent and spread it in the shade of a nearby tree. There was a dew of perspiration on her upper lip and some damp wisps of hair curling around her ears. She had small, perfect, pink-lobed ears. It had never occurred to me until now that ears could be extremely erotic. Her nose was faintly sunburned. She was a little disheveled now, from the heat and the windy motorcycle ride, but even more beautiful than when perfectly groomed.

"Shall we eat lunch?" I asked.

"No, not yet."

"Al fresco," I said. "Did you ever kiss al fresco, Pamela?"

"Never met the chap."

"Will you be my guest at the villa some night this week, for dinner and the rest?"

"How can that be? I'm just a lowly player."

"What do you mean?"

"Well, don't you know, your Alexander doesn't want any of the show business rabble anywhere near the villa except when we're performing. That was made quite clear."

"To hell with him. You'll be my guest. He won't dare say anything."

She shook her head.

"Anyway, there are already a lot of show business rabble staying at the villa, as guests of Alexander."

"But they aren't *rabble;* they aren't even actors or singers or whatever anymore, if they ever were. They're corporations. They're vast international enterprises. They're *stars.*"

"You're going to be my guest. Don't argue."

"Well, it might be fun."

"It will be; I promise."

"At the end of the week? The last night? It wouldn't matter if I were fired then."

"It's settled, then."

"Very well."

"What sort of program are you and your group going to put on?"

"Oh, theater pieces."

"Plays?"

"Sort of."

"Sort of plays?"

"Playlets. Actually, I'm not certain yet what we'll be doing. It depends. We're preparing a number of sketches. It's all secret, you know. I can't tell you much."

"Tell me all that you can."

"Well, it's strange, what we'll be doing. Rather cruel. Your friend Alexander is a cruel man, I think. We are being paid very well to perform public cruelties."

"Do you enjoy being cruel?"

"Theatrically?"

"Yes."

"I'm an actress. If the part is good, and the lines—I love being cruel. I'd rather play the bitch than anything. I don't often get the bitch parts because I'm young, and perhaps because of the way I look. But really, cruelty— I'll turn your hair gray in three acts."

"And if people are hurt by your performance?"

She gazed at me. "You're not so wet as that, are you?"

"No. I'm just trying to get to know you."

"By asking questions? You can't learn much about people that way. We all lie. You must intuit people."

"I'd like to intuit you," I said.

She smiled. "Intuit me, then. As long as you understand that intuition doesn't require the removal of clothing."

15

There was a note pinned to the cottage door when I returned:

> Jay—
>   We were disappointed that you weren't able to attend the reception last night. We hope you are not indisposed this evening. Cocktails at 7:00, dinner at 8:00. Black tie, if you will.
>
> A

Alexander's annoyance was encoded in the word "disappointed." The rest was irony.

I wandered over to the villa at seven-thirty. A frilly jet contrail arced across the cloudless still-blue sky. The sun had descended below the western highlands and the grounds were in shadow, but a dry, bitter-tasting heat remained. We needed rain. The island always needed rain.

I felt imprisoned by the tux, the starched shirt and the tie, the tight leather shoes, and was sweating and irritable by the time I passed through the gates and into what reminded me of the Bedouin idea of paradise—a lush oasis in a harsh desert. There was running water and bountiful fruit trees and succulent morsels of food borne about by obedient slaves and, here and there, everywhere, beautiful, compliant houris.

Maria greeted me coolly. Perhaps her spies had informed her of my afternoon with Pamela Bristol. She denied me her direct gaze and impish smile, and her normally musical voice was flat. She was especially lovely tonight. She punished me with her beauty.

And so, cool and remote, she led me around the patio and introduced me to those guests I had not met. We stood briefly chatting with each, and then drifted away to meet another. I met three dozen men and women within half an hour. Earlier I had skimmed some of the dossiers, and so I was able to assign capsule biographies to many of the names, but the faces tended to blur.

I exchanged pleasantries with the exiled African tyrant, Biki Benematale, an enormously fat man who was surprisingly genial; a Japanese entrepreneur and his tiny wife; Gypsy Marr, sullen and pale; a young Arab prince; politicians and the patrons of politicians; a famous English playwright; a Romanian sculptor; powerful businessmen, many of whom had formed a paranoid enclave near the waterfall; a handful of the European nobility; entertainers, world-famous singers and film actors and musicians; and—oddest duck of all—a palsied Nazi who had long ago been a protege of Reinhard Heydrich.

It was as though Alexander had carefully prepared guest lists for three or four separate parties, then said to hell with it, and invited everyone to this single disharmonious affair. But of course it had been deliberate, a childish kind of mischief, provocation. Now, in various ways, he would ignite this volatile mixture and in godlike serenity observe the resultant fireworks. It was a kid's stunt but intriguing, too, like pouring dozens of violently reactive chemicals into an original brew.

Konstantin was fairly drunk but still cheerful: the brooding, the contempt and anger, and, perhaps, the violence would come later. He was sitting alone at a patio table. There was a perfect lipstick imprint of a woman's mouth on his cheek.

"I've been meeting guests," I said.

"Haven't we all."

"A strange mix, isn't it?"

"A *mélange degenres.*"

"There is the party," I said. "And then there is the anti-party."

"The oil and the water."

"The assonance and the dissonance."

"The wheat and the chaff."

"Who kissed your cheek, Kon?"

"Some sex goddess or other."

"Where's the old man?"

"I don't know. But I do know that he's mad at you."

"Why?"

"Because you missed the reception last night. Because you're stubborn and aloof. Because you're not properly respectful. And because you took his motorcycle without permission."

"That was satisfying in an obscurely sexual way, Kon. Stealing his motorcycle was like screwing his mistress."

"Except it hurts more to have an unfaithful motorcycle."

I circulated, drifting with the tide, pausing to exchange platitudes with Jack and Louise Black, briefly discuss the bulls with Aguilar, be snubbed by Maria, and nod to Nigel Rye, who was involved in courting a handsome young waiter who clearly didn't appreciate Nigel's attentions and intentions.

Nico Krisos motored down the walk in his electric wheelchair and blocked my way.

"Beep beep," he said.

"Hello, Nico."

"Too busy to visit me, Jay?"

"Too important."

We shook hands; his grip was powerful, and I could hear my knuckles crack. He wanted to hurt me, but only a little, enough to establish what he no doubt thought of as dominance. Nico's hands, arms, shoulders, and torso were extraordinarily strong, overdeveloped, while his legs were as thin as a child's. Usually a blanket was spread over his legs, not for warmth, but to conceal his atrophied legs. He had been shot and partly paralyzed in Italy some years ago during a kidnap attempt.

"Jay," he said, "I want to talk to you."

Sure.

"Not now, tomorrow sometime."

I nodded. "What about?"

"My sister."

"Are you going to ask me if my intentions are honorable?"

"You're never without a cheap wisecrack, are you?"

"I guess not. Sorry."

"It's part of your laid-back California charm, I suppose."

"Nico, I'm not going to sit humbly while you lecture me about Maria. Instead, let's have a few drinks tomorrow and a game of chess."

"It must be tedious work to be so charming," he said. "Always *on*. Professionally charming."

I laughed. "A lot of people don't find me at all charming."

"Permanent guests have to be charming. Parasites, leeches, spongers can't do without the casual, oily charm and the quick smile."

"That's enough, Nico."

"You charmed Kon and you charmed Alexander and you charmed Maria and now I hear you're trying to charm my mother. But you never fooled me, Chandler. I've always known that you were just another hustler."

Nico had always been a sort of reduced version of his father, smaller though similarly built, bearlike; and less confident, less forceful, less cunning, less imposing, not *dangerous*. And now, very angry, he looked like the angry Alexander of fifteen years ago, except there was a petulant note in his voice and doubt in his eyes.

"I never cared that you hustled the family for your living," he went on. "It was a minor expense, like keeping good horses or stocking the wine cellar. You were always amusing."

"Nico," I said, "get your go-cart out of my way."

"Hustler, very well, it didn't matter. But gigolo—no. Maria, never!"

I threw my drink in his face (two women, eavesdroppers to Nico's tirade, hissed and recoiled), turned, and walked around the big fountain and entered another part of the gardens.

The story quickly circulated. A few minutes later Konstantin approached, handed me a drink, and said, "Let's get one thing straight—*I* never thought you were charming."

All of the valuable antiques, the pots and jewelry and sculptures and weapons, had been removed from the villa's great hall, and a snow white carpet, intended to save the parquetry, had been laid down wall-to-wall. There were many tables scattered around the room, most six- and eight-tops, but one long table, set diagonally in the center of the room, had chairs for thirteen. A Krisos whimsey? The carpet was white, and the drapes, the tablecloths, the grand piano mounted on an elevated platform at the east end of the room. The only color was provided by the vases of freshly cut flowers placed on each table. The room was too bare, too starkly white, until it filled with guests, and then the clothing—men in black, the women wearing gowns of many colors—established a balance. Even so, the place looked like the main dining room of a luxury hotel or cruise ship.

I had been assigned to one of the smaller tables, a four-top near the platform. The place cards informed me that my table mates were Gypsy Marr, Biki Benematale, and Alexander's fiancee, Francoise Créneau. The idea was to play a kind of musical chairs; we would change tables and dining partners each night, so that by the end of the week each individual would have dined with every other.

I sat down and watched the milling crowd search confusedly for their tables. The room's acoustics were poor; hushed laughs and words without context floated among the rafters. Some of the guests were already drunk, and I noticed that each place setting had five wineglasses, two for white, two for red, and a champagne flute. And brandy would be served with coffee. There would be indiscretions tonight, headaches tomorrow.

Biki Benematale, moving with the grossly fat man's ponderous shuffle, advanced toward the table. He did not weigh less than 350 pounds. His skin was as black as tar and now sheened with sweat. His head was huge, and his scalp was a tightly knit mass of gray curls. Benematale was the only man present who had dressed in white tie and tails. And he wore black fleece-lined bedroom slippers. I guessed that he had foot problems like many extremely fat persons.

He smiled and said, "Ah, Mr. Chandler, how pleasant that we are to dine together." His teeth were perfect, big and even and white, the kind that can easily uncap a bottle or crack a Brazil nut.

He squared up in front of the table, placed his palms on either side of the plate, and gradually lowered his bulk into the chair.

"I fear that I shall have to arise again, and again and again, when we are joined by the ladies. They are like jumping jacks. Glad I am tonight not to be posted to a large table, one that is decorated by four or six of the rising and descending creatures."

His bass voice sounded as though it had emerged from a mine shaft. His accent was British; the elaborate diction perhaps derived from old missionary texts.

"I am afflicted by a glandular disorder," he said. "Thus my adiposity."

He was in his early to middle fifties. He had not always been obese; photographs taken of him while he was still King Benematale showed a big man, overweight but not monstrously so. He had often been photographed on horseback in those days.

"Is it hellishly hot in here?" he asked.

"It's too warm, yes."

"Perhaps I should have jettisoned my vest this evening. Though, truth be told, I feel as naked and helpless as a cherub without my vest."

I assumed that he was talking about a bulletproof jacket and not a vestcoat.

"This is a most stupendous bash, Mr. Chandler, is it not? Look about. Everywhere one's eye pauses it alights upon still another illustrious personage, a star in the firmament of commerce, governance, aristocracy, or the arts, highbrow and low. But, if you'll forgive my boasting, there are none here so protean as I, as various. Scholar, musician, soldier—private to general—president, dictator, king, king in exile, king emeritus, you might say. And I do card tricks!"

His face smoothed and rounded, and he laughed, a jolly bass rumble that made me laugh with him.

"And what are your magnitude and coordinates in this great galaxy?" he asked.

"I'm just a small satellite," I said. "Or maybe an unplotted asteroid."

"Ah, a nobody. Wonderful! Whose nobody are you?"

"I'm nobody's nobody," I said. "I'm a sort of renegade nobody."

He laughed again, that infectious rumble, and he was about to speak when Gypsy Marr arrived at the table. We rose, Benematale slowly and with a significant glance in my direction; and no sooner were we seated than Francois Créneau approached.

We got through the introductions and the preliminary small talk and then divided into pairs: Benematale and Francoise began a conversation in French, and I turned to Gypsy.

"I've enjoyed your films," I said, though I thought they were terrible.

She nodded.

"Are you staying the entire week?"

"God, no. This is a bore."

"Well, the party just started. It will become interesting, maybe even exciting. Alexander will see that it does."

She shrugged. Tonight she wore makeup, not her professional mask, the whore's maquillage, but enough to emphasize her best features: her large round eyes and sullen mouth. Her lips looked puffy, as though she had been kissed hard a few minutes ago, or slapped.

"Why are they talking French?" she asked.

"They're discussing Paris. You can't reminisce about Paris in any other tongue. It just isn't done."

"Do you know French?"

"Very little."

"I've been there. It's a dirty city. It's cold and it's damp and it stinks and there's too much traffic."

There was something heavy about her, inert. Maybe it was stupidity.

"Are they talking about me?" she asked.

"No. They're discussing restaurants."

"Everyone here is dead. Look around. Dead."

"An interesting thought," I said. "Maybe this is hell."

She stared at me in a way that suggested that I, too, was a corpse; then she said, "Christ," and turned away. The waiter, a Greek boy from the village, arrived and took our orders. There was no regular menu, but we had a choice of three soups, half a dozen vegetables, four entrees, and so on. Gypsy did not like any of the available dishes. She sat slumped in her chair and in a querulous tone rejected this and that and everything, and finally ordered a tomato-and-cucumber salad. When the waiter asked if that was all the lady wanted, she dismissed him with a contemptuous gesture. Her surliness was a kind of aggression, an assault on the rest of us.

Two bottles of wine were brought, opened, tasted, and approved by Biki Benematale and then poured.

I wondered at Gypsy's enormous popularity. Sex goddess. It could not be all hype; there had to be some content inside the manufactured package. In person she was a fairly pretty, nicely built woman, but I detected no aura, no "charisma," no steady low-frequency emission of sexual energy. I thought that maybe what came through in her films and videos and concerts, what made her the object of so much lust and worship, was exactly the thing that repelled me now: her selfishness, her vast, infantile narcissism.

Just as the first course was being served, a servant brought me a note from von Rabenau.

16

Von Rabenau was waiting for me outside the gates.

"Come with me," he said.

"What is this about, Walter?"

"Walk."

"The escargots on my plate are getting cold."

"The corpse on your bed is getting warm."

We started across the grounds toward my cottage. There were lights burning upstairs and down, although I had left only the porch light on.

"Heinrich was checking the cottages' doors. Your back door was unlocked."

"Sorry."

"He went in. He was concerned about the security of the files."

"I'm sorry, Walter. It was careless of me."

"I don't know what's going on. Do you know what is going on around here, Chandler?"

"No. What's this about a corpse on my bed?"

"The dossiers were not disturbed."

"Good. But, Walter—"

"We'll bring you a safe to keep the files in. Can you remember to lock the safe?"

Heinrich was sitting at the bar that separated the kitchen from the living room. He had a bottle of beer in one hand and a cigarette in the other. He twisted and looked at us over his shoulder.

"Ah," he said. "You have apprehended the mad mutilator."

"Are you referring to me, Karl?"

"Chandler, we are very concerned about your appetites. We are sophisticated men and tolerant of deviant behavior, but this goes too far."

"Do you want a drink?" von Rabenau asked me.

"Do I need one?"

"I believe you do."

"Scotch."

"I'll have another beer," Heinrich said. Then he turned to me. "Americans! It's appalling. We Europeans are accustomed to reading about your bizarre, bloodthirsty entertainments, but this . . ."

"That's enough, Karl," von Rabenau said.

"What did you do with his epidermal envelope?" Heinrich asked me.

Von Rabenau gave Heinrich a bottle of beer and handed me the scotch. He was drinking cognac.

"Cheers," Heinrich said.

"He was flayed," von Rabenau said.

"Flayed?"

"Skinned."

I looked at him.

"Like a rabbit," Heinrich said. "I haven't found his skin."

Von Rabenau drank half of his cognac and put the glass down. "Come on," he said.

"I don't think I want to see this."

"It's not so bad."

"Like a rabbit," Heinrich said again.

I followed von Rabenau up the stairs and into the bedroom loft. Every light in the room was burning. The object was centered on the bed, centered in the hard glare. It lay supine on the satiny off-white bedspread.

"Karl couldn't find the skin," von Rabenau said.

"I heard."

It was the color of a side of beef, dark red, almost wine red except for the patches of remaining skin and the streaks of fat. Not all of the skin had been removed around the fingers and toes, the genitals, the nose and ears, the eyes. There was a sour, metallic smell in the room, unpleasant but not yet the choking stink of corruption.

"So somewhere there is a bag of fatty skin. I would guess that the skin of a man this size would weigh twenty-five to thirty pounds."

The man had been tall and lean; long arms and legs, long feet and fingers. You could see the taut lines of tendons beneath the flesh, bluish veins, and the clear outline of the rib cage.

"It's a very old torture," Walter said. "Flaying a man alive."

I vaguely recalled using the phrase "flayed alive" recently.

"But this man wasn't flayed alive. He was flayed dead."

"Who is it?"

"Look at him. His face—ugliness is more than skin deep. He was an old man, tall, maybe six feet four or five."

"Simon Rye."

"Yes."

"His corpse was stolen from the freezer—"

"And evidently wasn't completely thawed when flayed. It really isn't a perfect job of skinning, you see. There are a lot of deep nicks, bits of skin left here and there."

"It wasn't done here."

"No. You can see that there isn't much blood in the room. He was skinned elsewhere and brought here."

"Why?"

"Ask the flies."

We went back downstairs. Heinrich was gone. The smell lingered in my nostrils, my brain.

I said, "I suppose it would be foolish to ask why someone would steal Simon Rye's corpse from a freezer, skin it, and leave the cadaver on my bed."

"Foolish to ask me."

"Who would be capable of skinning a human being?"

"Morally? Or do you mean who would possess the skill?"

"Skill, then."

He shrugged. "A butcher. Anyone who has worked in a tannery or slaughterhouse. Fanners, shepherds. Many rural people would know how. Hunters—do you hunt, Chandler?"

"No."

"Never skinned a deer?"

"No. Have you?"

"As a matter of fact, I have."

We were quiet for a time, and then Walter said, "Well, don't let me keep you from your dinner."

"You and Karl are a funny team," I said. "Walter and Karl, the Krazy-with-a-K Krauts."

"I'll have someone come in and take away the carcass and scrub down your bedroom. And we'll have a new bed brought in, or at least a new mattress and bed linen. But we might not get it done tonight."

"I'll sleep somewhere else."

"Good night, Chandler."

"Does Nigel Rye know that his brother's corpse was stolen from the meat freezer?"

"Not unless you told him."

"I didn't. And so you not only have to inform him that his twin's corpse was snatched from a meat freezer; it was flayed. And the skin is unaccounted for."

Von Rabenau smiled. "It's the host's duty to inform Nigel Rye, don't you think?"

"Alexander might want to wait to see what further outrages are inflicted on Simon's remains before notifying Nigel."

"That's true."

After he left the room I went to the box containing the dossiers.

CONFIDENTIAL
Simon Trevor Rye
(?)

17

Precis of file 112-GB
Authority: Von R.
Compiler: ConInq-GB
Access: SR-0112-GB

(a) Subject "known" to have been born to Louis and Elizabeth Rye in the village of Crawley, Sussex. No birth records found in Crawley, the county of Sussex, or neighboring counties. No records found in England or UK. No record of parents, Louis and Elizabeth Rye. No record of twin brother, Nigel Basil Rye. (See file 113-GB.)

(b) No record of Simon Trevor Rye attending Harrow School or Christ Church College, Oxford.

(c) No data regarding Simon Trevor Rye in National Health Service records.

(d) No passport issued to Simon Trevor Rye.

(e) No trace of Simon Trevor Rye in Inland Revenue Service records.

(f) No record of military service for Simon Trevor Rye.

(g) No mention of Simon Trevor Rye in United Kingdom police files. No match of fingerprints.

(h) Simon Trevor Rye not known by Interpol.

(i) No record of Simon Trevor Rye having been employed by the British Museum.

(j) No record of Simon Trevor Rye having served as consultant to Sotheby's Auction House.

(k) No record of Simon Trevor Rye having been employed by the Oriental Institute at the University of Chicago, USA.

(l) All other agencies, institutions, and sources consulted during the course of this inquiry (materials available in complete file) unable to provide information re Simon Trevor Rye.

CONCLUSION: "Simon Trevor Rye" does not exist.

ADVISE: See file 113-GB (Nigel Basil Rye).

18

Precis of file 113-GB
Authority: Von R.
Compiler: ConInq-GB
Access: NR-0113-GB

No information available re Nigel Basil Rye.
See file 112-GB (Simon Trevor Rye).

19

The entrées had been served and new wines poured when I returned to the villa. I weaved in and out of the tables, glancing at faces, avid eyes and greasy mouths, and at the plates, partly eaten lobsters and fish and grouse and two-inch-thick steaks. Alexander, sitting at the head of the big table, looked reproachfully at me when I passed. And Nigel Rye, sitting halfway down the same table, was dismembering a lobster with precision.

"Ah, sir," Biki Benematale crooned when I sat down at our table. "You are back. I feared I might have to eat your beef. This is an extraordinarily high-quality beef, I assure you, and it would be a pity to waste it."

Francoise Créneau smiled at me. Gypsy was gone.

"I have a small appetite generally," Benematale said. "But I do believe I could have done justice to your beef."

"Where is Miss Marr?" I asked.

Francoise, still smiling, said, "She called me a frog cunt and Mr. Benematale a fat nigger cannibal."

"I cannot recommend her manners," Benematale said. "If you had been present, Mr. Chandler, she might have been equally severe in her judgment of you."

154

Francoise seemed very pleased with herself. I presumed that she had enjoyed the conflict with Gypsy.

Benematale was eating with great gusto. His appetite had not been disturbed by being called a fat nigger cannibal. His now-ravaged steak had just been seared top and bottom; it was really raw, and blood had pooled on the plate.

My steak was charred on the outside and pink within. I cut off a chunk and experimentally tasted it. It was indeed high-quality beef. After viewing the carcass of Simon Rye I'd thought that I might be a vegetarian for the rest of my days, but the steak was good, I was hungry, and my stomach did not confuse the sirloin with the flesh of Simon Rye.

"More wine, Jay?" Benematale said.

"Yes, thank you, Biki."

The salad came near the end of the meal, in the French style, and then there was fruit and cheese and, after that, coffee and cognac. Benematale withdrew two cigars from an inside pocket and offered me one. I did not light mine.

Alexander rose from his chair and made his way toward the stage. He was the ugliest man in the room, an ape in a tuxedo, and he was the most attractive man in the room. His vitality, his power, were evident in his expression and stride. Here was a man who feared nothing, who acted, who did not hesitate. He was only, sometimes, a fool when he talked.

I excused myself and went outside to smoke the cigar. Alexander would now deliver his Apollo and Dionysus speech. Apollo was a sun god, a god of light and reason, rationality and order. Dionysus, the wine god,

was a darker force; he represented the animal uncon-
scious, sexuality, art and ecstasy, and inspired drunken
revels. Each of us, Alexander would say, is a Dionysus
encapsulated by an Apollo. Both gods and what they
symbolize are true and good. One could not reject either
the Apollonian or the Dionysian without serious consequences. We are both. But. "But," Alexander would say,
"you have been invited to a Dionysian festival, and so
for one week Dionysus rules. Fill your wineglasses, all of
you. Raise them. Drink to Dionysus!"

The clusters of women below in their bright gowns resembled bouquets of flowers, and their voices chimed
like bells. The men blended into the darkness except for
a flash of cuff or a pale profile. Most of the guests had
come out for the evening's entertainment.

Floodlights placed high in the trees brightly illuminated the aerialists' scaffolding, the platforms, the high
wire and trapezes, and the spiderweb of netting. I sat
alone in the center of the highest arc of seats, almost at
eye level with the performers. They were Russian, three
men and two women, and they seemed unaffected by
the usual gravitational imperatives; they levitated, they
soared, and they were so good that the audience did not
appreciate the difficulty and danger.

I noticed that Biki Benematale was advancing toward me. He climbed as small children or the infirm
go up a steep stairway, always leading with the same
foot and often pausing for rest and balance. He lifted
his right foot to a step, lifted his left, hesitated, and then
proceeded on the same way to the next step. His black

face gleamed with sweat. His mouth formed an O as he exhaled.

Below and beyond him some workers were pushing a wheeled bandshell out onto the grounds; others followed with a baby grand piano. Maria was going to play for us.

Benematale continued on up the stairs in his ponderous shuffle. His eyes were large, his mouth opened wide—there was something desperate in his expression, fearful. But he kept on coming until he reached the top. He held the splayed fingers of his right hand over his heart. He tried to speak, failed, and smiled ruefully.

I slid over. "Sit down, Mr. Benematale."

"Is there—"

"I'll have one of the attendants bring us cushions and something cool to drink."

"Is there a breath—"

"Perhaps you ought to take off your coat."

"Is there a breath of air at this extreme altitude, Mr. Chandler?"

"I'm afraid not."

"Alas."

He remained standing for a while, breathing deeply, and then he cautiously shifted his center of gravity and slowly settled on the stone slab. I could smell his sweat mixed with a fruity cologne.

"Let me help you remove your coat," I said.

"No, no. Thank you, but a gentleman does not remove his coat in the presence of ladies."

All of the ladies were seated in the lower section of the theater and, anyway, would not have been much offended by the sight of Benematale in his shirtsleeves.

He said, "You are thinking that I am old-fashioned."

"A bit."

"Victorian. It is true; I confess to being old-fashioned. When I was a boy I learned from nuns, and the nuns in those days had many quaint notions. I am a chaste old maiden in some respects. Inside Biki Benematale reside the importunate ghosts of half a dozen prim, dry nuns. When a lady enters the room those nuns cry out, *Biki, elevate your corpulent self!* I obey. *Biki, do not remove your jacket in the presence of elegant ladies.* I obey. Those devoted, pious nuns also injected Jesus and Mary and the angels into my heart. They reside there still."

"That must be tedious," I said. "And tough on the arteries."

"Of course, those good nuns also injected Satan, evil, into my innocent heart."

"Coronary crowding, Mr. B."

"Have you ever observed, Mr. Chandler, how nearly every religion views knowledge as evil—the ultimate evil, in fact. From before Prometheus to beyond Adam and Eve. The nuns began my education. They gave me knowledge. And thus, sir, I was expelled from my lovely, wild African garden and thrust, willy-nilly, into the paranoid, Manichean, medieval European landscape of good and evil, crime and punishment, heaven and hell. I was cleaved asunder."

"The recital is about to begin," I said.

"Perhaps we'll have the opportunity to talk another time."

"Fine."

"And I may perform some of my card tricks."

"I'd really like that," I said.

His body trembled and laughter rumbled deep in his chest. "Sir, I think you are not the naïf you like to appear."

"You, too, Mr. B."

A spotlight stabbed out into the darkness beyond the bandshell and captured Maria in its center. She emerged from the trees and walked gracefully across the glowing emerald green lawn. She wore a full pale blue dress and high-heeled shoes, and her hair was gathered in a pony-tail. A ring, a necklace, and a small brooch glittered spectrally in the spotlight. Maria mounted the steps (lifting her skirt) and gravely advanced to the piano. She did not acknowledge the scattered applause. She sat down, at the same time sweeping her skirt beneath her, and for a moment hovered predatorlike over the keyboard.

"Ah," Benematale softly exhaled.

I felt sorry for Maria without understanding exactly why. Perhaps because she was rendered vulnerable by her sincerity.

She was scheduled to play short pieces by Chopin, Mozart, Tchaikovsky, and Liszt.

During the Chopin, Benematale leaned close to me and whispered, "Is the young lady left-handed?"

"No." At first I didn't understand the point of the question; then I said, "She recently injured her right hand, burned it, but not very seriously."

"Ah."

The audience was restless during her performance, moving about and talking, clearly bored, and the brief applause at the end was less than polite. Didn't they know who she was?

When she finished—angrily refusing to bow or acknowledge the meager applause—Benematale stood up and shouted, "Jolly! Damned good!"

When he settled back to his seat I asked, "Is she really?"

He glanced slantwise at me.

"You're a musician. How good is Maria?"

"Why do you say that I am a musician?"

"I've heard that you were. I read it someplace."

The spotlight followed Maria as she left the stage; then it was abruptly switched off and she evaporated into darkness.

"I once thought of myself as a musician, but that was a long time ago, and I've not had much time for music since."

"Well, what is your opinion of Maria's playing?"

"I enjoyed it tremendously."

"Are your nuns whispering, *Gallantry, gallantry*, in your ear?"

"They are, in fact."

"All right."

"What's next on the program. Let me see. Can this be so? Ventriloquy?"

"Maria performs all over Europe, not just Athens. Paris, London, Moscow, Vienna, Florence."

"Yes." After a long pause he added, "Of course her father is immensely rich."

"Is that it?"

"In my opinion the lovely Maria is quite good technically. Really quite accomplished. At first the play of her right hand puzzled me, but you explained that. But for me her music is redolent of . . . perspiration. The teachers, the study, the sweat, the yearning. Technically proficient, oh yes. But forgive me. She is not favored by the Muse. Call it genius, inspiration, passion, the Muse . . . she has not been favored. It's most unfortunate. She is a beautiful young woman; she has an arresting stage presence; she is honest; she is splendid technically; she no doubt has worked at music with a slavish dedication. But there is no genius. She has not been favored."

"I was afraid that might be the case," I said.

"But what do I know? I am just a fat nigger cannibal."

"Gypsy's a stupid bitch."

He nodded cheerfully. "Yes, and I shall probably end up in bed with the creature. Oddly, sir, being called a fat nigger cannibal is often a sexual gambit."

"Not in my world, Mr. B.," I said, and got to my feet.

His face rounded and bunched up and he began rumbling with laughter. He wiped his eyes and said, "Aren't you going to stay for the next act?" He consulted the program. "Mel and Miranda."

"I've seen them perform," I said. "They're marvelous."

I walked down the steps wondering if Benematale had, in passing, explained the difference between Maria and Gypsy: the one possessed every musical virtue except "genius"; the other was musically a savage but "inspired" while performing. Of course there was no comparison between the two musical forms, Mozart versus Marr, but maybe the same principle applied. Exalted muse or vulgar muse—Maria had been denied and Gypsy blessed. Same principle, separate audiences. For her audience, Gypsy, the slut, transcended herself. Maria always remained Maria.

20

A heavy steel safe had been moved into the cottage during my absence. A note from von Rabenau informed me that the dossiers were inside and that I should phone him to obtain the safe's combination. I was about to do that when the door was flung open and Maria rushed into the room. "Bastard!" she cried, and she removed one of her shoes and threw at me. "Traitor! You left during my performance." She removed her other shoe and threw it. "Son of a bitch!"

"I did not leave."

"You left in the middle."

"I didn't. That must have been someone else."

She glared at me, then said, "You *wanted* to leave."

"Maria, don't be crazy. I'm not in the mood."

She walked toward me. Her bare feet left faint moist prints on the tiles. "There's someone here with you. Is it that Pamela tart?"

"There is no one here."

She turned abruptly and ran up the stairs to the bedroom loft. I waited, half-expecting to hear a scream, but the corpse had been removed, and she came slowly down the steps saying, "Oh, Jay, I know I'm not great, but I'm good. I really am good."

"Of course you are."

"Don't patronize me."

"I'm not."

"Do you really think I'm good?"

"Yes."

"But then," she said, "what the hell do you know?"

"I know when a drink is called for."

"You drink too much. Everyone drinks too much. I drink too much."

"It's just for the duration of this damned party."

"Brandy," she said.

I poured two brandies and when I returned she was lying supine on one of the settees. She balanced the glass on her stomach.

"They didn't like me, Jay."

"Sure they did." I retreated to the other settee.

"No one listened, really listened."

"I listened. Biki Benematale listened."

"What the devil is a Biki Benematale?"

"He's an exiled African dictator."

"Oh, yes." She laughed.

"He knows something about music."

"My God, I am appreciated by a tone-deaf archaeologist and an exiled African dictator."

"Listen, why do you care what that international trash thinks?"

"I don't know. It hurts. I worked so hard and it means so much to me."

"Pick your audiences more carefully."

"I suppose."

"That's a Mel and Miranda crowd."

"Jay, I really am good. I'm a good concert pianist. There are better and there are worse. But I can play."

"Sure you can."

"It's just . . . Daddy's fucking money. No one will take me seriously. No one will ever really listen to me play. Because it's clear, isn't it, that Daddy's money has opened all of the doors. Alexander Krisos contributes two hundred thousand dollars to an orchestra, and soon after his spoiled daughter, Maria, is invited to perform. Those are the rumors. Daddy's money has made everybody deaf. Why for God's sake can't they just listen to me play?"

"Stop whining," I said.

She tilted her head and stared hard at me. "I saw you sitting with that whore at dinner tonight."

"Gypsy or Francoise Créneau?"

She smiled maliciously.

"Gypsy called Biki Benematale a fat nigger cannibal."

"Oh, Lord, will he gobble her up?"

"It isn't out of the question. He has a glandular problem."

"What did you think of her? Gypsy?"

"She seemed rather dull and frowsy to me."

"Did she?"

"What do you think of Gypsy, Maria? Musically."

"Well. When she performs she reminds me of one of those very clever New York female impersonators."

"I see what you mean."

"And what about Pamela Bristol—is she dull and frowsy?"

"Anything but."

"Bastard."

"Maria, what is the subject of this conversation? You, me, money, Gypsy, Pamela Bristol?"

"Now, Jay, tonight. Deflower me. This is your last chance."

"Who are you kidding? You ain't got no flower no more."

"That's true, technically."

"Technically."

"What's that?" she asked, looking at the safe in the corner.

"It contains books, papers."

"What kind of books and papers?"

"Archaeological mystifications."

"Jay, is Pamela Bristol prettier than I?"

"No."

"You liar! Do you think I'm blind? She's beautiful."

"You're much prettier than Gypsy Marr."

"I know that."

"But she has a more flexible pelvic structure."

"I have very strong hands and wrists," Maria said. "I could strangle her easily."

"You don't have to kill Gypsy. She'll kill herself eventually, one way or the other."

"I wasn't talking about Gypsy; I was talking about your Pamela."

"She isn't my Pamela."

"Did you sleep with her this afternoon, Jay?"

"I couldn't sleep; I was too excited."

"Did you screw her, Jay?"

"I showed her the temple."

"And did she show you her temple?"

"I didn't know you female persons regarded them as temples."

"Hers is probably a cathedral."

"I don't know what that means, but it's funny."

Maria placed her glass on the floor, hiked her dress up above her hips, and lifted her feet into the air. Her toes were pointed. She was wearing lacy blue bikini panties.

"I have nice legs, don't I?"

"Very nice."

"And I have a nice ass and a little waist and rounded hips and perky little breasts."

"And powerful fingers and wrists."

She laughed and lowered her legs. "We have so much fun together, don't we?"

"You make me nervous sometimes."

"I know why you won't make love to me. The incest taboo. You feel that you're a member of the family. My brother. But you really aren't my brother, Jay. We are unrelated by blood."

"We have no incest taboo in my family," I said. "The three-eyed Chandlers."

"Mother told me that she saw you today."

"Yes. We talked, sort of."

"She understands more English than she speaks. She likes you, Jay."

"I like her."

"She won't object to our marriage."

"That's a relief."

"I think she ought to take a lover."

"How do you know she hasn't?"

"No, not here on the island. Who is there for her?

There isn't anyone that she would care about in that way."

"How do you know?"

"She prefers to remain chaste."

"It's getting late, Maria."

"Anyway, Father would not tolerate it."

"Your mother is free to do as she pleases."

"But this is Greece."

"This is Greece, and it's late, and I'm tired."

"Father would kill her."

"Nonsense."

"You've never seen my father in a rage—not the fake rages he uses to intimidate people, a true rage. He's terrifying. He owns, Jay. That is what he does and who he is—an owner. He owns Mother, in his mind. She was once his and so she must always be his. He simply could not bear the thought of another man making love to her, possessing her. Smile all you want; it's true. That means he still loves her, in his way. Men are like that. Except you, maybe. Would you care if I let Aguilar make love to me? Imagine it. See it in your mind. We are naked and shameless. I embrace him with my arms and my legs."

"I'll kill you," I said.

"That's much better."

"I'll kill both of you."

"Bravo, darling."

"Come on, I'll walk you back to the villa."

"Carry me."

She was light at first, as I carried her down the steps and halfway across the park, but then she became heavier and heavier, and by the time we reached the gates I was breathing hard and trembling with fatigue.

"You're out of condition," she said when I had released her.

"I run every morning."

"You are out of condition for carrying voluptuous women around."

"Good night, Maria."

"Kiss me."

I kissed her lightly, but she pulled me close and pressed against me. We were sealed together from knees to mouths. Finally she stepped back and grinned at me.

"I know you want me, Jay. I could feel how very much you want me."

"I was thinking about Pamela Bristol," I said.

"No, you weren't. You were thinking about Maria's sacred temple."

She laughed, turned, and went through the gates.

21

BENEMATALE, BIKI

(Joseph Hope)

Precis of file 39-AFR
Authority: von R.
Senior Compilers: ConIng-GB
Access: Equator BB "Frere"-FRA
(Redline)
Coco-AFR
Sidi-AFR

Biki Benematale—"Tall Flute Player"—was the name given to subject during tribal circumcision (maturation) ceremony. Among the Ibinopal peoples a male child has many names: he is addressed differently by parents, grandparents, siblings, more distant relatives, unrelated members of his totemic clan, villagers of other clans, strangers of the same linguistic group, etc. A boy may have as many as forty names, including diminutives and augmentatives, all of which are "forgotten"—become taboo—when the child passes through the arduous initiation ceremony and emerges as an adult. (Consult the appended anthropological and ethnological studies of the Ibinopal peoples.)

BORN: June 1946 (according to tribal recollection), or August 1946 (records of St. Anthony's Mission School, where he was christened Joseph Hope).

As a second son, and thus not subject to the tribal laws of primogeniture, Benematale was permitted to attend the St. Anthony's Mission School at River Crossing as a boarding student. He is reported to have immediately impressed the teaching nuns with his high intelligence, energy, good humor, and piety. Those nuns still alive (see appended transcripts) who were consulted during this inquiry state that Joseph Hope was: "Altogether exceptional." "Studious." "Gifted especially in mathematics and music." "He walked out of prehistory, in a way, and into the twentieth century." "Near genius."

When Benematale was seventeen he received, through the intercession of the nuns and the colonial administration, a full scholarship to the national university. His exceptional qualities were recognized and encouraged by the university's faculty, although he was not popular among the students, particularly those involved in the anticolonial political movements. Benematale was regarded as a "ghost" (white man) because of what was seen as his pro-West, pro-Christian, pro-capitalist biases. His many political opponents scornfully referred to him as "the good African," i.e., the weak, sycophantic African.

Benematale once again proved to be a superior student (grade transcripts, test papers, teacher appraisal, and dissertation appended), although it appeared to his faculty adviser, Mr. B. P. Greffi, that Benematale was "topping out" in his mathematical studies.

In 1966, when Benematale was twenty, he received a scholarship to Trinity College, Cambridge, where he experienced the first academic failures of his career. There was no question of his intelligence or effort, but it became clear that the inferior quality of his prior education (mission school, provincial African university) had not prepared him to compete against the privileged, well-prepared students at Cambridge.

After two years, when it was apparent that he would not obtain a good degree (a first or even a second), Benematale dropped out of college and moved to Paris, where, for six years, he led a rather bohemian existence as a student at the Observatoire Français and as a musical performer in various Left Bank nightclubs. His group, called Nuit Afrique, played a modern jazz style deeply influenced by African rhythms and tempo. Later he left the group and concentrated his energies on the composition of classical music, again bringing an African musical sensibility to the Western form. During this period he composed many pieces of music, including four symphonies, one of which was performed by the Observatoire Français's student orchestra to high critical praise. His tutor at the Observatoire, the composer Georges Benoit, stated that Benematale was a gifted musician and composer and deplored his student's abandoning music, saying, "Only a few are capable of making significant contributions to the world's musical library; any clever hoodlum can become a dictator."

Excerpt from Unpublished Autobiography by Biki Benematale

How and why does a Hitler rise Phoenix-like out of the bloody ashes of post–World War I Germany? Why Adolf and not another of the 40 million Germans of the time? Why and how does a Biki Benematale rise out of the mud and stench of his little village to rule his nation and, in time, by his wisdom and example, lead the entire African continent out of darkness and into the brave, bright, great future. Africa is the future; Biki Benematale is Africa.

During the last three years of Benematale's residence in France, he became deeply involved with a clandestine (terrorist) organization called Groupe Militaire, the action arm of his country's minority political party, the Revolutionary Democratic Alliance. He was suspected of participation in several terrorist bombings, including one of the residence of his country's ambassador to France, and a failed attempt to destroy the Arch of Triumph.

In the autumn of 1974 Benematale was expelled from France. He returned to Malwinda and joined a guerrilla unit fighting in the west of the country. He enrolled as a sergeant, but his background in the respected Groupe Militaire, his intelligence and education, and an apparent talent for strategic and tactical thinking quickly propelled him through the ranks. Three years later, at the time of the army revolt and palace coup, Benematale was a colonel and well situated as chief of ordnance and logistics to maneuver during the power struggle since termed "the one hundred days of blood." Benematale ruthlessly eliminated his rivals and emerged as president. Two years later he declared himself dictator; and three years after that, king.

Observers state that during the first two years of Benematale's regime, he was serious about bringing enlightened government to Malwinda, he and his family lived simply, and he eliminated much of the official corruption, attempted to curb the power of the military, and tried to mediate between rival tribal factions.

Excerpt from Unpublished Autobiography of Biki Benematale

I governed compassionately for two years and

was thanked by my People with jeers and spittle. I ruled sternly after that and the People greeted me on their knees, cheering. Collectively the People are more good than bad; individually they are jackals. Give a man food for one day and he will bow and thank you. Give him food for a week and he will revile you and plot your death. The People respect only power. They worship power—know you a god who is not capricious and cruel? The People are valuable in the aggregate, worthless individually. Machiavelli said that the prince should be both a fox and a lion. I say, a fox, a lion, a serpent, a scorpion, a raptor. I say the prince should be a wind, a whisper, a plague, a conflagration.

There are many rumors concerning Benematale's behavior during his years in power: that he personally tortured political opponents and spies; that he held "cannibal feasts" for intimates; that he fed enemies to his collection of beasts, lions, and crocodiles, to be devoured alive; that he murdered his first wife and two sons during a "paranoid episode." Benematale denies all of these allegations. No hard evidence has been found to substantiate them. It should be noted that such monstrous crimes are routinely ascribed to all powerful African dictators.

Benematale does not deny that he is a sensualist, an orgiast, although he vehemently rejects the many charges of rape, finding particularly offensive the accusation that he is fond of raping nuns.

Excerpt from Unpublished Autobiography of Biki Benematale

I have been viciously criticised for being a sensualist. How do I reply to this charge? Yes! for God's sake, what man would not be a sensualist if he could? I have enjoyed the embraces of thousands of women, black and white and all the hues between, and I do not repent. (Nor do I consume a half-cooked thigh or ham after consummation.) It is my best hope to enjoy the firm embraces of an equal number of women in the future. But I have never, despite the slanders, raped women. It has never been necessary. Women enjoy me as much as I enjoy women. It is all quite glandular.

In 1984 a successful revolt by the army forced Benematale to flee the country. He was denied refuge by Great Britain, France, Belgium, the United States, and Canada and was ultimately granted a residence permit by Switzerland. (It is reliably reported that he escaped his country with more than $90 million in cash, jewelry, stocks and bonds, and bearer certificates.)

According to Benematale's autobiography, he expects that someday he will be called back to once again rule his country and, eventually, all of black Africa. "Some day my People will cry out to me, 'Father, come home. We are sorry, Father.' And I shall return in a chariot woven of gold and love and fire."

(a) The 800-page manuscript copy of Benematale's autobiography is available in the master file.

(b) Scores of Benematale's musical compositions are available in master file.

(c) Financial data are available in master file (redline).

22

The Harley-Davidson was wrapped around with cloth-padded chains and secured to a ring set in the concrete wall.

I drove a pickup truck down the cliff road and parked in an alley behind the church. The village was brightly lighted, ablaze, a glare that rose in a hazy dome above the rooftops and penetrated deep into the lanes that, like the spokes of a wheel, slanted toward darkness. The square was swarming with celebrants in various states of drunkenness. Music and shouts and laughter reverberated up and down the streets.

For half an hour I searched for Pamela; then I drove the truck up to the temple site. There were still many lights burning up at the villa complex, and the glow from the village erased the stars over much of the northeastern sky. I could still hear music and shouts, the urgent and senseless babble.

The ruin looked different now, not a graceful little temple to be, but a square patch of land strewn with marble rubble. I was almost sorry that Sophia Krisos had told me the truth. The reconstruction could have been completed in a few more months. But it did not belong here; it belonged at its original site. It was an act of vandalism to move the ruins to this island, this cliff. Of course, I should have known. I had so fervently wished the temple to be authentic that I'd subconsciously colluded in the deception. *My* little ruin, *my* archaeological project, *my* beautiful little classic temple.

The motives of the Krisos family didn't matter; this was a hoax, nothing more or less, and I was the pigeon. An expensive and elaborate hoax: what a lot of duplicity had been required, so many lies spoken and implied, so much bland treachery. Alexander, yes, this kind of manipulative stunt was in his character, and Nico, too, would enjoy the ruse, but Kon and Maria, the temple workers, the people who lived in the village, everyone . . . ? Only Sophia Krisos possessed the decency to expose the sham.

I walked to the edge of the cliff. Here is where Stavros Kamis had lost his balance, was poised for an instant between life and death, and then fell silently to the rocks below. Perhaps casualties must be accepted in a hoax of this complexity. You gave a generous pension to the man's family and went on as before.

Biki Benematale had paraphrased Machiavelli in saying that the prince must be both a fox and a lion. Very well. I was not any sort of prince, but I could play the fox, and the lion, too, when the time came.

23

It was after four o'clock when I returned to the cottage. The complex was mostly dark now, and sourceless shouts and laughter floated over the grounds.

I had intended to sleep on one of the settees, but I found that the upstairs room had been scrubbed and a new bed installed. A nose-stinging odor of soaps and disinfectants lingered in the air.

The French doors had been closed; I opened them and stepped out on the balcony. Somewhere out in the darkness a woman laughed. The telescope was mounted on the parapet, still aiming over the grounds toward the corrals, still sharply focused; the bulls were quiet, massed together, smooth black shadows partly enfolded by other shadows. The dry, hot air carried a faint sweetish odor of the animals and their manure. Even at this distance and in this poor light I was uneasily aware of their dormant power and latent rage. Their distant ancestors had been worshiped as representatives of the gods, godly powers; these animals were mostly regarded as cattle, cruelly slain meat.

I lifted the barrel of the telescope and scanned the

villa's facade; most of the windows were dark, a few glowed behind curtains and Venetian blinds, and one big square window on the top floor blazed with light. My view was of a bright cube. At the rear was a wall lined with shelves containing porcelain and ivory figurines, a chair upholstered in patterned silk, and an escritoire. There was no movement and I was about to swivel the telescope when a woman entered the frame. Maria. Her hair was free, drifting like smoke to her waist, and she wore a black nightgown that she proceeded to remove. Then she unsnapped and removed a filmy black bra, and last, with a dreamlike slowness, she pulled down and stepped out of her bikini panties. She moved with an artificial grace, a satiric eroticism. Naked, smiling, Maria turned and directly faced the window, the telescope, me. I had never seen her nude. Then, swinging her hips, she advanced to the window, smiled and waved, stepped aside, and the curtains were gradually drawn.

I laughed. Maria had been up in my bedroom briefly tonight and evidently noticed the telescope. She'd awaited my return. No doubt she had her own telescope or a good pair of binoculars. She had watched the cottage, knowing that an uncurtained window might prove too tempting for me. And then, at the right moment, she had entered the frame and commenced her whimsical striptease.

Suddenly the curtains were drawn back and Maria, still nude, curtsied three times, acknowledging my silent applause (and maybe the silent applause of other voyeurs), and then she stepped aside and drew the curtain on her performance. There were no encores.

I went downstairs, made a cheese sandwich and a

small salad, got a beer from the refrigerator, put everything on a tray, and carried it up to the balcony. Maria's
window was dark now. I pictured her lying beneath the
bedsheet, laughing at me and herself.

There had been a subtle change in the light: it was
still dark, still night, but the air now seemed to possess a
dull luminosity that presaged the coming of dawn.

I ate half of the sandwich and a few forkfuls of salad. There was no point in trying to sleep now; Aguilar
would expect me at the bullring in ninety minutes. Anyway, I wasn't tired; I was running on nervous energy,
adrenaline, and I'd probably continue to do so until the
party ended.

My eye caught a brief flash of light in the hills above
and beyond Sophia Krisos's cottage. I swiveled the
telescope and scanned the terrain until I found some
dull metallic gleams. Yes, trucks, three of them, two
ordinary pickups and a flatbed. Men—pale faces and
hands, shadowy limbs and torsos—were unloading a
big spool of insulated wire from the flatbed. Four men
carried it up an incline and then mysteriously vanished,
gradually blending into a darkness the telescope could
not penetrate.

After a few minutes they one by one rematerialized
and descended the slope. I recalled that there was a cave
mouth in that general vicinity. There were many cave
openings scattered around the island, most of them cemented over so that they would be no danger to children
or the roaming herds of goat. So then, that particular
cave had been opened and these workers, Krisos's men,
were secretively preparing it for—for what? One of Alexander's peculiar entertainments, no doubt.

24

Precis of file 91-DFR
Authority: von R.
Senior Compiler: Max-DFR
Access: "Barbarosa"

BORN: April 9, 1913, Berlin.

FAMILY: Father: Erich Joseph Leuger, a prosperous furrier whose clientele included many of the rich and powerful of pre–World War One Germany. Leuger lost most of his considerable fortune in the days following that war, and his subsequent business ventures failed. A Lutheran; Mason; accomplished international fencer with the epee (fifth place, 1936 Olympics, Berlin). Refused to join the Nazi Party despite the urging of his son Jürgen and the advantages of membership. Died July 21, 1943, of renal failure. Mother: Ilsa Maria Goeltzer, a violinist for the

Berlin Philharmonic Orchestra until the birth of her first son, Rainer. In 1939 she was investigated by the Gestapo for suspected "Jewish blood." Investigation halted by order of Reinhard Heydrich (see Nuremburg transcripts). Brothers: Rainer, born 1911, killed in battle, Italy, 1943; Ernst, born 1917, killed in battle, Russia, 1942; Lothar, born 1917, killed in battle, France, 1944 (posthumous Iron Cross).

EDUCATION: Jürgen Leuger attended the University of Berlin as a philosophy student under the tutelage of Dr. Wilhelm Mauch (see Nuremburg transcripts), who enlisted him in the Nazi Party. Good student.

MILITARY CAREER: Jürgen Leuger joined the Nazi Party in August of 1933; enlisted in the SS in 1935; was accepted for duty in the Reichssicherheitshauptamt (RSHA) in 1936. Lieutenant, 1935; captain, 1937; major, 1941; colonel, 1944 (British rank equivalents). Leuger served "with great distinction" in Belgium, France, Poland, and Russia and in Germany "defending the Fatherland."

In Russia he was subordinate to Otto Ohlendorf (see Nuremburg transcripts), who headed the SS Einsatzengruppen D (see Nuremberg transcripts).

The four *Einsatzengruppen* (special action groups) A, B, C, and D were detailed to eliminate all Jews and Communist Party members.

Elimination was effected by firing squad and by the use of specially constructed "gas vans." It is estimated that Group D, under Ohlendorf's command, was responsible for the murders of approximately ninety thousand men, women, and children. Jürgen Leuger was present and in authority during the killing of from ten thousand to fifteen thousand of the victims. (See Nuremburg transcripts.)

Leuger went into hiding after the defeat of the Germans, living in a small Bavarian village. He was discovered in 1947, put on trial in 1948, and sentenced by the German courts to twenty years in prison. In 1952 he was ordered released from prison by order of the Bonn government, having served four years for his crimes.

In 1953, after release, Leuger immigrated to Chile and established an import-export business, which eventually prospered. It is known that he was an intimate of members of the Nazi exile group centered around Bariloche, Chile.

In 1981 Leuger sold his business and returned to Germany, establishing a residence in Berlin, another in the mountains outside Munich, and purchasing a villa in Majorca, Spain, where he spends the winter months.

It is known that Leuger remains active in several organizations whose purpose is to provide financial, legal, and moral support to former SS and RSHA officers. He regularly attends reunions of the SS and in 1991 publicly accepted a citation and medal from his comrades.

It is known that he assumed the financial burden for the legal defense of Otto Eck (see Nuremburg transcripts).

It is believed that he contributes generously to neo-Nazi groups and causes.

Leuger's SS serial number is tattooed beneath his left armpit; the SS motto (My honor is my loyalty) on his right biceps.

In 1992 Leuger suffered a heart attack and was hospitalized for six weeks.

Leuger has for more than fifty years denied any involvement in Einsatzengruppen D and maintains that he has never, by word or action, caused harm to the Jewish people. He frequently states that he could not be an anti-Semite, since his mother was herself of partly Jewish heritage.

SEE: Index of Nuremburg transcripts

Nazi Party, SS, and RSHA documentation

German federal government trial transcripts

German documents effecting the remand of Leuger's prison sentence

Documents made available to us by MOSSAD

Intercepts of Leuger's correspondence with clandestine SS organizations

Article in the May 30, 1989, issue of *Der Speigel*

Photographs re actions of *Einsatzengruppen* in Russia

25

The mingled fragrances of the flowers and the women's expensive perfumes were cloying.

"Smells like a Chinese whorehouse," Kon said.

"I've never been in a Chinese whorehouse."

"All right," he said amiably, "it smells like a Chinese restaurant."

We were in the center of the crowded patio, drugged on the heat and variety of perfumes, submerged in a babble of voices speaking four or five languages, all of them together blending into a single incomprehensible tongue. Bass, baritone, tenor, soprano, alto, contralto . . .

A dye had been added to the fountain's circulating water, and so now it spewed a pinkish froth the color of cotton candy. Pink water, an indigo sky, heat, rich perfumes, flowers, and gowns that shamed the spectrum.

"I'm seated at a table with Gypsy tonight," Kon said.

"Are you wearing a cup?"

"The Nazi will be at your table."

"Jürgen Leuger? Your father has a curious sense of humor, Kon, inviting that man."

"Father's sense of humor is becoming curiouser and curiouser."

"There's something going on at the cave in the hills above your mother's place. Mysterious night doings."

"Curiouser and curiouser. Look, I've got to go. I owe many people apologies for my behavior last night. I don't recall who I offended, so I'll apologize to everyone and let them sort it out."

Maria was sitting on a marble bench near the entrance gates. She wore a white dress and white pumps. Her legs were crossed, her arms folded, as slantwise she watched me approach the bench and sit at her side.

"Well?" I said.

"Well what?"

"Just well."

"Never mind," she said, looking away.

"Never mind what?"

"Just never mind. Don't say a word."

"Maria . . ."

"Don't humiliate me, please."

"Of course I won't humiliate you."

"You'll tease me. That's humiliating. I had far too much to drink."

"I was only going to say that I saw the prettiest nymph last night."

"See? I knew it. That's teasing. I had too much to drink and I thought I'd play a little joke on you, catch you spying and make a joke out of it."

"And it was funny, too," I said. "And charming. And provocative."

"Do you really think so?"

"I really do."

"You aren't lying to make me feel better?"

"No."

"I was so ashamed when I woke up this morning."

"I glimpsed a nymph, that's all. And nymphs never feel shame."

"Provocative?" she said. "Really?"

"Yes. And now I'll always see you naked, Maria, no matter how many clothes you wear. Right now I can see through your dress, your slip and bra and panties, see your smooth lovely skin."

"You bastard!" she cried, laughing. "I knew it. Treachery."

"I can see your breasts and your pubic beard and your compact, perky derriere."

Laughing, she leaned forward and buried her face in her palms.

I left Maria to her girlish modesty and mirth and wandered around the patio, overhearing disconnected snatches of conversation.

"Two billion. That's pounds sterling, Jack—twelve zeros, not nine."

"I left it in the room."

"The room! Jesus Christ, one of the servants is probably wearing it now."

"Je ne me sense pas bien."

"Qu'aves-vous?"

"J'ai des vertiges."

"I don't gamble. I never gamble. Only fools gamble. My investors do the gambling."

"Lieber noch Untergang!"

"Why, that is a most fallacious assertion. You have lovely, globular breasts." (Biki Benematale.)
"Do you actually think so?"
"Most assuredly."

"Un monstre gai vaut mieux qu'un sentimental ennuyeux."

"Yo soy un marinero." (Aguilar, telling a woman that he was a sailor.)

"I saw you go off with the bastard."
"Nothing happened."
"You were gone two hours."
"Yes, but nothing happened."
"Like all the other times nothing happened."

Only a Japanese woman, Mrs. Shimatzu, and I were punctual: we sat across from each other at the table, a six-top not far from the stage, and attempted polite conversation. She said something that I could not understand, and I replied with a phrase that baffled her. Mrs. Shimatzu was a tiny woman. She wore Western clothes and makeup, and her sleek black hair had been chopped off in a gamine style, but even so she resembled a Kabuki actress or a woman in an old Japanese print. She spoke an English so queerly inflected and accented that it sounded like Japanese. Only now and then did a recognizable English word emerge from the murky staccato flow. I spoke slowly and clearly, but I could tell by her embarrassed smile that she understood me no better than I understood her.

"You have a legitimate grievance against your English instructor," I said.

"Ah ben wen chew bat fin," she replied, smiling uncertainly. Finally I saw Nigel Rye advancing toward us in his slouched, semispastic shamble. He fussily searched for his place card and then slowly lowered himself into the chair. He pursed his cyanotic lips and blinked at us like a tortoise.

"You," he said. "F-f-friend of the f-f-family. Mr. what?"

"Chandler."

"Won't you introduce me to this l-l-lacquered doll?"

"Mrs. Shimatzu," I said, "this is Nigel Rye. Nigel, Mrs. Shimatzu."

She smiled and nodded shyly.

Rye inclined his head and spoke to the tablecloth: "So pleased, really, honored . . ."

"How is it going, Mr. Rye?" I asked.

He screwed his face up into a grotesque pout and then petulantly drawled, "Not altogether s-s-satisfactorily, actually. These Greek boys are extremely elusive; they aren't at all b-b-behaving as Greek boys are supposed to. I've found my own Alcibiades, but he is being very n-n-naughty."

"You may find yourself in a cistern," I said.

"B-b-bloody nonsense!"

"Like your brother, Simon."

"Oh, really, b-b-bloody s-s-stuff!"

Nigel Rye and Mrs. Shimatzu were to be dinner partners, the one outrageous and the other unintelligible; I looked forward to listening in on their conversation.

Louise Black and Jürgen Leuger arrived one after the other. Louise, "Poochy," was gorgeous with her red-gold hair and jade green eyes and a decollete that revealed most of her lightly freckled, creamy breasts. She addressed Nigel Rye as Lord Barley, but with a sly smile ("Ah, Mrs. Brown!" he cried, lurching to his feet.)

Jürgen Leuger was a very thin, erect old man whose facial skin was like scar tissue, very taut and glossy. He half-bowed to each of us before sitting down. His trembling hands, which he folded on the table, were deformed by arthritis and speckled with liver spots. His eyes, though, were a clear dark blue, and his voice was steady.

"So," he said, "I think we speak English, not French, at this table."

"You may s-s-speak Japanese if you wish," Nigel Rye said. "Please d-d-do."

Evelyn Callisto (Callisto the name of her eighth, most recently estranged, husband) was last to arrive at the table, last to enter the hall, and we all rudely stared at her as if examining a marvelous archaeological relic—which in a way she was. She waited for me to pull out her chair and then sat down in a queenly way. Her jewelry pulsed and glimmered in the candlelight: a diamond necklace and a diamond bracelet, a diamond ring with a stone as big as an acorn, a square-cut emerald ring and emerald earrings, a carved ivory brooch of a unicorn with ruby eyes.

She apologized for being late—"I'm always late"—and smiled, apparently unoffended by our greedy interest. Evelyn Callisto had not appeared in a significant movie in twenty years, and yet she remained a super-celebrity, a star, a notorious femme fatale: the tabloids recorded every act of virtue, the commission of every sin; the succession of husbands and lovers; the intervals of drug and alcohol addiction and periodic rehabilitation; the details of her cosmetic surgeries, her fund-raising for worthy charities—her soap opera life in general and in all its particulars.

I lied to her as last night I'd lied to Gypsy. "I like your movies very much," I said.

"Thank you," she said in her strained whiskey voice. "But most of them were trash. I've always wanted to do Shakespeare."

Leering, Nigel Rye said, "And I'm certain that the B-b-bard, were he alive, would like to d-d-do you."

"I wouldn't say no." Then, after a smile and a comic frown: "I can't remember ever saying no."

She was about sixty-five but appeared ageless; that is, neither young nor old, but rather one of those creatures that science fiction writers call androids. The cosmetic surgeons with their knives and liposuction and abrasion techniques and silicons and other black arts had reconstructed an imperfect version of the woman when she was twenty-five. Nigel Rye had referred to Mrs. Shimatzu as a lacquered doll; Evelyn was doll-like, too, a smooth plasticine replica that was almost, but not quite, like the original.

Louise Black and Jürgen Leuger were placing their orders with a waiter. Mrs. Shimatzu captured Nigel's attention with a volley of Japanese-English that sounded

like, "Gitso bin cho po bin ato." ("Indeed!" Rye cried.)
Evelyn turned to me. "You're Konstantin's friend,
aren't you? The one who's going to fight a bull."

"Did Kon tell you that?"

"Kon, Alexander, others. Alexander, you know, is
one of my oldest and dearest friends."

I said, "There's a conspiracy to get me to make a
fool of myself in the bullring. Alexander started it by
buying me a young bull and spreading word that I was
going to fight it. It won't happen."

"I had a long affair with a bullfighter years ago.
Miguel Navarro—Miquelito."

"I've heard of him."

"He was very good. But then the bulls ruined him. I
mean, he was badly gored in his genitals and was never
able to perform after that, in the ring or in bed."

"That's the kind of fate I'm trying to avoid."

"We tried everything, even a dildo, but you know,
that wasn't very satisfying to either of us."

"G-g-god, I adore s-s-smutty talk!" Nigel Rye shouted.

Evelyn obliged him by beginning a monologue
concerning her futile attempts to arouse the mutilated
matador; the neglected Mrs. Shimatzu self-consciously
plucked at her napkin; Leuger was explaining, in a ponderous German way, the workings of some mechanical
device to Louise Black.

Later, when the first course had been served, I
heard Leuger say, "I see, Mrs. Black, that you are eating smoked salmon. But you would call it lox, perhaps?
Jewish food. I find the notion of Jewish food very curious. Salmon—Jewish food? I do not think that salmon
swim in the Dead Sea."

We all looked at him.

"Latkes—potato pancakes? No, no, I don't think so. And borscht, surely that is Eastern European. Herring? Please, herring do not swim in the Dead Sea. I think what is called Jewish food is actually European food."

"I don't know," she said. "I never thought about it."

"There are no salmon in the Dead Sea. No lox."

"Very well," she said.

But Leuger was not ready to surrender his pedantry, his obsession.

"It is difficult to say who was the more seduced—Europe by the Jews or the Jews by Europe. But the Jews, an Oriental race, in Europe became more European than the Europeans. You absorbed our culture as a sponge absorbs moisture. Our music, our literature, our science, our philosophy, our ways, even our foods. Lox do not swim in the Dead Sea."

"Have some wine, old boy," Nigel said.

Mrs. Shimatzu looked anxiously around the table; she sensed the tension but could not understand the cause.

"All of us here will s-s-stipulate that lox do not swim in the D-d-dead Sea."

"Please, do not misinterpret my words. Do not be deceived by my reputation. That is all lies and half-lies. No one admires the Jewish race more than I. But, as I was saying, the Jews entered Europe and Europe entered the Jews. Isn't it a curious thing, Mrs. Black, how many Jews have fair hair and blue eyes? As you do. Fine golden hair and light skin and green eyes. You won't say those things are a part of your Jewish genetic inheritance."

Louise glanced around the table, searching for an ally, a sane face.

"I don't understand," she said to Leuger. "I'm not Jewish."

"Not wholly," he said.

"I'm Irish and Danish mostly, with some Swedish."

He smiled.

"I wouldn't mind being Jewish. But I'm not."

"I estimate that you have one-eighth to one-quarter Jewish blood. There is a type of facial asymmetry that is particularly Jewish."

We studied Louise's face for asymmetry.

"It is a matter of millimeters," Leuger continued, "the eyes a bit close together, one frequently smaller and higher than the other; a mouth that is not quite straight, and which often possesses a rather sour expression; a face that in pure Jews is virtually as wide as long; ears set a little lower than is normal in Europeans; and of course the famous Jewish nose."

"Oh, really, r-r-racial quackery, how b-b-bloody b-b-boring."

"Perhaps one of your grandparents concealed his or her heritage," Leuger went on, ignoring Nigel Rye.

Suddenly, in a voice almost shrill, Evelyn said, "Who are you?" Then: "Oh, it must be that the fucking Nazi."

She lifted her glass and, aiming carefully, threw the wine diagonally across the table into Leuger's face.

He recoiled, sat perfectly still for a moment, then lifted his napkin and gently patted his face dry.

People at the nearby tables were staring at us.

Leuger carefully folded his napkin along the original creases, placed it on the table, rose to his feet, bowed to each of us in turn (an especially low bow to Evelyn), and then with an absurd dignity walked across the hall and out the door.

Nigel, smirking demonically, said, "He behaves like a man who has a glass of wine thrown in his face every evening at d-d-dinner."

"I hope I didn't splash any wine on you, honey," Evelyn said.

"No," Louise replied.

"That's why I selected a white wine, in case I splashed you—it doesn't stain as bad as a red wine."

"I wish you wouldn't have done that," Louise said.

"I had to."

"I really do wish you hadn't."

"But I had to. I was Jewish once myself."

"Asymmetry indeed," Nigel said. "B-b-bloody astigmatism!"

The many high floodlights were focused down into the arena now, and the perfect circle of dark gold sand sparkled with tiny mica and pyrite crystals. All of the other lights in the complex—the villa, the cottages, and outbuildings—had been turned off so that the bullfighters might not be distracted or temporarily blinded at a critical moment. They would be isolated in a globe of radiance; the viewers, as if excluded more by the fringe of light than the two fences, were immersed in the insect-humming, bat-fluttering dark.

Today the corrals and adjacent areas had been covered by an enormous canopy. A helicopter was parked behind the villa. I knew that one of the villa's rooms had been converted to an emergency surgery and that Aguilar's personal physician had arrived on the island. If one of the toreros was seriously gored he would be rushed to the surgery for treatment and then, if necessary, evacuated to a hospital on the mainland.

Maria and I sat one-third of the way up in the steep half-bowl of the theater. Our sight lines were good, with no blind spots except for one patch just beyond the inner fence. One could sit closer to the action in a regular bullring, in the *barrera* or *contra barrera* seats, but even so, the theater provided a much better view than I had expected.

There were perhaps a hundred men and women scattered around us in the darkness, some of them drunk, some bored, some engaged in sexual rituals, but all of us—it occurred to me—all of us fools. We, not the killing of bulls, were the true spectacle.

Earlier I had seen Karl Heinrich, armed with a rifle, lounging beneath the trees. He was to be our protector in case one of the bulls escaped from the arena or corrals. A bull could easily jump the five-foot-high *barrera* fence into the passageway—many did—but clearing the eight-foot-high outer fence was not likely, though possible; bulls were amazingly agile for all their weight.

A bar had been set up on the upper rim of the theater and servants circulated, bearing trays of drinks. Maria accepted a glass of wine; I took a beer.

"How many bulls is Aguilar going to kill?" Maria asked me.

"Just two this evening. Two more on Friday."

"And you'll be fighting your *torito* Friday night?"

"In your dreams."

"Coward," she said.

"If you say so."

"Liar," she said scornfully. "You said you were a bullfighter. You lied."

"I never said that I was a bullfighter, and I wasn't. I was an *aficionado practicante.*"

"*Cobarde practicante.*"

"Maria, give it up."

"Do it, Jay, fight and kill your *torito,* and then come to me drenched in bull's blood and take me."

"I'll think about it."

"Better yet, come to me in the form of a bull, like Zeus, and rape me."

"Zeus, as I recall, turned himself into a swan."

"That's all right, too."

One of the two gates on the far side of the arena opened, and Aguilar and his assistants entered. They walked casually across the sand. There was not the usual parade, no trumpets, no posturing; they strolled through the brightness, slipped behind the *barrera,* and in a businesslike way began arranging their gear—capes, muletas, the leather sword case, *banderillas,* water bottles. Since this was an exhibition and not a formal *corrida de toros,* Aguilar was dressed in what was called the *traje corto:* boots, tight trousers with slightly flared bottoms, a white silk shirt, a waist-length black jacket, and a flat-brimmed Córdoban hat. His men, though, wore their usual outfits.

"Have you ever seen a more handsome and dashing man?" Maria asked.

"Every morning when I shave."

"In your dreams," she said. And then: "Here comes your kraut friend."

A shadowy form was ascending the steps toward us, and for an instant I irrationally thought the "kraut friend" might be Jürgen Leuger; but then von Rabenau slipped into the aisle and sat next to me.

"Come along, Chandler."

"Go away, Walter," Maria said. "Can't you see that we're occupied?"

"Sorry. Chandler?"

"Is this important?"

"Yes."

As we descended the steps a gate opened on the far side of the arena and a bull erupted out of the chute and into the white glare. The tossing hump on his shoulders was thickly swollen. His eyes and curving horns and black coat reflected gleams of light. He paused briefly in the center of the ring, all of his speed and power and aggression tightly coiled, explosive—he looked like a magnificent sculpture—and then he saw motion behind the *barrera* and charged.

26

Crowd noises, cheers and jeers, and the percussion of hooves on the hard earth gradually diminished. The upper sections of the trees in the little park glowed emerald in the floodlights. Von Rabenau, refusing to speak, led me through the park (past a pair of his lounging "commandos") and around the back of the villa to where his Land Rover was parked.

"What is it this time, Walter?"

"Get in."

He did not switch on the headlights until we began to descend the steep switchbacks of the cliff road. Ahead I could see a halo of light above the village, and to my left the moon-frosted sea. Little bursts of foam swiftly expanded into long white combers that cracked loudly as they hit the reef. The sky remained clear; the star-hazed Milky Way arched from horizon to horizon, a galactic bridge.

"Find another flayed cadaver, Walter?" I asked.

"I'm quitting," he said, his voice raspy with fatigue. "I'm through at the end of this week. It isn't worth it. Alexander is mad. The entire family is mad. They've all been deranged by money and power. Karl wants my job—well, he can have it, and good luck to him. I have enough money saved. I'll retire to Spain or Portugal. What do you think, Chandler?"

"There are already too many retired Germans in Spain and Portugal."

He smiled faintly. "Italy, then."

"Same story, too many Germans."

"All right, then. Florida or Arizona."

"Too many Americans."

The party for all those who had not been invited to the Party was still in progress, wilder and noisier than last night, tending toward anarchy now. There was a desperate note to the gaiety, hostility waiting behind the raucous good cheer.

"Smile," Walter said.

Shining faces, oddly alike in their stupid blankness, stared in at us. Were they resentful, angry, joyful? I couldn't tell. I looked for Pamela but did not see her. There were only a few women on the streets, none of them Greek.

"Keep smiling," Walter said. Then: "I would not care to drive through this rabble in a limousine tonight."

The crowd thinned, the conflicting music (Greek, pop, rock) faded behind us, and we drove along the harbor quay (Alexander's moored yacht brightly lighted and strung with pennants from bow to stem, but apparently unoccupied except for the crew), and around a slight curve to an isolated four-story apartment building against the cliff wall.

On the elevator Walter said, "No, not a looted corpse this time, Chandler. A fresh one, still warm."

"Ah," I said. "Good."

He smiled with clenched teeth, roughly combed his hair with his fingers, and obscurely said, "Justice delayed is justice denied."

The elevator doors opened into the sitting room of a large apartment. There was a stink of feces in the room: the hanged man had emptied his bowels.

A pair of young village policemen quickly rose from a sofa when we entered. One of them held an open bottle of Metaxa.

"You are needed in the village," von Rabenau said. "Tell Dr. Demetrios to come here immediately. Go. And leave the bottle."

"Fools," he said when they were gone. Then: "Stinks, doesn't he? Shit his trousers. They say a hanged man ejaculates when he dies, but I don't see any sign of that, do you? Well, he was old, dried up, didn't even have that last consolation."

It was a big room whose French doors and balcony overlooked the village roofs and harbor. Beige carpeting, a mix of old and new furniture, watercolor paintings on the walls, doors leading to the bedrooms, bathroom, and kitchen.

Von Rabenau picked up the Metaxa bottle and carried it to the drink cabinet. "Brandy?"

"Yes," I said. "Walter, why was he staying here? He was a guest."

"Think. Count. There are far more guests than cottages and rooms in the villa. The overflow was stashed here and at another place. They didn't mention it to the other guests, of course."

There was an overturned chair on the floor. Leuger,

his head bowed penitently, his arms straight and his toes pointed downward, slowly and for just a few degrees twisted clockwise and then counterclockwise. He had become a smelly sort of pendulum.

Von Rabenau gave me a glass of brandy. "Cheers," he said.

Leuger had cut a length of cord from the Venetian blinds, tied one end to the ceiling light fixture, fashioned a noose, and stepped off the chair into oblivion.

"Look," I said.

On the coffee table was a half-empty bottle of beer and a plate containing half a sandwich and a few black olives.

"This guy had a glass of wine thrown in his face at the dinner table, left, came here and ate a little, and then hung himself."

"Do you feel sorry for him?" Walter asked.

"A little, I suppose."

"Have you read his dossier?"

"Yes."

"And you pity him, even while knowing what he had done."

"All I saw was a queer old duffer whose hands trembled."

The cord was deeply buried in the flesh of Leuger's neck. His eyes bulged, his complexion was dark red, almost purple, and his jaw, his lips, were slack.

"*Requiescat in pace,* do you think?"

"I threw a drink in Nico Krisos's face last night."

"Christ, did you? Was that smart? There's a lot of nasty in Nico."

"I know."

"And after all, Chandler, he is a cripple."

"Walter, why did you bring me here?"

"Remember, you are my eyes and ears."

"Fine. I heard Leuger espouse his demented theories of Europe and the Jew, the Jewish physiognomy. I saw Evelyn throw a glass of wine into his face. I saw him leave the table, leave the dining hall. There. You have the testimony of my eyes and ears."

"Odd, don't you think, that a man who had endured the general execration of humanity, the knives of his own conscience—if he had one—the nearly total psychic exile of the mass murderer . . . odd that he should finally kill himself because of a social snub, a splash of wine?"

"I don't know. Maybe he was exhausted. Maybe his health was poor."

"Really, Chandler, do you believe that men like Leuger kill themselves?"

"Hitler did. Goring did. Goebbels did. Himmler did."

"Yes, but out of remorse? Because of social ostracism?"

"Christ, I don't know and I don't care."

Von Rabenau stopped the corpse's slow twisting.

Leuger's dinner jacket, wetted to remove the wine stain, was folded over the back of a chair.

"Alexander killed him, of course. Or had someone kill him. I'd guess that he did it himself."

"Get some sleep, Walter. It's what it seems: a suicide."

"Really? You said you read Leuger's file. Was it the abbreviated version?"

"All the files you gave me are abbreviated."

"But you read the file, you know about this man's

connection with Greece, with Alexander, and you still say that this was a suicide?"

"There was nothing in his file about Greece or Alexander."

"Ah." Von Rabenau tapped at his front teeth with a thumbnail. "Alexander has been in my computer, erasing. Have you read Alexander's file yet?"

"No."

"Read it. And while you read it, remember that Jürgen Leuger commanded an SS unit in Greece, in the Peloponnesos, in a village called Saint Spyridon, in the winter of 1940. Then tell me that this was a suicide."

"All right, Walter. I'll read the file. Now will you give me a ride back to the villa?"

He fished in his pocket and threw me the keys to the Land Rover. "I have to wait for the doctor."

Maria was sitting alone at a table in the patio, near the fountains, whose reflections scattered pink bubbles of light over her dress and hair. A man and a woman— Konstantin and Gypsy—were sitting close together at a table in the shadows, whispering furiously.

I sat across from Maria and tasted her drink— lemonade.

"What was that about?" she asked.

"One of Walter's whims. How was the bullfight?"

"So-so." She appeared to be in one of her sulky moods, or perhaps, like the rest of us, she was merely very tired.

"Tell me about it."

"The bulls were no good. Enormous *mansos*. Aguilar did all he could with them—more, really, than was safe. The crowd naturally didn't understand that kind of work, mostly *piton á piton*."

"Well, maybe the other bulls will be better."

"Maybe. Were you off seeing your Pamela?"

"No. Walter and I had a drink in the village."

"Did another corpse show up?"

"What do you mean?"

"Oh, come on, Jay; everyone knows that Simon Rye was murdered, and that his body was stolen from the meat freezer and found skinned on your bed." She paused to smile maliciously. "And the other man, the photographer or whatever he was, who was killed by the bulls. Those are the prime topics of gossip around here. That and who is screwing whom."

"And who is screwing whom?"

"From what I hear, Jay, everybody is screwing everybody else. Except you're not screwing me."

"We're the exception to the rule. How did that story about Simon Rye's flayed cadaver get out?"

"Secrets can't be kept on this little island."

"Some secrets are kept very well here."

"Cryptic utterance. What do you mean?"

"Nothing."

She finished her lemonade, leaned back, and sighed. "Take me to the village. Maybe they're having fun down there."

"It may be turning into an ugly sort of fun."

"All the better."

"I didn't sleep at all last night. Watching nymphs and such. I'm going to bed now."

"Fine. Perfect. Go."

I awakened just before dawn and aimed the telescope toward the hills beyond Sophia's cottage: lights again, and trucks, and men furtively working.

27

Aguilar devoted all of the morning workout to instructing me on techniques that I didn't need or want to learn. When I protested once again that I was absolutely not going to fight the *novillo* Friday night he merely shrugged and said, "Extend your arms; stretch; lengthen the pass."

He believed that I was adequate with the cape but required much more schooling in the muleta.

"No *naturales,*" he said. "*Derechazos* only."

The *derechazo* was a right-handed pass performed with the sword spreading the muleta; the *naturale,* basically the same pass on the left side but without the sword and consequently with a smaller, limp muleta, was far more dangerous.

"The goons in the seats won't know the difference."

He also worked on my punishing passes, *piton apiton* (horn-to-horn) techniques, and *remates,* and passes that freeze the bull in place and passes that release him.

"Not too ugly, El Poeta," he said.

There was no shade here, no refuge; we stood in the center of the arena with the sunlight burning down and

the ring of earth like a griddle underfoot. It was a desolate African sky, an African heat. My eyes burned with
sweat, my shirt and shorts were soaked, and I had a
feeling of vertigo. If I had eaten breakfast this morning I
might have vomited now.

The scars on Aguilar's legs were a stark glossy white
against the suntan.

"How many bulls have you killed?" he asked.

"Seventeen. The eighteenth sent me to the infirmary."

"So few?"

"One too many."

"Were you bad at the killing?"

"No. Actually, I had good luck at it. It was a messy
business once, but I never had any fiascoes like some of
my friends."

"Killing is mostly a matter of confidence. You were
confident."

"Yes, but that was a long time ago."

"I learned something about killing in slaughterhouses.
I bribed the workers to let me practice killing market cattle
with my sword. Of course it isn't the same, but you learn
where to place the sword, the exact spot and the precise
angle, and how you'll hit bone if the animal isn't correctly
squared. I killed a great many cattle. Many bulls, too, more
than a thousand, and perhaps three hundred *novillos*."

"Bovines can hardly be glad to see you coming."

"Nor I them. Let's see how you look with a sword in
your hand, El Poeta."

After the workout I walked down the ridge road toward
Sophia's cottage. The dust was ankle-deep and as soft as

ashes. Small lizards, buried in the dust, erupted and scurried off into the brush when I approached. I saw birds that, from a distance, appeared injured, broken-winged and flopping, but they were just taking dust baths. The land and encircling sea looked flattened, stunned by heat and glare, and a dirty brownish smog haze rimmed the horizon. Plants and cacti were more gray than green, parched yellow in spots, and the sparse grasses had turned to straw.

But Sophia's place remained an oasis in the sere desolation, an acre of green.

She was working in her garden when I arrived. Her hair was covered by a red bandanna, and she wore a full black dress that fell to her ankles, straw slippers, and dirty cotton gloves. She smiled and straightened when she saw me.

"Ho!" she cried. "It's you!"

"It is I, Ho," I said.

She removed the right glove and offered me her hand.

"You said you like men to stink," I said, "and so I have come here stinking."

She jokingly sniffed the air. "Not so stinking. Hungry."

"And thirsty."

"Yes, I think so."

I sat on a bench in the cool aqueous light of the little arbor. A few arrows of light pierced the lattice and the leafy vines. Bees were still busy looting nectar from the tiny bell-shaped flowers.

Sophia, in three trips (she refused my offer of help) carried in trays containing plates, utensils, glasses, and coffee cups; a pitcher of water and a pot of coffee; a sliced melon and some oranges and plums; and finally a loaf of fresh bread, butter, and honey.

While we ate I told her an abbreviated version of events at the villa, alluding to the sexual intrigues, the petty maneuvering for position, the feuds, and I told her about Jürgen Leuger's suicide. She already knew about Simon Rye and the by now almost mythical paparazzo.

"Terrible," she said. "Every year. Terrible things."

I mentioned my seeing lights late at night in the hills beyond her cottage; Sophia said that she had once or twice heard the sound of vehicles, machinery, and once—pointing at the floor—"Down there!"

The caves were very dangerous. Hesitantly, searching for the English words, she told me about a French team of "cave people" who years ago had come to explore and chart the cave system. There had been some sort of accident, a rockfall, perhaps, or flooded chambers—she was vague—and two of the six Frenchmen had been lost in the deepest caverns, and their bodies never recovered.

After eating, Sophia went into the cottage and returned with a battered old photo album. Inside were badly focused pictures of Alexander and herself when they were young and poor (Sophia lithe and pretty, Krisos even then a man whose stance and expression signaled danger), and later, better-quality photographs of Maria, Kon, and Nico when they were children— bright, happy rich kids.

"Why you don't bring Maria?" she asked.

"I'll bring her the next time I come."

"Yes. Tomorrow."

"Tomorrow, perhaps."

"Tell them. Maria, Konstantin, Nico. Come see mother."

"I'll tell them."

*   *   *

Alexander was sitting on a bench in the little park that separated the villa from the cottages. His strong face was blandly inexpressive now, neutral. He wore a white panama hat, a light-weight linen suit and white silk shirt, but no tie, no socks, and sandals instead of shoes. He looked like a character in a John Huston film, maybe a new member of the *Maltese Falcon* bullies.

I sat on the grass, my back against a tree trunk, and lit a cigarette.

"So you're still smoking."

"And so are you."

"Cigars are different."

"Were you waiting here for me?"

"Waiting? No."

"I was visiting your ex-wife."

"Yes?"

"I like her."

"So do I," he said dryly.

"But I don't understand why she chooses to live this way, on this island."

"It puzzles me as well."

"She says it's so she can see her children more often."

"Yes."

"But her sons and daughter spend only a few weeks a year here."

"That is true."

"And even then they rarely visit her."

"Yes. Well . . ."

"Jürgen Leuger killed himself last night. But you know that, of course."

"Of course."

"That's three, and it's only Wednesday."

"Are you blaming me?"

"I think you are partly responsible."

He smiled and cocked his head.

"You're a bad man, Alexander."

"But you've always known that. If I had been a *good* man I'd still be in the Peloponnesos, ignorant, foolish, unable to care properly for my family, always a little hungry, always tired, a poor herdsman or farmer, my life barren and my pride ruined, the helpless victim of anyone more powerful than I, less *good,* an impotent old man, Jay."

"Virtue is its own reward," I said, and we laughed together. He said, "You missed the bullfights last night."

"Thanks to Walter."

"They weren't very interesting."

"You could have made them interesting by buying bulls from a first-rate ranch. These bulls are virtually impossible to work with any artistry."

"But I don't care about artistry. I'm more concerned with watching the primal contest, seeing if a man can subdue and dominate his fear rather than merely subduing and dominating a stupid beast."

"'The only beast is the crowd,'" I said, quoting Blasco Ibáñez.

"The problem is Aguilar. He's too skilled, too experienced, too courageous. Now, to watch a man of marginal skill and courage face those very big and difficult bulls—"

"You're not talking about me, are you, Alexander?"

We laughed again.

28

Aguilar was late for our morning workout. I waited in a crescent of shade on the east side of the ring, inhaling the odors of the bulls and the dry air that again today smelled of dust and bitter herbs and pollution—a smoky haze dimmed the sun and veiled distant islands. It was as if great fires were burning somewhere over the horizon. The high-pressure system remained centered over the Libyan plateau, and you could taste the accumulated poisons, see them in your discolored phlegm when you spat.

"Filthy air," Aguilar said when he arrived.

I told him that I had changed my mind about fighting the *novillo* tonight.

He studied my expression. "All right. But why?"

"Maybe I'm bored."

"That *novillo* will unbore you quickly enough."

"Maybe it's a gesture—punctuation, full stop. My life is going to change soon."

"Alexander said that you would finally agree to fight the *novillo.*"

"Alexander knows a lot. But there's a lot that he doesn't know."

"Get the muleta. We'll make it a slow, easy workout. You don't want to breathe these gases too deeply."

Afterward we sat beneath the trees in the park and Aguilar talked about the bulls. He mentioned their vision. The vision of the bovines was peculiar, not at all like a man's. To a certain extent each eye functioned independently of the other. That's why you always tried to interest, compel, the outside eye, the eye farthest from your body. The vision of each eye was basically conical, like a flashlight beam spread out over the ground. This is a simplification, but true enough. There were blind spots in a bull's vision, particularly one four or five feet directly in front of the bull and low—that's why you often see toreros kneel there with their backs to the tired animal; they were invisible. It was a trick predicated on the species's odd vision. "Don't think about the animal's temperament," Aguilar said, "or his intelligence—he has none. Think about his vision: what is he seeing? More important: what is he failing to see? Forget the horns. It's the eyes, always the eyes. And movement; a bull is virtually blind until an object moves."

And he talked about terrains, the bull's terrain and the man's, the complexity of terrains in a perfectly circular arena—where is the bull aggressive and where does he become defensive? For example, he will usually swerve away from the fence and toward the center of the ring, which is why you rarely worked a bull when he was between you and the fence. And yet sometimes, and you had to recognize it, a bull preferred to wage combat in *suerte contraria*.

Aguilar had a great deal more to tell me, but I didn't

want to hear any more. I got to my feet. "You make it sound very difficult," I said.

He smiled. "It really isn't terribly difficult," he said. "Only that the penalty for ignorance can be severe."

Back in the cottage I locked the door, closed all of the blinds, and turned on the air-conditioning unit. The room cooled quickly, and the filtered air smelled less strongly of chemical pollutants. I sat in the humming cool breeze and thought.

I intended to fast the twelve or thirteen hours until the bullfight—twenty hours after my last meal. My stomach and intestinal tract would be empty then in case I received an abdominal wound. Aguilar's surgeon, Dr. Medina, would have his work simplified.

Tight clothing, nothing to snag on a horn tip: a blue polo shirt tucked into old jeans, jogging shoes, and a red bandanna folded and wrapped around my forehead as a sweatband. And for a touch of color, a bit of dash. Red for dash, red for blood, red for the hell of it.

I sat at the kitchen counter and drank glass after glass of orange juice.

Fighting the *novillo* was stupid of me, of course. Bravado. There hadn't been time to train properly. And he was awfully big for a *novillo,* just a few months away from being considered an adult bull; and he came from a ranch notorious for the difficulty of their stock; and too the fight was to take place at night in a makeshift arena, with the makeshift infirmary one hundred yards away.

At eleven o'clock Maria came to see me. She rattled the doorknob and then tried to peer in through a crack in the blinds, calling, "Jay? Jay?" After a while she went away.

I didn't know where I was going, just that I was leaving this place, these people. It had been a mistake to come here. They were not, as we all except Nico pretended, my family. I had been summoned by them—the temple was a pretext I'd welcomed—and now perhaps in subtle ways I was being dismissed.

I had been temporarily co-opted by the Krisos family, not corrupted. It wasn't their wealth alone that drew me to them, but their vitality and bold eccentricity and the sense that soon, within minutes, one of them would do something daring or funny or dangerous or simply surprise you with a gratuitous insult or spontaneous kindness.

When relaxing, like now, they were as willful and anarchistically free as feral children. Paradoxically, few persons were more disciplined that the Krisos family members: Maria was a slave to her music, Alexander worked eighteen-hour days for weeks on end, Kon and Nico were deeply involved in their father's business affairs, and even Sophia Krisos spent her years laboring like a peasant.

Sometime after noon Jack Black pounded on the back door and shouted something about lunch in the back gardens. Poochy would be present. Jack pimped his beautiful wife in a harmless, chaste way; used her to attract company. Wealth had abraded rather than polished Jack. He was an ignorant man, a bore, and consequently isolated in a gathering like this.

An hour later Biki Benematale arrived on the porch. He, like Maria, rattled the doorknob and attempted to peer in through a slit in the Venetian blinds. Perhaps he could see me in the dimness of the room, perhaps not, but he, like the others, seemed to believe that I was present.

"Mr. Chandler, my friend, are you there? It is Biki. You remember Biki, do you not?"

He moved to another window, pressed his face against the glass.

"It is I, Biki. I must have a word with you, sir."

He was a huge shadow against the glowing yellow of the blinds.

"Are you not receiving guests at this time?" He giggled and continued down the porch to another window.

Finally he said, "Very well then, Mr. Chandler. I shall leave my card."

As I was leaving the cottage that evening I found his large gold-embossed calling card pressed between the screen door and the jamb.

General Biki Benematale
D.C.B. / Knights of Tumba / B.M.E.
Gnostic Mysteries (Master) / Societe du LeRoi
K.R.C. M.B.O. / King (deposed) C.O.E
et honeurs comparable

29

.

We could hear the people in the theater on the hillside above us, sense the weight of their boredom and hostility, but all of them were concealed by a curved wall of darkness. They were safely anonymous while we were encapsulated in the bright glow of the floodlights.

Smoke haze was incandesced and textured by the light. It was not thick enough to much affect visibility, but it increased the mood of dreamlike isolation.

I experienced a quick series of associations: we were striding across the bottom of a cloudy crystal ball; we were like insect specimens pinned by light and critical eyes; we were the accused in an arena of harsh judgment.

We slipped into the passageway between the *barrera* and the high outer fence. My mouth was dry and tasted chalky; my tongue felt swollen, inert—a slab of flesh. Tension had narrowed my vision and skewed perspective. Aguilar saw me repeatedly blinking, grinned, and said, "Calma, El Poeta, calma."

I had asked that my *novillo* be released first. I wanted to get it over with quickly. I didn't want to stand here numbly and watch Aguilar's six-hundred-kilo monsters thunder around the ring, splintering fence planks with their horns, goring horses and maybe men. My nerve probably wouldn't last longer than the fifteen or twenty minutes necessary to work and kill the *novillo*.

Aguilar's men were stationed at various points around the arena. They would run the bull when it entered, and they would be prepared to rush out to help me if I was tossed.

I was aware of the impatience of the viewers above me in the darkness; then the gates were opened and the *novillo* exploded into the arena. He looked very big to me, enormous, and mystically potent. I had seen adult four-year-old bulls that were smaller. Black, with curving black horns that lightened to ivory as they tapered to points. He was as quick as a quarter horse. The fenced circle of earth reverberated like a drumskin to his hooves. He showed no hesitancy, no timidity—he was far more eager for the battle than I.

Aguilar's men, flapping their capes one after the other, drawing the *novillo's* charge, ran him twice around the perimeter, and then Aguilar stepped out into the ring. He passed the *novillo* three times without much style. He didn't want to detract from my performance with a display of his superior skill.

He returned to the passageway and said, "He's a cupcake. Be nice to him."

I entered the glowing smoky haze and cited the bull from about thirty feet. He charged immediately. My veronica was a little too slow, and a horn tip caught and almost tore the cape out of my hands. He turned quickly, almost falling, and came back before I was fully prepared. I retreated a step and managed to flag him past, but too close, the horn missing my leg by a couple of inches. Aguilar shouted something about "angles." I'd lost the bull on my second pass, and now I had to run after him and regain his attention.

The *novillo* was a little slower than when he entered the ring, and my two passes, even though sloppy and defensive, had given me confidence. I passed him with four more veronicas that felt very good, almost as slow and smooth as practice passes, and then I turned him sharply and stopped him with a media veronica.

"Not too bad," Aguilar said as I moved behind the fence.

I heard boos and whistles, and for a moment I believed they were intended for me; but then I saw the mounted picador enter the ring.

Aguilar did not think that I was prepared for the tricky business of leading the bull to the horse, and so he did it himself, swiftly, casually, and again without style. The bull took two hard pics, staggering the horse both times. He did not break away when the steel entered his flesh, but kept charging, leaning in, fighting to get at the horse and rider.

Then José, Aguilar's *peon de confianza,* went out and placed three pairs of sticks.

I got the muleta and the lightweight false sword.

"He's developing bad tendencies," Aguilar said. "He's beginning to search. Don't work him close; give yourself a margin. And make your faena brief—he won't remain honest much longer. Do you understand?"

I nodded.

"Keep his face buried in the cloth."

"Okay."

"And use your right hand only. No *naturales*. Nothing fancy. Don't get rabid out there."

"All right, all right."

"Don't stray toward the center of the ring. Stay close to the *barrera*. We'll be just a few yards away in case something happens."

"Christ," I said, "is there anything else?"

He grinned and slapped my shoulder. I could see that he was worried.

The animal was hurt now, and tired and slow. He would not charge from a distance. I had to shuffle cautiously forward until entering the area he was defending. He was conserving his remaining strength; he wanted to be sure. I stamped my foot, inched closer, stamped again. His back and shoulders were bloody from the pics and the banderillas, and a small mushroom of blood pumped out of the pic wound.

Then I entered his range and provoked him into charging. He was very slow and still "honest," and I linked five *derechazos* into a continuous series, the last pass *en rondo,* 360 degrees. Twice he came so close that my jeans and shirt were smeared with his blood, and the clattering bandilleras whipped against my ribs. His nostrils foamed. His exhalations were soft huffing explosions, like the sound of gasoline fumes bursting into flame, and his hoofbeats seemed to vibrate in the air all around me, humming.

I walked a few yards away to rest him for the next series. The crowd was cheering. I felt exhilarated, invincible.

"*Cuidado!*" Aguilar called, seeing that I was losing control of myself, becoming "rabid." "Be careful!"

But I was in a kind of delirium: I knew that my passes had been good, perhaps very good, slow and suave and close; and they had given me an emotion that I was not yet willing to surrender.

I removed the sword and approached the bull with the muleta in my left hand. Just a few *naturales,* I thought, three or four, and then I would square him up and kill him.

"No!" Aguilar said. He was angry.

I had to move close to the bull, less than a yard away, to provoke a charge. It was the same as before with the first two passes, but on the third the bull stopped in midcharge, veered in toward me, and tossed his horns into the cloth. The flat of his left horn struck me hard on my right thigh. I got rid of him with a clumsy *paso de pecho* and walked over to the fence, disappointed to have spoiled the emotion of the good series of passes with that near tossing.

"Sorry," I said. "I should have listened."

José held out the leather sword case and I withdrew the heavy curved sword and handed him the fake.

"Do you want me to kill him?" Aguilar asked.

"No, hell no."

"I think I should."

"No."

"Don't try to place the sword correctly. Spear him low and at an angle; go for the lungs."

"Should I punish him first?"

"*Matalo,*" Aguilar said. Kill it.

The animal was very defensive now. He stood quietly, head low, smeared with blood and saliva, and for the first time I pitied him.

I furled the muleta and profiled, aiming down the length of the sword, and then moved forward. The bull seemed to follow the sweep of cloth. The sword hit bone and flexed, bowed, and with a pinging sound recoiled and rose spinning into the smoky light above. At the same time I felt my body being lifted, effortlessly levitated, and I was soaring. Flash thoughts: Was I seriously gored? Would the sword cut me—or even pierce my body—when it fell? Would the bull drive a horn into me, my head or chest, before Aguilar and the others arrived? It happened very quickly in real time, for those watching, but I had been abruptly plunged into torpid dream time.

And then I was on the ground (with no sense of impact), on my back, digging my heels into the earth and trying to squirm away. But he was on me, driving his horns left and right, spraying saliva and blood, and I could smell the beast, blood and sweaty hide and hair, a thick, sweet stench, and his hot breath in my face. Capes were flashing all around, but he wouldn't leave me. Then Aguilar was kicking him on the nose, kicking hard with the pointed toes of his boots, and finally the bull was distracted.

Aguilar's men wanted to carry me out of the arena, but I fought them off and limped over to the passageway.

My clothes were soaked with blood. Bull's blood or my blood, I couldn't tell. There was no pain. I was numbed, dazed, as if just awakened from a deep sleep.

"He got you," José said.

"Where?"

He pointed to a ragged tear in my jeans.

I backed against the outer fence, lowered the jeans, and cautiously probed the wound. It was a ragged, bleeding hole the size of a half-dollar on my inner right thigh, a few inches below the old scar. Still no pain. I inserted my index finger into the hole, and when I removed it there was blood up past the second knuckle.

"*Puntazo*," José said.

Out in the ring Aguilar had twisted the bull with a few punishing passes and was now squaring him for the kill.

The wound had come when I'd been tossed, but to my amazement the bull hadn't gored me afterward, while I'd been lying helplessly on the ground. Perhaps he had been too eager.

"*Puntazo*," José said again. "You were very lucky."

The word meant a jab or stab, a slight wound caused by a penetrating horn tip; while a *cornada* was a deeper, serious wound.

Now Aguilar profiled, went in, and buried his sword to the hilt. A great hemorrhage of blood gushed out of the animal's mouth and nostrils, bright, foamy lung blood. He staggered away, walking slowly toward the far side of the arena, toward the gate through which he had entered.

I pulled up my trousers. José, holding my arm, led me around the passageway.

"*Un puntazo, solemente*," he said. But it was more than a *puntazo* while less than a *comada*.

The bull fell, got up, and slowly continued his weary trek to nowhere—perhaps toward a remembered pasture.

Just before we left the arena Aguilar dispatched the

bull with a single stroke of the *descabello*. He fell over onto his side, legs stiffly thrust out.

Dr. Medina probed and cleaned the wound, stitched it closed, bandaged it, gave me an injection of penicillin and an antitetanus shot. He said the wound was not very serious, less than three inches deep and with the single trajectory. The femoral artery had not been touched. He thought that I might have a couple of cracked ribs, though, and so he tightly wrapped my chest with tape. He assured me that the other minor lacerations and the bruises would heal quickly.

"I saw it all," he said. "Your luck is phenomenal."

He was a brutish-looking man with gentle hands and a soft voice.

"A little hole. Nothing to worry about. But don't let it become infected."

He wanted to tell me about the really serious horn wounds he had treated: deep thigh gorings with four or five trajectories, (each trajectory fouled by dirt and manure); severed femoral arteries, severed femoral nerves; horns that had entered the groin and penetrated the abdominal cavity; pierced chests and crushed skulls; emasculations; horns that had driven up through the anus and colon and ripped the intestines . . .

The pain was becoming severe now, in my leg and ribs, my back, everywhere, and I felt a postadrenal nausea.

My vision dimmed when I stood up. "Do you have something for the pain?"

He was surprised. "Pain is natural," he said. "You must endure pain. I don't believe in painkillers."

"I do," I said.

He reluctantly gave me a jar containing a dozen capsules of a morphine compound.

"Thank you, Dr. Medina."

"For nothing."

"Your fee?"

He waved away the thought of a fee.

"Good-bye, then."

"See me tomorrow. And, my friend, stay away from the bulls."

30

I was awakened by the sound of someone opening the cottage's front door, and a moment later I heard footsteps on the stairway. The bedroom lights were turned on, and Maria approached the bed.

"Oh, poor baby," she said, and she sat on the edge of the bed and smiled down at me. Wisps of smoky hair lay aslant her cheek. "Does it hurt terribly?"

"It's a mortal wound."

"First you were mediocre, then fairly good, then you were very good for a minute, and then you were mediocre again, and then you were flying."

"That sounds about right."

"I was so scared when you were on the ground and the *torito* was after you. I thought he was going to eat you alive. He was hooking at you left and right, left and right, and from the theater it looked like the horns were going into your body. Did you hear me screaming? I thought, *My poor dear Jay, that* torito *is turning him into lace.* And I shrieked."

"Don't call him *torito* anymore. He was a *toro.*"

"Let me see the wound."

"It's bandaged; you can't see anything."

She abruptly lifted the bedsheet and looked at me. "You're naked," she said.

"Maria . . ."

She removed the purse slung over her shoulder and took out a bloody cloth napkin. "I had one of the men cut this off your *torito*." She unfolded the napkin and held up a bloody triangular ear.

"Take it with you when you go. It'll draw flies."

"Not as many flies as Simon Rye, I bet."

"Maria, I'm in considerable pain, I'm groggy . . . Thanks for stopping by, but . . ."

She stood up and began undressing. It was not like the night when I had watched her perform a slow, comic striptease; there was nothing coy or playful about her now, no posing. She was neither hurried nor slow, neither shy nor bold; this was the simple shedding of clothes.

"It's impossible," I said. "I've got a bloody hole in my thigh, and cracked ribs, cuts and bruises."

She snatched away the bedsheet and retreated to the French doors. "Ha!" she cried. "*Torito!* Come little bull."

"Stop clowning. Go away."

"And so the lovely nude *torero* enters the arena of tragic fate."

"*Torera,* not *torero.* Feminine noun."

She performed half a dozen passes with the bedsheet, hissing "Olé!" each time. They weren't true *veronicas,* but were graceful because Maria was naturally graceful.

"Is the *torera* pretty, Jay?"

"I think so."

"I can see that you think so."

I said, "The other night you were ashamed of your

little striptease. Now you're prancing around the room like a veteran tart."

"Now the piccing," she said, looking around for something that might serve as a pic.

"No, Maria, no pics."

"The timid bull begs to be spared his rightful pics. The *banderillas*, then."

She dropped the bedsheet and dramatically posed as a *banderillero* preparing to place the sticks. She stood straight, back arched, on her toes, with her arms raised overhead. Her index fingers—the *banderillas*—pointed at the ceiling.

"Ha!" she said. "*Torito!*" And then she ran in little circles, approaching and retreating, approaching again, and finally leaning over me and stabbing her index fingers into my navel.

"And now the second pair of sticks."

"No more sticks," I said. "The sticks hurt."

"What a pathetic *toro*."

"Come here, Maria."

She smiled. "But you're in such pain, and so groggy."

"You are a tease."

"It's time for the third *tercio*. The muleta. The kill."

"Come here."

"Is it time for the *torera* to impale herself upon the bull's horn?"

"It's a dubious image," I said. "But yes."

She came over to the bed. She was ready. She had readied herself, and me, with her provocative *torera* dance. Moving gently, careful of my taped ribs and bandaged thigh, she straddled me and settled downward, taking me into herself.

"Ah," she murmured softly. "At last, you bastard."

31

ALEXANDER STELIOS KRISOS
(Alexandras S. Kristopoulos)

Precis of file 1-Hellas
Authority: A. Krisos
Senior Compiler: Von R.
Access: Krisos von R.

BORN: February 6, 1933, on a farm two kilometers from the village of Saint Spyridon in the Peloponnesos (Arcadia).

FAMILY: Father, Stelios Panagiotis Kristopoulos, a contract farmer, was executed on November 19, 1940, by a special unit of the German RSHA—Amt. IV. Kristopoulos and nine other resistance fighters were killed by firing squad in the village of Saint Spyridon (pop. 245). The area population was gathered and required to witness the executions, then herded into the

231

church, which was set on fire. Alexandras Kristopoulos, then six years old, was one of three survivors of the massacre. Mother, Anna Kristopoulos (nee Alexiou), perished in the fire, as did her three other children: Konstantin, 10; Nico, 9; and Maria, 8.

Following the massacre Alexandras (like many children orphaned by the war) came under the protection of the church. He was moved to Tripolis, where he attended school from December 1940 to April 1947. No school records exist. Persons interviewed stated that he was an unexceptional student except for a facility in languages: he learned to speak colloquial German from the occupying troops and later acquired English from British soldiers stationed in the vicinity during the civil war that erupted after liberation. It was also stated that throughout these years he was a rebellious child who many times was severely disciplined by secular and church authorities. No details. Alexandros received less than seven years of formal education.

In the spring of 1947 he was expelled from school and placed with "foster parents" named Maglaris, subsistence farmers who welcomed the cheap, virtually slave labor available through the program. Alexandros, like other similarly placed youths, was evidently very badly treated by his "stepfather," half-starved, compelled to work long hours, and expected to sleep with the livestock. He was often beaten.

In the summer of 1949, when he was fifteen,

Alexandros attacked and seriously injured his guardian, Tasia Maglaris. (See appended police report.)

Alexandros evaded the local authorities and escaped to Athens-Piraeus, where he lived "criminally" (A.K.) for six months before procuring forged merchant seaman's papers. It was in Athens that he extra-legally changed his name, first to Khristos ("the annointed one") and later, while securing the forged documents, to Alexander Krisos. (The name change has never been formalized.)

For three years he served as a deckhand on a number of ships sailing under "flags of convenience," Greek-owned but registered in Liberia and Panama. During this period his ships called at many ports in the Mediterranean, Red, and Adriatic Seas. On three occasions he was arrested for smuggling: Naples, 1950; Marseilles, 1951; Tel Aviv, 1951. Twice he avoided punishment by bribing local government officials and once (Tel Aviv) by escaping police custody and stowing away aboard an Italian vessel. Krisos does not deny his smuggling, but characterizes it as "petty": cigarettes, perfumes, handguns, and antiquities "genuine and counterfeit, mostly the latter" (A.K.).

In late 1953 Krisos and a partner whose name has never been disclosed leased a small freighter and, at Port Said, Egypt, loaded aboard forty tons of arms and ammunition (British, German, Italian) that had been salvaged from the desert battlefields of World War Two and stored at various sites in Egypt and Libya. These were mostly small arms, antitank weapons, explosive materials, but also included were several armored vehicles and some artillery pieces.

"Americans say that it's the first million dollars that's hardest to earn. For a poor Greek, it's the first twenty thousand" (A.K.).

Krisos continued to deal in arms, legally and illegally, during the ensuing years. He has mediated advanced arms (aircraft, missile, and antimissile systems, etc.) transfers between many countries while acting on behalf, separately, of the United States, Great Britain, the Soviet Union, France, and others. And he has also clandestinely purchased "salvaged" weapons from different war zones (Korea, Vietnam, Iraq) and transshipped them to factions in Africa, Latin America, and the Middle East. It is alleged that Krisos assisted Pakistan in the procurement of materials essential to the manufacture of nuclear weapons. It is alleged that Krisos assisted Iraq in the procurement of materials essential to the manufacture of nuclear weapons. It is alleged that Krisos assisted South Africa in the procurement of materials essential to the manufacture of nuclear weapons. Krisos denies these and similar allegations.

In 1956 Alexander Krisos returned to Tripolis and married Sophia Maglaris (see file 2-Hellas), then sixteen, daughter of his former guardian, Tasia Maglaris. Their union produced three offspring: Konstantin, 1959 (see file 3-Hellas);

Nico, 1962 (see file 4-Hellas); and Maria, 1965 (see file 5-Hellas).

In 1981 Krisos "adopted" Jay Francis Chandler (see file US-121), a close friend and classmate of Konstantin Krisos. This adoption was not formalized in either the United States or Greece.

The marriage between Alexander and Sophia Krisos was dissolved in June of 1983. The former Mrs. Krisos has not availed herself of the considerable monies and properties granted to her by her ex-husband.

Up to the time of his divorce, Krisos led a quiet, reclusive, almost austere life for a man of his wealth and power. However, in the middle 1980s there was a sudden and radical change in his personality and "lifestyle." (See appended psychological reports and analyses.) In the words of family members and business associates he became "flamboyant," "eccentric," "unpredictable," "devious," and "rather sinister." Tabloid gossip linked his name with film actresses, dancers, a member of the British royal family, titled members of the European aristocracy, and the "international jet set." Previously known as an extremely frugal man, he soon gained the reputation among business associates as foolishly generous, imprudent, a spendthrift. He spent money lavishly and presented friends and acquaintances with expensive gifts. He bought residential properties in London, Paris, New York, and Monaco and purchased an entire island in the Aegean Sea. His annual island parties have become the subject of many scandals (and several pending lawsuits).

Also during these years (to present), Krisos periodically "vanished" for a month or six weeks, laboring as a stevedore, serving as a deckhand of tramp freighters (none of Krisos registry), traveling alone by motorcycle through parts of Africa (the Sudan, Morocco, Tanzania), etc.

Major Investments (Known)

(1) Arms manufacture. Arms purchase and resale. Arms sales mediation.

(2) Resort properties in Europe and America.

(3) Gambling casinos in Europe, Asia, the United States, and the Caribbean.

(4) Shipping. (A fleet of nine cargo ships and four oil supertankers.)

(5) Oil and precious minerals. (Eartheme, Ltd.)

(6) European and American film production and distribution.

(7) "Communications." Newspapers, television and radio stations, in the U.S., Great Britain, Canada, Australia, and Germany.

(8) Computer manufacture. (TEMPO, GB.)

(9) Rocketry, satellite placement. (SpaceTime Consortium.)

(10) Electronics manufacture.

Extremely Confidential

Dual approval (A.K., von R.) required for access to appended files on these and other investments.

ESTIMATED ASSETS: $23,000,000,000 (23 billion U.S. dollars.)

LITIGATION: Litigation—national, corporate, and private—is active or pending against Alexander Krisos (and his assigns) in fourteen countries.

HEALTH: Excellent. (See appended medical reports.)

MEMBER: International Olympic Committee; Greek National Olympic Committee; Consulting Secretary of the World Health Organization (UN); Special Delegate to the United Nations; Greek Ambassador at Large; Chairman, African Charities; Chairman, Liberate Cyprus Action Group; Chairman, Socratic Fund; First Councilor, Greek Economic Affairs Committee; Associate, World Population Council; board member, Hellenic Language Association; board member, Mediterranean Trust. (See appended files for complete list of Alexander Krisos's social, charitable, fraternal, and corporate positions. See appendices for list of honors and commendations.)

FAVORITE QUOTE (paraphrase): Friedrich Nietzsche: "Money is beyond good and evil."

32

A low-pressure system moved into the area early Saturday morning. Smoky thunderheads veined with lightning rolled across the bleached sky, and by ten o'clock it was raining. It rained for five hours, and when it stopped the air was clean and sweet and cool.

There was a pocked and stained marble statue of Silenus placed among some lemon trees in the villa's patio. He appeared eager to leap out and assault the passing female guests. Silenus, an ugly, drunken, lustful creature with goat legs and stubby horns, had been fondly and humorously appreciated by the ancient Greeks. It was said that Socrates resembled him.

Konstantin, holding a flute glass of champagne in each hand, was standing next to the sculpture.

"What a repulsive, debauched satyr," I said.

"He is, isn't he?"

"I was talking about you."

"Oh."

"But hung like a stallion."

"Thank you."

"I was talking about Silenus."

"Oh."

"Why are you lurking around Silenus, Kon? Is it a form of advertising?"

He nodded. "Pubic relations."

"Give me one of those glasses of wine."

"Can't. Saving it for my lady."

"Gypsy?" I laughed. "Your lady?"

"My amour. My heart and soul. My mate. My epiphany. Here she comes now. Hello, darling."

"If it ain't the Three Stooges," Gypsy said with a crooked smile. "Curly, Moe, and Big Balls."

"Isn't she wonderful?" Kon said to me.

Gypsy was pretty this evening in her special, campy way; she looked like the kind of whore who hangs out at not-quite-fashionable beach hotels and ski resorts. A whore on the way up or on the way down.

She accepted a glass of wine from Kon and turned to me. "You didn't have a clue, did you?"

"What?"

"You didn't have a clue when you were out there dancing with that bull."

"I did all right."

"Sure. He drilled a hole in you. I was cheering for the bull."

"That's isn't very original. Lots of people boast about cheering for the bulls."

"And the bull won."

"Yeah? That bull is steaks and roasts right now. That bull is hamburger."

She leaned over and patted Silenus's stone genitals—

"For luck"—and then she and Kon sauntered away.

I was surprised to see Sophia Krisos there. She was dressed formally but in an old-fashioned style, in black, with pumps that resembled orthopedic shoes, and her hair was elaborately done up in a series of diminishing coils held in place by pearl-headed pins. She wore no makeup, no jewelry except for the hairpins and a string of carved ivory beads.

She approached me with a smile, gave me her hand, and said, "Chay! Hello!"

"Hello," I said. "What are you doing here?"

"If children don't come you, you go children." She gestured toward a bench where Maria sat (looking like a penitent schoolgirl), with Nico nearby in his wheelchair. Nico glared balefully, his upper lip reflexively peeled back in a silent snarl. I was startled to see that Nico hated me so much.

Sophia smiled, gave me her hand again, said, "Very good, Chay!" and returned to her son and daughter.

Alexander had again exiled me to a fringe table. There were six of us: two "entrepreneurs" and their severe wives, a gaunt Russian ballerina attired mostly in white plumage, and I. It was a slow, dreary dinner. The men communicated with each other in a numerical code (Dow Jones, Standard & Poor's, Futures), while their wives complained—complained about the villa's "hard water" and how it virtually ruined one's hair, complained about the incompetence of the servants, complained that Alexander had not scheduled a Grand Ball for this, the final night. The avian ballerina (was she wearing her *Swan Lake* costume?) told me Chekov short stories as if they were factual and had happened to her. It seemed that she had spent much of her youth gliding over the snowy streets of Saint Petersburg in a horse-drawn sleigh.

My ribs and thigh wound ached; I was struck mute with boredom.

After coffee and cognac had been served, some performers came onstage and presented a series of skits that lampooned certain guests, but gently—no one was seriously humiliated, no carnal outrages exposed. Pamela did a parody of Gypsy. She was dressed and made up like her and wore a white-blond wig, and she danced like Gypsy (frantic and awkward) and sang like Gypsy (a singer with her lungs full of helium).

I left the dining hall before Alexander could rise and make a speech.

Biki Benematale was sitting on a patio bench. He offered me a cigar, and we sat silently for a time, smoking; then he asked, "Did you find the revue amusing, Mr. Chandler?"

"Mildly. I thought it would be crueler and funnier."

"Crueler, at any rate. I feared that Biki Benematale's avoirdupois would be mocked."

"I found your calling card, Mr. B."

"Ah, yes. Some of us were going to take a launch out to a sandy island for a picnic today, and I wished to invite you."

"I'm sorry I missed it."

"It was canceled because of the weather."

We smoked complacently for a time, fogging the air, and then Biki asked, "Do you plan to attend the tragedy tonight, Mr. Chandler?"

"Tragedy? A theatrical production, I hope."

"Indeed. An original tragedy in the Sophoclean mode, so I have been told. I have been hearing strange rumors all week."

The ash on Biki's cigar was now more than two inches long and drooping toward his dinner jacket.

"Watch your ash, Mr. B."

He gave me a puzzled look, and I pointed at his cigar.

He flicked the ash on the ground, raised his eyebrows, and commenced a deep, rumbling Biki laugh, exhaling pale smoke, his gigantic belly quaking, and finally he wiped his eyes and said, "Indeed, sir, we must all watch our ashes around this place!"

The bullring and corrals had been dismantled and removed and the theater's performance area restored. Fitted into the open end of the horseshoe curve of the front row seats was the orchestra, originally the "dancing place," a ring of about fifty feet in diameter, whose perimeter was made of raised, fitted stones. Behind the orchestra was the *proskenion,* a level platform above some steps; and behind that the *skene,* which tonight was constructed to represent the facade of a palace. There were three doors on the facade, the largest in the center, and a stylized colonnade in front.

The light technicians were setting up their equipment at the top of the theater when Biki and I took our seats. Alexander must have finished his speech, for some of the guests were drifting over the grounds toward us. It was dark now, and cool, and you could smell the spicy wet vegetation and earth.

"Are you familiar with Greek tragedy, Mr. Chandler?"

"Not very," I said.

"Strangely enough, sir, while a child at mission school I learned to read the Greek called Koine. That was so that we could study the New Testament in the original language. And later, while at Oxford, I learned to read classical Greek moderately well, and I have since struggled through many of the tragedies. But let me confess at once that I prefer the vulgar comedies of Aristophanes to the tragedies, which are quite extravagant emotionally, and sometimes cause me to giggle inappropriately."

A boy came by and gave us programs.

Characters in the Play

OEDIPUS, king of Thebes
JOCASTA, the wife of Oedipus
POLYNICES, elder son of Oedipus
ETEOCLES, younger son of Oedipus
ANTIGONE, daughter of Oedipus
HAEMON, adopted son of Oedipus
TEIRESIAS, a blind prophet
CHORUS OF THEBAN ELDERS

The Scene

The Royal Palace of Thebes

The players were listed on the reverse side; Pamela Bristol was Antigone.

Biki studied the program. "This is most confusing, Mr. Chandler. I can't see what dramatized myth

is going to be presented this evening. And look here—
Haemon, adopted son of Oedipus. But Haemon was
the son of Creon, brother of Jocasta and eventual suc-
cessor to the throne of Oedipus, and the lover of Antigone in the *Antigone*. Perhaps this is to be some sort
of pastiche."

"I suspect that we can ignore the classical associations tonight, Mr. B. Just think of them as members of
the Krisos family."

"Really?" He glanced again at the program. "Ah.
Then Alexander is King Oedipus and Jocasta is his wife,
Sophia."

"Ex-wife."

"So, Polynices is Konstantin, Eteocles is Nico, and
the lovely Maria is Antigone. But then who is Haemon?"

"I am Haemon."

He grinned, and wriggled in gargantuan delight. "I
smell a delicious scandal, Mr. Chandler."

"So do I, Mr. B. So do I."

Guests continued to materialize out of the night. I saw
Kon and Gypsy, Evelyn Callisto and her newly recruited
entourage, Sophia and Maria and Nico, the shambling
Nigel Rye, the Blacks and the Shimatzus, everyone. Soon
the first four or five rows of seats were filled.

Alexander, alone (I could not recall seeing the Cre-
neaus, father and daughter, for several days), took his
place in the front-center section once known as the
throne of the priest of Dionysus. Kon and Gypsy sat a
row below me and a dozen yards to the right; Sophia,
Maria, and Nico were at the theater's extreme left side,
the *parodos*.

At ten o'clock all of the lights were switched off for

several minutes, and when they came back on the cast and chorus were lined up along the elevated *proskenion.* They wore masks, though not the anonymous, agonized masks of classical tragedy: these were superbly crafted faces that both resembled and caricatured the persons represented. Each mask exaggerated a vice or character flaw in the Krisos portrayed: Alexander, an enormous pride, hubris; Nico, spite and self-pity; Kon, dissolution, with greed and violence half-concealed by an ingratiating smile; Maria, sly vanity; and Sophia—the cruelest portrait and the most unjust—stupidity, the face of a vacuous rustic.

This, then, was how Alexander viewed his ex-wife, his sons and daughter, himself. For there could be no doubt; this was Alexander's party, his theater. The actors he had hired wore the masks he had ordered crafted, and they would recite the lines he had commissioned (or written himself). And so of course his mask was the least satirical, the character flaw only an excessive pride, which he probably regarded as a high virtue. Pride is a vice that wears a noble expression.

Biki was tugging at my arm. "Oh, dear, Mr. Chandler—is that you?

The mask caricaturing my face (Oedipus's adopted son) puzzled me. Clearly, it was an enlarged and somewhat cartoonish version of my face, but no vice or depravity was evident on its (my) expression, no ambition or greed or lust or hatred, no true passion of any sort. It (I) was watchful, a rather bland cypher—a spy, perhaps, an intruder into the lives of the Krisos family, a usurper. Was that how Alexander saw me? It really was not an offensive likeness. Or was it? It could be that Alexander regarded the absence of passion as a weakness greater than any vice.

The masks of the twelve men of the chorus were identical, and so were their gowns.

33

When the lights came on again the blind prophet Teiresias, tethered by a rope to a small boy, was standing on the palace steps. Oedipus entered through the *skene's* middle door.

OEDIPUS/ALEXANDER

Teiresias, old and frail, from youth blind, led around by a boy as a boy leads a colt, yet he has the power to summon kings. His strength is his weakness. I am here, Teiresias. They tell me that you have again dreamed the future.

TEIRESIAS

The blind man's dreams are dark and strange, peopled by shadows whose crimes unfold contrary to the will of the dreamer. What others call a gift, I name a curse.

OEDIPUS/ALEXANDER

Friend, I know that the dreams invade you unbidden and unwelcome. Teiresias is not the incubator of the dark dreams, only the medium through which the Dead speak. Let them speak, then.

TEIRESIAS

I dreamed of a great and noble boar brought to bay in a nighttime forest. The boar was old, with hoary bristles and armed with blunted yellow tusks, but his courage was undiminished. In my dream he is surrounded by dogs, half of them dead, disemboweled by the old boar, and further ringed by five human figures fearfully brandishing their spears.

OEDIPUS/ALEXANDER

So you have dreamed of a hunt. So . . . ?

TEIRESIAS

The language of dreams is like a foreign tongue, Oedipus. One must learn the Scythian vocabulary before one can understand the Scythian's rude speech. It is the same with wordless dreams, vapors, in which one thing often stands for another. As a Scythian word corresponds to a word of Greek, so might a noble boar represent a noble king in the dialect of dreams.

OEDIPUS/ALEXANDER

Do I understand you, Teiresias? This hoary, dog-killing pig is King Oedipus?

TEIRESIAS

I believe it to be so.

OEDIPUS/ALEXANDER

Our dreams, true and false, rise like a contagion from the Underworld. We know that the shades, whose afterlives are no more than a dream of a dream, send blind Teiresias visions that soon or late come true. But cannot even wise and honest Teiresias be deceived by these vapors?

TEIRESIAS

I pray that it is so, Oedipus.

OEDIPUS/ALEXANDER

Good friend, surely you have intercepted a dream intended for a fool. A Scythian fool.

TEIRESIAS

I pray that it is so, Oedipus.

OEDIPUS/ALEXANDER

Every hunter respects the courage and ferocity of the cornered boar. I myself wear the scars of such encounters. But noble, Teiresias? A noble, kingly pig? If the beast in your dream were a great old bull . . .

TEIRESIAS

It was very dark in the forest of my dream, inhabited by the shadows of shadows, and so confused was the melee that I might have seen falsely. Yes, perhaps it was indeed a mighty bull.

OEDIPUS/ALEXANDER

A bull can be a god. A boar is a boar; an old pig is an old pig.

Now, for the first time, the audience responded: Sophia Krisos laughed freely (pompous Oedipus was being mocked), and Biki rumbled, and then others joined in with a laughter that betrayed a certain nervous tension. The crowd did seem absorbed in the play despite its crudely analogous nature and the stilted language, the fake poetry. Perhaps the audience believed that this was to be a comedy.

Teiresias then described his prophetic dream in detail: of the five figures "fearfully brandishing their spears," two were women, one old and the other young, and three were men, one of whom had been crippled in battle and another who was a son of Oedipus, but not by blood. Teiresias and the chorus, when it entered later, knew that the murderous five were Oedipus's own family, but Oedipus refused to believe it: the dream was a slander, a lie—no man had a more loyal and loving family than he. If Teiresias dared to repeat his loathsome dream he would be forever exiled from Thebes.

Oedipus and Teiresias exited, and the chorus entered half-singing and half-chanting. They proceeded to the orchestra circle and, still sing-chanting, commenced an intricate maneuver that reminded me as much of military close-order drill as dance.

The chorus, in strophe and antistrophe, melodramatically called upon the gods (mighty Zeus, Delphian Apollo, wise Athena) to witness their anguish and warned of the gods' anger and the consequences to Thebes should Oedipus not soon awaken and expel the vipers that warmed at his hearth, warmed at his bosom. The vipers were named Hatred, Envy, Ambition, Vanity, and Ingratitude, and they were even now preparing to fulfill old Teiresias's dreadful prophecy.

And the chorus revealed that both Oedipus and Haemon (Jay) had as infants been abandoned on remote hillsides, to perish there, but:

CHORUS (SINGING)

. . . thus the infant Oedipus, saved by a wandering shepherd and raised as a prince in the palace of King Polybus of Corinth, remembered his debt to the gods and so himself rescued a doomed infant whom he named Haemon and raised as a prince in his own palace. The circle is closed.

The lights were extinguished for a few minutes, and when they came on again some painted panels representing an interior room of the palace were placed in front of the *proskenion*. Jocasta, holding a long bronze dagger, addressed her son Polynices.

JOCASTA/SOPHIA

Your father Oedipus is old and weak, a braggart and fool, king only in name. You do not see strength in him, only the memory of strength. Have no fear, Polynices. His muscles are slack and his bones brittle; your dagger will slide as easily into his suet as into a pig's. You have killed pigs?

POLYNICES /KONSTANTIN
Enough to know that even the fat old boars still have tusks.

JOCASTA/SOPHIA
All that he was you now are; all that he is you should be; all that he possesses is rightfully yours.

POLYNICES/KONSTANTIN
This is not the time. Soon, when the time is right.

JOCASTA/SOPHIA
(Scornfully) Tonight drink three more cups of wine than usual and, drunk, approach the king from behind; or drunker still, if you must, send the dagger home while he sleeps.

Finally, Polynices agreed to participate in the murder of his father that night.

In the subsequent, nearly identical scene, Eteocles (Nico) is persuaded by his mother that *he* will become king after the murder and his brother, Polynices, will be exiled.

Then Haemon is summoned to her presence and he too (like Polynices and Eteocles) is promised the throne. He denies interest in the royal succession, but does not denounce the planned murder or expose the plot to Oedipus. He indifferently observes all that follows.

Antigone (Maria) casually, almost absentmind-
edly, acquiesces in the parricide, and then dreamily
recites a list of the things she will buy with her share
of Oedipus's wealth: great horses, priceless jewelry,
exquisite gowns . . .

Alexander, sitting alone in the section reserved for
the priest of Dionysus, intently watched the play. He
was very still, expressionless except for an occasional
brief, private smile.

I noticed that Sophia frequently leaned close to Nico
or Maria for a translation of the dialogue and choral
strophes, then she would lean back and watch until once
again confused by the English. She appeared to be completely unperturbed by the portrayals, amused, but both
Maria and Nico were obviously furious.

Pamela Bristol played Antigone/Maria as a vain, devious—at heart vicious—bitch. She had learned to faithfully
mimic Maria's walk and voice and sometimes-affected gestures. She spoke most of her lines in a sullen, spiteful tone.

Kon, loosely sprawled out in his seat, smoking one
cigarette after another, watched the play with a sort of
weary irony. His eyes were half-lidded, his mouth now
and then curved into a contemptuous grin. Gypsy, next
to him, was bored and sleepy.

The play's climax took place in the palace room,
while the agitated chorus marched around the orchestra
and chanted commentaries on the vileness of the characters and the ghastly action.

For a moment I thought the final scene would be played
farcically. The entire Oedipus/Krisos family was gathered
together. (Biki softly protested that no more than three
characters ever appeared together in classical drama.)

OEDIPUS/ALEXANDER

Stop. What do you have concealed in your robe?

JOCASTA/SOPHIA

What I have always revealed to you when you asked, and opened to you at night when you asked: my body, surely as familiar to you as your own; this body that safely carried your sons and daughter and delivered them to you strong and whole. Shall I reveal it to you one more time? *(She approaches OEDIPUS while reaching to untie her robe.)*

OEDIPUS/ALEXANDER

Teiresias, I have wronged you.

JOCASTA/SOPHIA

Here, Oedipus. This belongs to you. *(She withdraws the dagger and plunges it into OEDIPUS' abdomen.*

OEDIPUS/ALEXANDER

Polynices? Eteocles? Where are you? *(He crouches, blood spreading over his robe.)*

JOCASTA/SOPHIA

(JOCASTA removes the bloody dagger and holds it aloft.) Polynices, it is safe now; the old boar is weakened. Don't hesitate. Do it.

POLYNICES/KONSTANTIN
Farewell, Father. Sleep well. *(He takes the dagger from JOCASTA and thrusts it into OEDIPUS.)*

OEDIPUS/ALEXANDER
(OEDIPUS groans and staggers away.)
Eteocles?

The actor portraying Oedipus evidently wore some kind of thick padding (perhaps lined with cork) beneath his robes, as well as bags containing a blood-colored fluid, because each thrust of the dagger brought forth another gush of blood, and soon his white robe was soaked. The right hand of each assailant was bloody, too. You could hear the impact of each stabbing, observe the force exerted—it really looked like murder. Some members of the audience involuntarily gasped as the dagger penetrated "flesh." Up to now the play's action had been detached and stylized; this sudden bloody realism was a shock.

The chorus was chanting and marching in an accelerated, frenzied way.

ETEOCLES/NICO
(He limps forward, accepts the dagger from his brother, stalks OEDIPUS across the room, and stabs him in the back.) You would not listen to me. If only you had listened.

ANTIGONE/MARIA
The dagger! Quick, give me the dagger! *(She*

eagerly takes the dagger from her brother and stabs OEDIPUS leaving the blade in place.)

JOCASTA/SOPHIA
Haemon. We are waiting.

HAEMON/JAY
(He advances and removes the knife from the back of OEDIPUS. OEDIPUS groans deeply, shuffles forward, and finally collapses.)

JOCASTA/SOPHIA
Haemon?

HAEMON/JAY
He is dead.

JOCASTA/SOPHIA
Corpse or not, bloody your hand, Haemon.

HAEMON/JAY
Very well. *(He leans over and plunges the dagger three times into the motionless body.)*

34

The actors and the chorus retreated quietly into the darkness behind the *skene,* while the still-masked corpse of the slain king remained sprawled in a spotlight that gradually dimmed and then was extinguished. There was no applause. The players did not return onstage and remove their masks. We sat in absolute silence for perhaps thirty seconds, and then there was a rustling and a murmur as we arose and drifted away from the theater.

People were baffled by the grotesque performance and what it revealed about the Krisos family individually and as a unit, and what might be inferred about Alexander's mental state. Few in the audience were familiar with classical Greek tragedy, and so they'd missed the references and the often-comic parody. Most left the theater disturbed, annoyed. This drama certainly had not provided anything resembling Aristotle's catharsis. Tensions had been increased, not dissolved; the emotions aroused had not been dissipated by "terror and pity"—the conflict portrayed onstage was at least partly true, real, dreadful, and unresolved. We had witnessed an exhibition of disease; a familial pathology. It was almost like watching the actual ravings of a disintegrating family, participating in patricide. That so much of it had been presented comedically only made it stranger.

Evidently Biki had been wholly entertained by the play: he shouted to the crowd at large, "Jolly good! The fate of kings is often like that!"

I got an unopened bottle of Scotch whiskey from the cottage and drove down the muddy, rutted ridge trail to the temple. It was raining again, but lightly, a fine mist that fell like dew. Pinpoint lights on the nearest island were ringed by foggy coronas. The earth smelled sweet after the rains, alive. All around me the dark sea surged and ebbed; below, at the base of the cliff, the small waves advanced and expired in a foamy sizzling whisper.

I drank a cup of the whiskey and then proceeded to destroy the temple. I tipped the altar stone into the sea. The lintel shattered when it fell; the graceful columns toppled slowly at first, steeply leaned as the drums separated, and then collapsed with brittle cracking noises and wisps of marble dust. I worked for an hour, and when my little temple was once more a ruin, a scatter of marble chunks and chips, rubble, I sat down and drank another cup of whiskey. Fog, a damp, clinging mist, billowed in off the sea. Visibility was reduced to thirty or forty feet.

Two years of hard work; two years of deceit; two years of my life consumed by Alexander's selfish whim and the complicity of his family and the islanders.

But that was not wholly true, or maybe not true at all: I had greatly enjoyed my two years in Greece, my work of restoring the temple, my friendship with the family—I'd be twice a fool if I permitted my present anger to repudiate the reality of the past. It really had been a good two years. And what did I have to show for it? A good two years.

Pamela Bristol arrived half an hour after midnight. She walked up from the village. The rain and fog muffled sound, the darkness absorbed form, and I didn't realize that she was present until I heard her voice. "Jay? Is that you?"

"Pamela? Hello."

"I thought I might come up here and sleep in your tent. It's ghastly in the village."

She was standing thirty yards to the south, dimly silhouetted against the dull glow of fog.

"I have some whiskey," I said. "And there's another deck chair in the tent."

"I didn't mean to disturb you, Jay."

"I need disturbing. I'm glad you've come."

She walked forward. She wore shorts and a gray wool Shetland Islands sweater that was beaded with droplets. Her bare legs gleamed.

I went into the tent and returned with a folding chair and another metal cup.

"Will you give me a lift back to the village later?"

"Of course. But you can stay tonight in the tent. I'll go to the cottage."

She sat down next to me and experimentally sipped her whiskey. "This is awfully good stuff, isn't it? Though I don't know that drinking it from a tin cup improves it."

There was just enough light for me to appreciate her exquisite profile. Her face seemed to glow faintly, like an ivory cameo, and her hands, too, floated palely in the darkness. She smelled of lavender soap and wet wool.

"It was very brutal, wasn't it?"

"Very."

"Are the people anything like that? Konstantin, Maria, all of them. You."

"In part, I guess. The play isolated certain characteristics and then exaggerated them. Flaws were magnified, virtues ignored."

"Yes, but satire does that, don't you think? Accuracy, fairness, balance—those aren't the duty of satire."

"That's true."

"Did I remind you of Maria?"

I laughed. "A demonic Maria. Maria with the better half of her soul amputated. But if you mean, did you physically resemble her, yes. Your walk, gestures, even your voice were Maria's. And that sly sideways glance of hers. Yes."

"I studied hours and hours of film and videotape of her, from home movies in her childhood to tapes recorded as recently as last Tuesday. We all studied very hard for these parts."

"And were paid well."

"Very well. Are you disapproving?"

"Only a little."

"We discussed this a few days ago, remember? About the performer and the necessity of cruelty."

"I remember."

"Anyway, you came off very well. I mean, the character who more or less represented you came off well."

"I'm not so sure about that."

"May I have more whiskey?"

"I'm sorry. Of course."

It was pleasant, after the hot, stagnant, smoky days,

to sit outdoors in the fog and gentle rain, drinking whiskey and talking, acutely aware of each other and knowing that we would sleep together tonight. I sensed her willingness. Acquiescence was implicit in her posture, her lack of tension, and the husky intimacy of her voice.

"I needed something to drink. One becomes incredibly high after a performance like that, a little demented, perhaps, and it takes a while to return to the everyday. Life is never so intense as theater, is it? So condensed and focused? Probably you felt similarly last night after fighting the bull."

"No. All I felt was pain and regret."

She laughed. "Going into the ring with that animal was either very brave of you or very foolish."

"The latter."

"Am I talking too much?"

"No, not at all. No."

"If so, you may still my hurrying lips with a kiss. Or with another cup of whiskey."

"First one, then the other," I said.

We sipped whiskey and talked, prolonging and intensifying the sexual tension between us, until it became as painful as pleasurable, and then we went into the tent and undressed. I lit a kerosene lantern so that I could see her. I spread a thick foam pad on the floor and covered it with an opened sleeping bag.

When I awakened, the lantern had burned out. We lay close together in the darkness, my face buried in her fragrant hair. I could hear her slow, deep breathing, feel the smooth warmth of her buttocks and back. I wanted to waken her but decided against it—let her sleep; there was time.

The chill fog had thickened; a fine mist still fell. The air was drenched with moisture. Sound carried freakishly through the stillness; I could hear the dull clanging of a distant bell buoy but not the sibilance of the sea one hundred yards below.

I was still drunk, the rock was wet, and the night and fog reduced visibility to near zero; even so, I had ascended and descended the cliff face so many times that I did not hesitate now. I knew every hand and foothold, every detail of the route.

The sea was fairly calm in the deep water far offshore, and warm in comparison to the cool air. I drifted outward on a gentle current. The water was black as obsidian. Billows of fog rose like smoke and drifted away. I could no longer hear the irregular clanging of the bell buoy. The soft crashing of the surf was all around me, onshore, at the twin promontories, on the many reefs and islets. It was disorienting; a weak swimmer, one prone to panic, could easily become "lost."

Then above me and to the south a bright shaft of fog incandesced. A light from somewhere near the village was shining diagonally into the sky. It tilted farther upward, slanted down toward the horizon, then lifted again. A car was climbing the cliff road.

I began swimming in toward the little beach. Halfway there I paused to rest and saw that the glowing shaft had leveled to the horizontal and was now moving across the plateau toward the temple, the tent, Pamela.

By the time I reached the beach the light had halted

directly above, and glowing fog boiled out beyond the jagged edge of the cliff's rim. Pamela was screaming.

I climbed hurriedly, carelessly. After being in darkness for hours, the radiance above was half-blinding. My ribs ached. The wound on my thigh had torn open. Pamela was screaming. It was not the scream of an actress, not the kind of scream you heard in movies or on television; this seemed pitched beyond the range of the human voice, and to emanate from some deep old animal source.

I scrambled the last few yards to the plateau, dizzied by pain and effort, sickened by the whiskey I'd drunk.

A car was parked just south of the temple. Its engine still ran; I could hear it and smell the bitter exhaust. The headlights brilliantly illuminated the fog and, for an instant, as I rose to my feet, seemed to freeze the action, petrify the two forms. Pamela screamed and pleaded in an incomprehensible muddle of words. Her nude body was streaked with blood. Maria had surprised the sleeping girl and pulled her out of the tent, dragged her over the sharp marble fragments, and now the two of them— Pamela supine, Maria crouched—were struggling at the edge of the cliff.

Maria ignored my shout. I rushed forward, broke her grip on Pamela's wrists, and pushed her away. And when she silently, furiously returned (her expression like that of the mask Pamela had worn tonight), I slapped her twice and pushed her back against the car.

And it seemed again as if time halted for a heartbeat, and I saw the three of us as we might be viewed from outside the globe of incandesced fog: a bloody nude woman sprawled on the rim of a steep cliff, a naked man leaning over her, and a few feet away—flanked right and left by blazing headlights—a tall, attractive, fully clothed woman whose malicious smile seemed a commentary on the entire mad tableau.

Maria, unrepentant, still smiling in a cold, satisfied way, got into her car and drove across the plateau toward the village.

Pamela was in shock, hysterical in a numbly child-like way (she sobbed and hiccupped like an inconsolable eight-year-old). I soothed her as well as I could, cleaned most of the blood from her skin, dressed her, and drove her down to the hospital. There were dozens of abrasions and lacerations over her body, most on her right side and back, some on her breasts and abdomen. A few of the cuts were deep and required sutures.

PART III

THE UNDERWORLD

35

Some of the guests had stayed over an extra day in response to Alexander's invitation to "visit the Minotaur in his labyrinth." He promised a fine brunch in Echo's Cavern, gifts, entertainments, surprises and games, adventures.

We gathered on the slope below the cave's mouth at nine thirty. The Blacks were there, Jack and Louise, the Shimatzus, Evelyn Callisto (dressed and bejeweled as if for a coronation), Biki Benematale, Nigel Rye, and Gypsy Marr.

Kon and Maria were there, too, and I'd heard that Nico would be arriving with his father. Evidently the nasty portraits of them in Alexander's play hadn't caused a schism in the family. They were tolerant of each other's random and calculated cruelties. The Krisoses were a strange family, always it seemed on the verge of disintegration, but still a family. They distrusted each other while distrusting the world and outsiders even more.

Maria, wearing slacks, sandals, and a loose white blouse, walked toward me. Her smile was tentative and bold at the same time; she wished for my forgiveness but was prepared to be defiant if it weren't granted.

"How is your Pamela, Jay?"

"Terrified. She left the island."

"She's an awfully silly girl. Last night she screamed and screamed. She screamed like a dog that had been run over."

"Pamela's afraid of heights," I said. "But even so, what a silly girl, wanting to live so desperately. I'm sorry she embarrassed you with her vulgar display of emotion."

"I'm serious. She screamed and she fought, but she was weak—muscles like pudding."

"Whereas you have strong hands and arms from so many years of piano practice."

"Yes. You aren't *really* mad at me, are you?"

"Maria, you tried to murder a woman."

"All right. But I didn't think of it as murder, killing, death. I was in a rage. She was me in Father's despicable play; she was Antigone. And then the bitch went off with *you* after impersonating *me* on the stage."

"I can see that. But, Christ, Maria, to try to kill her . . ."

"Oh, I know that was wrong. Of course it was wrong. Try to understand. I guessed that she was with you, I knew it, but to go into the tent and see her lying asleep there, naked, so very beautiful . . . and the tent bright with the car's lights, and the tent smelling of you both, of sex, the tent where you loved *her* who had so viciously pretended to be *me* a few hours earlier—well, you do understand, don't you?"

"No, Maria."

"You will understand. Honestly, you will if you look at it from my point of view."

"What if I hadn't arrived in time? What if you had succeeded in dragging her off the cliff?"

"That would have been terrible. I'd be sorry for the rest of my life. But, Jay, who would know?"

"I would."

"Yes, but, Jay, you're one of us."

"Am I?"

"Of course you are. Don't be silly."

Biki Benematale was outfitted in a tailored safari suit that was complicated by belts, epaulets, ammunition loops, brass buckles and buttons, and lines of starched pleats. There was enough fabric in the jacket alone to rig a fair-sized tent. Beneath the jacket he wore a ruffled white shirt and a regimental striped tie. Biki was sweating, and his face shone like raw oil.

"So, Mr. Chandler," he said. "We descend into the Underworld. What and whom will we find there? Hades himself, legions of desolate shades, Cerberus, the three-headed dog, perhaps even Eurydice mourning her Orpheus?"

"Nothing that ordinary, Mr. B.," I said.

The inside of his mouth looked like an open wound. He revealed his mouth and his great square teeth and, quaking with laughter, said, "You are a jolly fellow, sir. I do very much enjoy your company."

Nigel Rye, squinting into the bright sunlight, appeared almost as cadaverous as his late twin: his long, bony face was yellowish, his hair dry and weedy, and the lids of his jaundiced eyes (the whites nearly orange, the pupils murky) slowly opened and closed, like a reptile's.

"Good morning, Mr. Rye," I said.

He responded with a kind of weary rage. "Who are you? Do I know you?"

"We've met," I said.

"I doubt that. What do you want?"

"Only to wish you good morning."

His gaze was slantwise, sly and satirical. "Oh, d-d-dear boy! How s-s-sweet of you to greet a lonely old man. Really. What a chirpy lad you are! And good morning to you, d-d-dear fellow. Yes, yes. Why, you're as cheerful as the perky little b-b-birdies. Oh, my, yes. Here," he said, pointing to the oblong hollow between jaw and cheekbones. His skin had a greasy, translucent texture, like parchment. "Here, won't you kiss a lonely old man g-g-good morning?"

"Not on your life," I said.

"Shoo," he said. "Who are you, anyway? The good-morning b-b-bird? F-f-fuck off."

Separate from the group, intensely alone, were Kon and Gypsy. They hissed at each other. They were both angry persons, angry nearly all the time, potential terrorists. Gypsy, dressed like an actual gypsy today in a brightly colored long patchwork dress, was sitting on top of a powdery white boulder. She wore gold earrings and gold finger rings and loops of linked-gold necklace. Kon had not changed clothes; he still wore his tuxedo, rumpled now, and the bow tie dangling. They quietly hissed and snarled at each other, cobra and mongoose.

They wanted to be alone. I approached over the slanting, stony, ashy soil. "Here comes the chirpy jaybird," I said. "Good morning, good morning."

Their expressions were at first hostile, then blank.

"Here comes the bullshitter," Gypsy said.

"Bullfighter," Kon said with a wry smile.

As I walked downslope the sunlight angled directly

into my eyes, and their forms became shadows rimmed by a liquid glow. I shaded my eyes with a palm. Beyond them the plateau was a wavery blue, and farther on the sea glittered blue and green and silver. Rain had been forecast for later in the day, but there was no sign of it now.

"How did you like the play last night, Kon?" I asked.

"I loved it. It made me feel good. How did *you* like it?"

"I was disappointed that I didn't use the knife on the living Oedipus."

"Maybe there'll be other opportunities."

I turned to Gypsy. "And did you enjoy the play?"

"It sucked."

"You know, Gypsy, there's always a danger that one will eventually become the role she plays, if she plays it too long and too well. I guess that's happened to you. You really are Gypsy Marr now."

"A cunt, you mean."

"That's close."

"A whore."

"Closer."

"Trash," she said, grinning at me.

"That's it."

Alexander, Nico, and a male nurse arrived in a large van. The nurse removed a folding wheelchair from the back, carried Nico to it, and with difficulty pushed him up the slope to a level area in front of the cave entrance. Nico remained expressionless during this procedure, but I was sure that he was humiliated by our silent watching, our thank-God-it's-not-me pity.

Alexander followed them up the hill. His skin was

waxy-looking, and there were bruised crescents beneath his eyes. But his fatigue was not evident in his stride, his posture, or the bold force and timbre of his voice.

"Good morning, my friends," he said. "It's cool inside the cave. Shall we enter?"

36

The cave opening and the first forty feet were so narrow that we had to proceed single file, hunched over, moving along the passage like a many-segmented animal. Maria, behind me, kept her hands on my waist. She breathed rapidly, and I recalled her terror that day when she'd become lost in the seaside caves. The tunnel was dimly lighted by candles set into niches in the walls. Candles were to set a mood, I supposed, since a rubber-insulated electrical cord ran along the cave floor. There was stone rubble scattered around, and the ceiling and sections of the walls had been shored up with thick new timbers. The rock was gray-black and had many facets, as if it had been chiseled rather than formed by the boring and smoothing action of water. I had no particular fear of enclosed places, but this cave spooked me. Perhaps I was infected by the fears of the others.

The passage expanded into a roundish pocket in the rock, large enough for us to stand erect. A tunnel on the far wall led to the left and downward. There were dozens of candles burning on the floor and walls, so many shining all around us, from every angle, that we did not cast shadows.

Alexander's voice, naturally deep and resonant, was greatly amplified in the echoing stone room. His voice, and the absolute confidence expressed through his voice, had a hypnotic effect. One was tempted to surrender to his strength and will.

"Let us rest a moment," he said, "adapt ourselves to the labyrinth. It isn't so terrible. Look above you."

On the ceiling were some primitive-style paintings of bulls and hunters. Ocher and black and rust, with dark outlines, they reminded me of the cave paintings of Altamira. In one, three hunters were throwing spears at a wounded bull; in another, a bull was goring a hunter. There were half a dozen paintings, all of them beautifully colored and executed.

"Imagine," Alexander said. "Twenty thousand years ago an artist entered this little room and, by the smoky light of oil lamps, using pigments derived from earth and roots and blood and charred wood, he recorded the hunt."

"Nonsense," I said.

Alexander, smiling faintly, turned to me.

"They were painted this week."

Everyone, it seemed, looked at me with disapproval; I had broken the spell, spoiled the game, exposed Alexander's charming little fraud. But I could not remain silent. I had to openly protest. I felt impelled to resist his magnetism, his insidious persuasion, his claim on our minds and wills. My voice sounded thin and querulous in comparison to Alexander's resonant baritone.

"Jay," Alexander said, glancing around the room,

"is quite literal-minded. Yes, these wonderful paintings were done during the last week by an artist whose name you would recognize. The paints are still wet. I wasn't trying to deceive you, only to give you a small pleasure and a sense of wonder. There are more such harmless amusements ahead. We can expect Jay to cry hoax."

I sensed that they were on Alexander's side, except for Biki Benematale, who had not ceased gazing at the ceiling and now said, "The paintings are indeed beautiful, Mr. Krisos. But the bulls are not bulls, you know; they are steers."

The next tunnel was long and inclined downward and to the left, hooked to the right, left once again, doubled back upon itself, snaked on for an indeterminate distance before leveling off and opening into a big chamber—the first of the expected caverns. I was confused about directions now and not sure how far we had descended. The weight of the earth pressed in on our bubble of space. I felt, or imagined, a pressure on my eardrums. There did not seem to be enough oxygen in the dank, cool air. But worst of all was the way the cavern vibrated with distorted sounds—hummed, groaned, tinkled, softly roared. The scuff of a shoe, a whisper, a cough reverberated through the vast space and continued to echo long after the original sound had ceased.

"This," Biki said quietly, "is like entering the digestive tract of a monster."

Nigel Rye sniggered. "Always thinking of your b-b-belly, eh, B-b-biki?"

The cavern was electrically lighted, but dimly, with torch-shaped fixtures mounted high on the walls. There was not much color. The friable limestone felt slightly greasy to the touch, and ranged from a dull pearl gray to striated slabs of black.

Among the diverse echoes, one rang clearer than the others, though it was no louder: a remote woman's voice softly intoning, "Farewell, farewell . . ."

The dim lights were placed so that we could not determine the dimensions of the cavern; all of the boundaries were obscured by darkness. But my senses told me that it was huge.

"I call this Echo's Cavern," Alexander said. "You all remember the myth of Echo, don't you? Of course. Echo was a very lovely nymph. Hera falsely believed that Zeus was in love with her, and so Hera made Echo mute except for the ability to repeat what others said to her."

Again we heard the soft, bell-like woman's voice penetrate the persistent hum of echoes to say, "Farewell, farewell . . ."

It sounded like Pamela's voice, recorded and broadcast through concealed speakers. Maria looked at me; she, too, recognized the voice.

"Echo, you know, was hopelessly in love with Narcissus, who didn't care at all for her, or anyone. He loved his own beauty too much to love another. When Narcissus was dying he called out to his reflected image, 'Farewell, farewell . . .'"

Pamela's voice again softly emerged out of the surrounding darkness: "Farewell, farewell . . ."

The electric lights were controlled by a rheostat and now brightened so that we could see that the cavern, though large, was not so huge as the acoustical qualities had led us to presume. It was oddly configured, a sort of octagon gone mad, with unequally proportioned and angled slab stone walls slanting inward and upward to form a vault high above.

And visible now at the far end of the chamber was a large blue-and-white Persian carpet upon which were arranged a buffet table and separate groupings of tables and chairs. The tables were covered by linen cloths, set with crystalware and silver and bone china, and one of the two white-jacketed servers was moving among them, lighting candles. There were many more place settings than people; apparently Alexander had expected more of his guests to join the cave tour.

The buffet contained a variety of food delicacies, cold and heated, and buckets of iced champagne set on tripods were placed at each table.

Alexander brought his plate of food to the table where Biki and I sat. He was pale, hollow-eyed, near exhaustion.

"You omitted a good deal of the Echo-Narcissus myth, sir," Biki said.

"I was afraid of being a bore, Mr. Benematale."

"What? No, you are never a bore, sir. Nor a boar, b-o-a-r," Bike said with a smile. "No. Bores are predictable. Bores are obvious. I must tell you how much I have enjoyed this week as your guest. I don't believe I have had so much fun since I was King Benematale. You are a most gracious and attentive host, Mr. Krisos, and I sincerely hope that someday you will be kind enough to permit me to reciprocate."

Alexander inclined his head.

"Perhaps," Biki continued, his eyes glowing with good humor, "perhaps on that occasion I, too, can prevail upon Mr. Chandler to engage a dangerous wild beast in combat."

"My specialty," I said. "Consult my agent for fees and schedules."

Kon and Gypsy, their profiles raptorlike and stabbing, were quarreling again, or scheming.

Alexander filled our glasses with wine. "Jay hasn't yet said whether he has enjoyed the party."

"It isn't quite finished, is it?" I said. "But so far it's been a fine party for the survivors."

Maria, Nico, and Evelyn Callisto were sitting quietly at one table; Nigel Rye was alone at another; and the Blacks and Shumatzus, none of them eating or drinking, were off in the shadows.

Only Biki and Alexander were at ease in this cool, dank, echoing cavern. Their appetites were unaffected. They ate and drank and chatted as casually as if comfortably seated in the villa's dining hall. Soon, no doubt, Biki would withdraw his leather cigar case, and he and Alexander would squint at each other through the rising smoke and knowledgeably discuss world affairs.

The rest of us were suffering from claustrophobia in varying degrees, with Maria, Evelyn Callisto, Mrs. Shimatzu, and Louise Black most seriously affected. The four women seemed to increase and reinforce each other's fear. Each appeared as if she were pensively awaiting the arrival of some as yet unidentifiable, but certainly hideous, entity. They looked at you without seeing. Each had what has been described as the thousand-yard stare. Mrs. Shimatzu jerkly glanced around with a shy, tortured smile. Maria's face was taut, almost deformed by anxiety. They watched; they listened. They had turned themselves into receptors. It was as if their shared panic had made them acutely sensitive to frequencies and light waves not perceptible to the rest of us.

Alexander noticed the spreading panic and quickly rose to his feet. He said that it was reasonable to experience fear in a place like this. Of course. Every person was susceptible to claustrophobia. But he wished to reassure them: "The caves are very safe, our route carefully mapped and prepared. The electric system is reliable, with a new generator and a backup generator in the event something should go wrong with the first. So, please, enjoy our little journey in the Underworld. Some fear is to be expected; indeed, it contributes to the pleasure of any adventure, but do not submit to panic."

Alexander's voice was deep and richly confident, as always. His smile was condescending. He was, as always, the bully, but you had to know him well to be aware of it.

When he believed that the women had been shamed and convinced into going on, he said, "However, if any of you wishes to leave now, why then naturally you must do so. Spiros and Thansassis have finished their work for now, and will guide you to the surface."

Evelyn Callisto said that she was feeling quite ill. Not afraid, oh no, just . . . ill. Louise Black and Mrs. Shimatzu also wanted to leave, and so of course their husbands decided to accompany them.

Alexander was disappointed: his expensive and elaborate preparation of the cave, his wonderful entertainment, was not a success. Only four guests remained now: Biki, Nigel Rye, Gypsy, and I; plus his daughter and his two sons. Alexander required a large audience and one less cynical about his ways. People had to be a little gullible to respond properly to his magic. He needed to elicit surprise and admiration, awe.

Maria started to leave with the others, hesitated, then turned back.

I went to her and said, "Go with them."

"I'm all right."

"No, you're not. You're terrified."

"Father would be angry if I left."

"Father can go to hell. You must leave."

"Do you have a flashlight, Jay?"

"No."

"I do. I knew that I couldn't ever be lost in darkness again, and so I brought a flashlight. Just in case."

"A good idea. Give it to me, and go now."

"And I took some of the candles. Six of them. Do you think I should take more? We can get out of here, can't we, Jay?"

"Of course. But you should leave immediately."

"No, really, I'm all right, because I have the flashlight and the candles. If anything happens we'll have enough light to find our way out of here, won't we?"

"Yes."

"Jay, you don't hate me for what I did last night, do you?"

"No, Maria."

"I'm so sorry; honestly I am."

"It's okay, Maria."

She embraced me fiercely, with all her strength, as much out of her present fear as from relief and affection. Her skin was moist and cool, and there were tears on her cheeks.

37

Three tunnels exited the cavern; Alexander pushed Nico's wheelchair into the largest, which was wide enough for us to walk two-abreast. The passage was lighted by spaced electrical "torches" with their flame-shaped orange bulbs. A line of roughly spun yellow yarn was strung out along the stone floor. Alexander was taking us to the "Minotaur's lair." The yarn, then, represented the thread that Ariadne had given to Theseus so that he might find his way out of the Labyrinth after killing the Minotaur.

The tunnel twisted and looped, always descending, narrowing at points and then expanding again. Here and there small subsidiary tunnels—most too pinched to allow entry—angled off into darkness.

I tried to imagine three-dimensionally the terrain we had so far traversed, the caverns and the linking chain of tunnels, but I was thoroughly disoriented. My sense of direction, normally quite good, was hopelessly confused now. Nor could I estimate how deeply we had penetrated toward the island's core. Fifty feet? Two hundred feet? And along with the loss of an interior compass, my perception of time had been radically altered; it seemed that we had been underground for many hours, which was absurd, but subjective time had been accelerated, and each minute was like ten.

The tunnel leveled and then we abruptly emerged out onto a ledge placed high on a cavern wall. This chamber was fairly brightly lighted, and we blinked and squinted until our eyes adjusted.

The ledge was about twenty feet long and ten wide, and at least thirty feet above the floor. The concave ceiling formed a dome overhead. It was an oddly proportioned stone chamber, almost an oval, with smooth stone walls and a sandy floor. For a moment I assumed that water had carried the sand here over the aeons, but then I recalled that we were in Alexander's labyrinth and this was the "Minotaur's lair."

The surface would not be composed of sand alone; a layer of soil or clay would have been laid and compacted and then a thin layer of sand spread over that. Tons of soil and sand carried or wheeled through the cave system and deposited here. Alexander's men had been working longer than just the past week.

Two tunnels led out from the base of the cavern, with both entrances blocked by heavy wooden gates whose frames were bolted into the rock. And there were two boulders on the floor, placed so that a man could quickly slip between boulder and wall. It was insane. Theseus and the Minotaur. Aguilar and the Spanish fighting bull.

Alexander pushed the wheelchair up to the rim of the ledge. The muscles in Nico's hands and forearms tensed. It would not occur to Alexander that his son, paralyzed from the waist down, helpless here, might be frightened by the height.

Maria and Nigel Rye pressed back against the wall; no doubt they, too, had a touch of vertigo in addition to the claustrophobia.

"I'm sure all of you are familiar with the story of the Minotaur," Alexander said.

The echoes in this chamber were flat and muffled.

"Remember? King Minos's only son was killed by a bull while he was a guest of the Athenians. In a rage, King Minos defeated Athens in war, and demanded that every nine years Athens must send seven young men and seven young women to Crete, where they were forced down in the Labyrinth, to wander lost in the tunnels until one-by-one they were found and devoured by the Minotaur."

And then, from one of the gated tunnels below, we heard a clatter of hooves and a great echoing bellow.

Alexander smiled at the timing.

"The young hero Theseus volunteered to be one of the Minotaur's victims, and he sailed with the others to Crete. You know that Ariadne fell in love with Theseus and gave him a ball of thread so that he might find his way out of the maze. You know that Theseus killed the Minotaur, and that he had many further adventures, and ultimately became king of Athens."

Alexander turned to Biki. "Did I leave anything out?"

"Quite a lot," Biki said. "We should remember, too, that the Minotaur was the monster offspring of King Minos's wife, Pasiphae, and a noble, beautiful bull."

Smiling, Alexander said, "Of course. Anything more?"

"Sir, I do not like this. It is a very dangerous thing."

"Killing Minotaurs has always been risky."

"I shouldn't like to see anyone hurt."

"Not even the Minotaur?"

"Kill the f-f-fucking Minotaur!" Nigel Rye suddenly shouted. "And let's get out of these t-t-tombs."

"Theseus!" Alexander called loudly.

One of the gates was opened from the inside, and Aguilar stepped out into the cavern. He was ridiculously dressed in thonged sandals, tunic, and a pleated short skirt that had been tucked and tied into a sort of loincloth. The glossy round scars on his thighs were exposed. He was dressed like some of the figures you saw on old Greek pots.

"Dear boy," Nigel said.

Gypsy laughed.

Aguilar walked to the center of the arena and looked up at us. He carried a sword in his right hand, the muleta in his left. "You're a fool, Aguilar," I said.

He looked at me and winked. "Theseus," he said.

I wondered how much Alexander had paid him to perform this mad stunt. Not enough, no matter what the amount. The cavern's floor was too small to safely work a bull, and there were only the two escape points, behind the boulders, and Aguilar was alone down there, with no one to help him if he were tossed. I hoped that at least the bull had been damaged in some way, slowed, drugged, bled, half-crippled . . . anything.

Aguilar ironically bowed to us, turned, and walked over to unbolt and swing open the other gate.

"Go, Minotaur!" Gypsy yelled. "Rah-rah-rah." Her peal of laughter, ordinary enough if heard outdoors, sounded like the shriek of a madwoman here in the cavern.

We heard the tapping of the bull's hooves. He entered at a walk, his head up and the tossing muscle swollen. He was the biggest of the bulls, more than six hundred kilos, with wide asymmetrical horns. Aguilar was standing quietly with his back against the wall.

I stepped to the lip of the ledge and waved my arms to attract the bull's attention while Aguilar closed and bolted the gate. He nodded to me and then slipped behind one of the big boulders.

The bull slowly circled the cavern's floor. Front and hindquarters were poorly coordinated. He stumbled and nearly fell. He was drooling clear saliva. Tranquilized animals usually drooled profusely. The animal's courage and fighting will remained, but he had been slowed, rendered less dangerous, by the drug.

"Olé, Minotaur!" Gypsy cried.

Aguilar had studied the bull during the time it had been confined in the corrals, and he watched it closely for a minute now, and then stepped out from behind the boulder and tested it with a few chopping passes. It followed the cloth well enough. Aguilar had its attention. He looked very confident. He cited it from about three yards, and halfway through the pass the lights went out. The darkness was absolute. It was like being abruptly transported from one medium to another; the darkness possessed weight, it seemed, density.

"Light!" Aguilar shouted.

A great gust of warm air, a wind that tugged at my clothing, blew out of the tunnel and into the cavern, and immediately afterward a distant thunder reverberated through the cave system, breeding new thunders and echoes that I could feel as pressure on my eardrums. There was a smell and taste of rock dust in the air.

"*Luz!*" Aguilar shouted. "For Christ's sake, light!"

Thunder continued to resonate endlessly through the cave's arteries, branching out, penetrating deeper and deeper until the noise was all around us, above and below, everywhere. Even so, we could still hear Aguilar's desperate shouts.

"Light! Light!"

Nigel Rye, a few yards away from me, was coughing violently. A woman, Gypsy or Maria, wailed. Someone else—Nico—was shouting in Greek.

"Light!"

And then a bright cone of light shot down through the dust-clouded blackness just as the bull was driving a horn into Aguilar's thigh. The horn slipped in smoothly, deeply, and with a twist of its massive head the bull tossed Aguilar halfway across the cavern. The animal was on him at once, driving a horn into his abdomen, then his thigh, hooking and lifting, and Aguilar, looking broken, disjointed, was hurled against the rock wall.

Gypsy screamed. Nico was still shouting incomprehensibly in Greek. There was just enough peripheral light for me to see that Alexander had left the wheelchair at the rim of the ledge (the cause of Nico's panic) and was advancing toward the flashlight, Maria.

Down in the cone of light the bull continued to hook and maul Aguilar's bloody corpse. His skull had been crushed. His abdomen had been torn open and loops of intestine were strewn across the sand.

Biki stepped forward and began pulling the wheelchair back from the rim. Gypsy turned away and buried her face in Kon's chest.

The bull left Aguilar finally and trotted twice around the perimeter, as if taking victory laps, and then it lowered its head and trotted toward the left gate and, with two tremendous blows of its horn, splintered the planks, broke through, and clattered away down the tunnel.

Alexander had the flashlight now.

"Stop!" he said. "Stop at once!"

For an instant I foolishly believed he was shouting at the bull.

"There will be no more hysteria," Alexander said. "No panic. Do you hear me, Nico? Kon, stop that foolish woman's whimpering."

He directed the flashlight's beam directly upward. The concave ceiling was now illuminated; the pit in darkness. We waited, frozen in the spilled light. The rest of us had been rendered helpless by the savage mauling of Aguilar; only Alexander remained strong.

It was quiet in the cavern now except for the clatter of the bull's hooves receding down the tunnel, and a persistent soft humming and crackling that was perhaps the tenth-generation echo of the original thunder.

"I shall," Alexander said in a loud, commanding tone, "leave the flashlight burning for one minute. I suggest that you all move away from the edge, perhaps sit with your backs against the wall. Try to find a reasonably comfortable position."

When we had obeyed, he said, "All right, then," and the vertical column of light vanished and we were once again submerged in blackness. I saw a series of retinal flashes, then nothing, and I realized that one only very rarely experiences total darkness. This blackness seemed more than the mere absence of light, a negative; it was a *thing,* as the wind is a thing, or the cold. And it confused my other senses. Sound possessed an unfamiliar, menacing quality. And I felt as if the ledge inclined steeply downward and I was in danger of sliding those few yards and then falling thirty feet into the pit. The ledge was level, I knew that, but nevertheless the sliding sensation remained.

Each of us was isolated in the crepitant blackness until Alexander spoke. He waited until our anxieties were nearly intolerable, and then he said, "Our situation is not as serious as it may appear at the moment. I'll describe our position and our alternatives. Be calm. Have courage."

38

Alexander spoke calmly and persuasively, but there was still a hint of the bullying tone in his voice, a latent anger. He was the wise, tolerant general now, rallying his troops; perhaps soon, if disobeyed, he might become the cold, brutal general. His low, confident voice, more than his words, gave us courage. He was our hope, our leader. Our center. The timbre of his voice, the almost-lyric inflections, united eight disparate individuals into a unit. (Later, Biki ironically remarked that it was as if God were speaking to us out of the original darkness and chaos.)

"I have Maria's flashlight, an invaluable object. Do any of you others have a flashlight, matches, cigarette lighters?"

Both Gypsy and Kon had lighters. I had a cheap, half-empty Bic.

"I have matches," Biki said, "perhaps two dozen of them. They are special matches I use to light my cigars, four inches long, made out of cedarwood, with a low-phosphorus igniting agent." Maria did not mention her small hoard of candles, and I didn't give her away.

Those half-dozen candle stubs, whether burning or concealed in her purse, were her sanity.

Alexander told us that the flashlight, lighters, and matches were communal property. They were to be used only in special circumstances, serious need. He did not expect to see an unnecessary spark of light. Our lives might well ultimately depend on a single, last flare. If there were any selfishness in this matter, he intended to confiscate the lighters and matches.

"You understand, don't you?"

"Mr. Krisos," Biki said cheerfully, "is the acknowledged keeper of the flame."

I suspected that Alexander was quietly elated by this disaster. No, not the disaster itself, but the opportunity it now provided for—his favorite words—"challenge, a testing, extremes." Certainly he regretted Aguilar's death. If there had not been a cave-in, if the lights had not been extinguished . . . Still, a man of courage like Aguilar, a man of action, a man who courted danger, knew something about luck, about consequences. I was sure that this would be Alexander's reasoning: not self-exculpatory, exactly, but detached.

We were mutually reliant, he said, self-reliant as a team, but there were others who at this very instant were organizing rescue efforts. Drilling equipment and a crew would probably be on-site by this evening or early tomorrow morning. The drilling should prove relatively easy; limestone was a fairly soft, often friable, kind of rock.

He presumed that the cave-in had occurred in the primary shaft and a few of its branches. It was likely that Echo's Cavern was intact; the drillers might choose to bore a shaft from the ridge directly down into that chamber. We would see.

He was unable to account for the collapse; an engineering group had been working for weeks to shore up the previously dangerous sections of tunnel and had declared it quite safe. Perhaps there had been an earthquake, perhaps an explosion of some undetected volatile gases.

The cave system, Alexander continued, had been three-quarters explored and mapped. A copy of the map was in Walter von Rabenau's computer files, and would be useful in planning the rescue efforts.

"I have studied the maps," Alexander said, "and remember the salient details."

Some years ago a society of French cave specialists had spent several weeks on the island, exploring the cave system for both sporting and scientific purposes. Unfortunately, there had been an accident before their work had been completed, and so the map, while valuable, did not reveal some of the cave's more remote tenacles.

The French team had reported a surprisingly large and intricate network. Certain portions of the chart looked like an illustration of a human's arterial and venous system. Many tunnels were too small to enter or had been blocked by old cave-ins; there were cul-de-sacs and fissures. Other tunnels, though, were as big as the rock tubes in a city's subway system. They had found one cavern, deep with bat guano, as big as a Gothic cathedral; smaller chambers whose accreted mineral deposits looked like gardens of crystalline flowers; pools of freshwater; stone conduits running swift with water either fresh or salt; and the fossils of extinct marine animals.

It seemed that the entire island and much of the surrounding submarine terrain were riddled with caves. The island, of course, had once been a part of the seabed.

In their published report, the French society had listed three exists from this, the central cave system: two were water-filled tunnels that ended in the seabed some distance offshore, which of course could be navigated only with the use of diving equipment; the other, a narrow cleft in the cliffs on the south side of the island. Unfortunately, this last exit was discovered during a rescue attempt, was not confirmed, and so was not incorporated in the maps.

And island legend told of two poorly equipped youths who, in the 1920s, had entered the main cave on a Thursday and the following Sunday emerged from a crevice in the cellars beneath the church (even as the parishioners were praying for their safe return).

So there were exits from the labyrinth, probably many more than were known and charted.

And there was freshwater: though the surface of the island was arid, rain percolated down through the limestone strata and collected in pools and subterranean streams. It was probably raining outside at this moment, and several days of rain had been forecast.

"And so we shall not suffer from thirst. With freshwater we can survive for a very long time. And if Echo's Cavern is intact, why then we have the food left over from brunch, quite a lot of food, some water, and even wine."

"And candles," Maria blurted.

"That's right, candles as well. So, you see, a calm, rational appraisal of our predicament shows that it is not as desperate as it first appeared. We have each other, and friends working on our behalf up on the surface. Panic is the enemy. Despair is the enemy. Weakness is the enemy. Now. Do you have any comments or questions?"

After the ensuing silence, he said, "Very well. I shall now go up the tunnel and proceed until I can go no farther. I'll use the flashlight very sparingly, and so may not return quickly. All right, then? Good."

He switched on the flashlight, picked his way among our sprawled bodies, and entered the tunnel.

Our optimism had been fashioned from the strength and conviction in Alexander's voice, and in his melange of facts, conjectures, half-lies, and omissions. As soon as he left, our sickly fear returned, and each of us was again isolated.

Alexander had not mentioned the two Frenchmen who had never been found, whose bones still lay somewhere in the catacombs below. The "island legend" was almost certainly just that, legend, a boys' prank and a village myth. Another of the reputed exits was unconfirmed and had been omitted from the society's map. Two more passages were flooded and required diving gear to traverse.

Gypsy had not been cowed by Alexander: there was a click, a little flame erupted in the darkness, and she lit a cigarette.

Soon we heard Biki's half-suppressed belly laughter, like a lion's rumble in the cavern, then a match spurted, and he expelled a long, satisfied, "Ahhh."

The cigar smoke was sharp and sweet and overlaid the odor of manure (the bull had defecated) and the faint, bitter stink of blood and viscera from Aguilar's mangled body.

Alexander returned after about forty minutes. He said nothing about the tobacco smell. He was sorry to report that Echo's Cavern was half-filled with rubble and the tunnels leading up to the hillside were blocked, buried. So then, there would be no food supplies, no water or precious candles. Still, Echo's Cavern remained partly open, and the ideal place for the rescue team to drill their shaft.

"I hope, sir," Biki said, "that the shaft is large enough to accommodate Biki's girth."

We laughed. Alexander had returned and we felt better in his presence.

"I looked at my watch a moment before arriving back here," he said. "It was twelve fifty then—about one o'clock now."

We had been in the cave for only three hours.

"I suggest that we rest, conserve our energies. Sleep if possible."

"Father," Maria said softly, "would you turn on the flashlight for a while—thirty seconds? So that we can orient ourselves."

"Indeed," Biki said. "It does seem, sir, that with extended periods of darkness one has a tendency to drift away. I mean, there is an actual physical sensation of floating off in space. It dizzies me. It's like being one of those astronaut chaps, but no longer attached to his space vehicle. And if I, with my avoirdupois, can float away, what about the others?"

Maria's voice was small and urgent, pleading. "I need to see where everyone is, and to look at the walls and ceiling. The space squeezes smaller and smaller when it's dark. Please."

I had experienced both Biki's weightless floating and Maria's sensation of advancing walls, compressant space.

Alexander, reluctantly, I think, switched on the flashlight and slowly played the beam over the scooped walls and concave ceiling. We looked at each other, fixing positions, studying the dimensions of the cavern. It seemed very important to know precisely where each of us was in relation to the others, and to memorize the configuration of our rock capsule.

Nigel Rye was awkwardly slumped at the far end of the ledge. Alexander switched off the light.

"Turn that back on for a second," I said.

"No. Enough of this childishness. It's dark, that's all. Control your imaginations."

"Something is wrong with Mr. Rye."

Alexander switched on the flashlight.

Simon Rye's long, bony jaw was slack and his half-lidded eyes were gluey, unreflective.

Alexander leaned over him. "Dead."

"The p-p-poor old d-d-dear," Biki said.

39

Twice in the next few hours there were heavy rumblings followed by the clatter of falling rocks. One stone slab the size of an automobile fell from the cavern roof and shattered in the pit below. Alexander briefly shone his flashlight, and through a cloud of rock dust we again saw Aguilar's bloody remains. The Grecian tunic and skirt increased the surreality of the scene—this place was a kind of objectified madness.

I had been raised in California and was familiar with earthquakes. The sensation was not the same here, underground, but I was pretty sure that there had been an earthquake and these were the aftershocks. It was impossible to judge the severity of the quake and its subsequent tremors.

Biki, always the pedant, talked about the destruction of ancient Minos by earthquake and the theory that Crete was the site of Atlantis. "A short reference in Plato, you know, is the only source for all of the Atlantis quackery."

Gypsy complained of thirst. Maria implored her father to shine the flashlight every now and then. But mostly we were silent, isolated by darkness and fear. We waited for the aftershock that would destroy the cavern and bury us beneath a million tons of rock.

About twelve hours after entering the cave we heard the first shuddering crash of the drill.

"There," Alexander said. "You see?"

The noise was transmitted through the tunnels and into the cavern, where it was amplified to a tremendous din. We had to shout to be understood. Shock waves traveled through the earth, and chunks of stone crumbled and fell from the walls and ceiling. The drilling cadence never varied: a booming thud every two and one-half seconds, twenty-four times a minute, *thud,* and the multitude of echoes, *thud*. It was like being imprisoned inside a gigantic bass drum.

Some time later the pounding ceased, but a muted throbbing in my ears continued at the same tempo.

"They're adding a length of shaft," Alexander said. "Or maybe changing the drill bit."

During the silence we heard sounds down in the pit. Alexander switched on the flashlight and approached the rim of the ledge. I followed him. The bull had returned. He stood motionless, enormous, tranquil, in the conical beam. His eyes reflected an amber glow. He was either unaware of us or indifferent to our presence. The blood on his horns had dried and darkened. He slowly walked over to smell the corpse, lifted his head, shook his great horns, then turned and trotted back down the tunnel.

Drilling resumed a few minutes later.

The temperature and humidity in the cave remained constant; it was fairly dry and somewhere around seventy degrees. Nico complained of a chill. He was constrained in his movements by his paralysis and the wheelchair. He had been sitting in the wheelchair for many hours now, and his discomfort must have been extreme, but he didn't complain of that, only the chill. He had a blanket, and Kon removed his tuxedo jacket and gave it to him, and yet he was cold.

I managed to sleep despite my bed of rock and the shuddering thud of the drill and the gravity of our situation. It was a shallow but true sleep, swarming with dream images that immediately vanished when I awakened. Oddly, I slept during the concussive pounding of the drill and woke up during the quiet intervals.

"Indeed," Biki said during a temporary cessation of the drilling, "is it not quite natural that so many religions have placed their hells underground. We have Hades, of course, which you might call the prototypical hell, though without the fires and sadistic tortures, and without Virgil's circles—simply being confined in the Underworld was terrible enough for the Greeks. Hades, you know, was both the name of the hell and the name of the Olympian who ruled there. Recall Antigone's anguished lament: 'Tomb, bridal-chamber, eternal prison in the caverned rock . . .' Recall also her words: '. . . I go living to the vaults of death.' And doesn't Antigone also say that she will be wed to the Lord of the Dark Lake, who is Hades, who is Death? Yes."

"Won't someone shut him up?" Gypsy said.

"And we know," Biki went on, "that the many heavens are located somewhere above, in the sky, on mountaintops, among the stars. Where the light is brilliant and the air pure. But this is not for lovely, brave Antigone, who is—"

The resumption of drilling aborted Biki's gloomy lecture.

I awakened abruptly. I could hear Nico shouting in the pauses that separated each concussion of the drill. The sudden shouting and the agony in his voice were terrifying. The darkness, our blindness, intensified every emotion and at the same time prevented us from understanding and acting. Then Alexander turned on his flashlight, and we saw that Nico seemed to be suffering some sort of convulsion. His upper body was distorted—arms bowed, hands curling, shoulders hunched—and his face was a mask of pain. Kon and Biki rushed to him, and for a moment it looked like a brutal assault, a beating, but they were only trying to straighten his arms, relieve the great muscular tension. The overdeveloped muscles of his arms, shoulders, upper chest, and back had cramped. He howled as they lifted him out of the wheelchair, laid him supine on the rock floor, and commenced kneading and plucking at the spasmed muscles. At first they were unable to straighten his arms. The drill thudded down, shaking the earth, and Nico howled, and the drill descended, and at last the cramps were partly relieved, though Nico remained in considerable pain.

During another break in the drilling Biki filled the hostile silence and darkness with his voice, telling us the myth of Orpheus and Eurydice. Orpheus, he said, was a great musician, nearly the equal of the gods, and nothing and no one could resist his magic when he played the lyre. He fell in love with the beautiful Eurydice, and they were married. But soon after the wedding she was bitten by a snake and died. Orpheus was inconsolable. He could not bear his grief, and so he journeyed to the Underworld, and with his lyre and singing he charmed all who were there, the three-headed dragon-dog Cerberus, the Furies, even Hades and his wife, Persephone. They could not resist Orpheus's music or the power of his love for Eurydice, and so they returned her to him on the condition that he would not turn and look back at her until they had left the Underworld.

And so Orpheus and Eurydice made their way through the stone tunnels and dark caverns toward the sun. Orpheus left the cave first and, in his exultation, turned to see Eurydice, but he was too quick, she had not yet exited the cave, and so she was returned to Hades. Eurydice had only enough time to say, "Farewell . . ."

Orpheus, in despair, went off and roamed alone through the wilderness, playing his sad and beautiful music.

After a while Gypsy said, "You're a cheerful old shit, aren't you?"

I could hear Biki, sitting nearby, humming with suppressed laughter.

"Did I leave anything out, Mr. Krisos?" he asked.

"Yes, Mr. Benematale. You left out the maenads."

"Ah, yes. The maenads, Miss Marr, were bands of drunken, crazed women, followers of Dionysus, who rampaged like packs of wolves through the wilderness. They tore animals to pieces and in a frenzy ate them raw and bloody. Orpheus's suffering finally ended when he was hunted down and torn apart by maenads."

"You're really sick," Gypsy said with loathing. "Sick people, all of you."

There was a pause in the drilling about every ninety minutes. The silence itself then had a quality of noise, a crackling like radio static and a soft, irregular drumming. It was during one of the quiet periods that we heard Nigel Rye moan. That is, gases escaped his body in a long, soft, bubbling moaning sound.

"Huh huh huh!" Gypsy said in a kind of chant. "Huh huh huh." And then she became hysterical, cursing and shouting incoherently, and she attacked Kon with her fists. Kon and Biki subdued her. She went on with an unceasing stream of invective, but quieter now, in a flat tone. Then she wept.

Alexander and I dragged Nigel Rye's body across the ledge and dumped it over the side.

Drilling did not resume after the fourth interval. Alexander suggested that perhaps the rescue party had broken through into Echo's Cavern. We waited, but the silence persisted for many hours.

Alexander flicked the flashlight on and off. "We've been in the cave for thirty-five hours," he said.

I was surprised; it did not seem that long, almost a day and a half. It was nine o'clock Monday evening now. We were beginning our second night in the cave. Time itself seemed unreliable, erratic. The seconds and minutes viscidly dragged, but the hours accumulated with bewildering rapidity.

"It may be that there has been a mechanical failure," Alexander said. "It will be repaired soon."

We were not reassured. The metronomic crashing of the drill had been our link with the surface, the world, life. Its cessation was a blow to our tentative courage.

"I think," Alexander said, "that it is time to reconnoiter the lower tunnels. We need water. Nico's cramps were probably partly due to dehydration."

"I'll go with you," Kon said.

"No. There's no advantage in two of us going."

"But what will you carry the water in?" Biki asked. "We have no containers."

"First I'll find the water, Mr. Benematale. And then I'll guide you to it."

Alexander went up the tunnel leading toward Echo's Cavern and returned a while later with a coiled length of the rubber-insulated electrical cord. One end was secured to a rock outcrop above the ledge, the other end tossed down into the pit. Kon held the flashlight while Alexander cautiously descended. The corpses looked two-dimensional, as if projected onto the ground by the flashlight's beam.

The loose end of the cord was drawn up, and the flashlight—still burning—was tied to it.

"Easy," Alexander said.

The flashlight was lowered.

"Very well," Alexander said.

"Don't go," Maria said.

Alexander ignored her, or perhaps he had not heard. He crossed the pit.

"Alexander," I said, "stick to the right-hand tunnel. The bull is loose in the other one."

He turned. "Actually, the two tunnels merge some forty yards ahead. There's a barrier at the intersection, but since the bull so easily destroyed the gate here, he won't be stopped by the barrier."

And then Alexander dryly added, "Jay, maybe you can tell me what I should do if I meet the Minotaur."

"I don't know," I said. "Try a *paso de pecho.*"

He laughed. It was a genuine laugh, hearty and free, with no strain in it. Alexander was eager to go exploring.

40

Alexander did not return.

Kon had a watch, and every now and then he flicked his cigarette lighter and announced the time. An hour passed, two, three, four hours. But that was surface time, calibrated to the movements of the Earth and stars, while we existed in the limbo of underground. Eventually Kon stopped looking at his watch.

The temperature was moderate and so we did not sweat much, but precious moisture was lost with each exhalation. We all suffered from thirst, Biki most of all.

"They say that our bodies are composed mostly of water. Ninety percent? If so, then the entity you know as Biki can be measured in hydraulic terms. X number of gallons at *y-psi*. Biki is a reservoir which requires prompt replenishment."

He remained cheerful despite his extreme thirst.

"You have heard of those blind fishes and amphibians that live in caves. Blind, because there is no light, and so vision would be useless. Some species are albino as well as blind, since skin pigment is unnecessary where there is no sun. Blind albino fishes and amphibians. Do you think, do you think"—he was trying to delay his laughter—"do you think that our descendants will be blind albinos? Miss Krisos? Miss Marr?"

Finally he said that he was going off to look for water. We could not dissuade him. If he must choose, he said, he would rather be quickly and messily killed by the Minotaur than suffer a prolonged, agonizing death by thirst.

Maria lit one of her candles. I doubted that Biki would be capable of descending into the pit, electrical cord or not, but he was an agile man despite his size, an athlete, and he easily made his way down.

He smiled up into the candlelight. "The horns of the Minotaur?" he said. "The horns of a dilemma."

"Wait," Maria said. She gave me the burning candle stub, reached in her purse to select another candle, and threw it down to Biki.

"The lady presents me with the gift of light!" Biki said.

He lit the candle with one of his matches and, his huge shadow spread over ground and rock wall, advanced to the right-hand tunnel. He opened the gate and turned for his exit line.

"Farewell," he said in a falsetto, mimicking Echo and Eurydice, and he went through the gate and into the tunnel. We watched the light gradually fade and then wink out. Darkness again, thick and humming.

Biki did not return.

I slept intermittently, uncomfortably, and dreamed of water, fountains of sparkling water, lakes and rivers, glacial streams, and I drank and I drank, but I could not quench my thirst. I didn't know how much time passed.

It didn't matter. Time was irrelevant.

"I'm going," I said.

"Don't be stupid," Kon said.

"I'm going."

"Our only chance is to be helped from the surface."

"And where are they, Kon?"

"Our only chance. Be patient. We're all thirsty. We're all sick of waiting."

"I'm going."

"Going where? To the same place as my father and Biki?

Think, for Christ's sake. Wait. That's all we can do."

"Let him go," Nico said. "Let the son of a bitch go."

Nico was still in considerable pain, his shoulder, his wrist, his back.

"Jay," Kon said, "wait. Just wait."

"Let the bastard go!"

"Jay . . ."

"I'm going," I said.

"I'm coming with you." Maria.

"Yes. All right, come with me."

Maria had the candle stubs, four of them after giving one to Biki and leaving another with Kon, Nico, and Gypsy. She was rich in light. Maria was fabulously wealthy in the only coin valued down here: light.

She unbolted and opened the gate, and we entered the tunnel. I held the candle. The hot wax burned my fingers. We slowly moved forward. Both of us were thinking of the "Minotaur." The candle burned with a pale, quavery light, expanding our shadows, and after the many hours of total darkness it hurt my eyes. The cave walls were rough, fractured. There was stone rubble scattered over the floor. The cave snaked forward for fifty yards and then merged with the other tunnel, doubling in size. The barrier that Alexander had mentioned had been destroyed, was now just splintered planks and metallic debris. The bull was loose. The Minotaur.

We went on. The hot wax burned my fingers. Our footsteps, our exhalations, were amplified. The nearly circular tunnel swarmed with shadows. It was like advancing down the barrel of a gun.

The temperature was the same as before, but I was chilled now. Maria held my free hand. There were fissures in the walls, cracks that perhaps opened into other tunnels or ended within a few yards. We kept to the main cave. I did not care to squeeze into one of those narrow fissures, entomb myself. The candle's thin blade of light wavered, elongated and shrunk, issued a vibrating glow. It was comforting, surrounded by stone, to touch warm flesh, Maria's hand. The dripping candle wax burned the fingers of my other hand. Our distorted shadows walked with us, crouched, gestured. Light and shadow, stale air that smelled and tasted of rock. Maria's palm was sweaty. We moved and we listened. We listened for the tapping of the bull's hooves, for Alexander's voice, for Biki's, for the sound of dripping or running water.

We descended. The cave branched. We entered the larger of the two tunnels, which farther on divided again, and there were more holes and fissures in the walls, more choices. Perhaps I was wrong to always choose the easier route. There was no way of guessing which passage might lead to water, to light. There were so many choices; so many possibilities we hadn't the time to explore. Each opening we passed was a lost hope.

The shaft descended more steeply than the others, curving gradually to the left, and narrowed until it was no bigger than an ordinary hallway. The walls were schisty and streaked with stone of another color and composition. The tunnel narrowed farther, and we had to move single file and in a crouch. Maria wanted to return. The candle stub was less than two inches high now. The passage closed to a vertical crack. I smelled a damp exhalation from ahead. Maria protested when I continued to advance on my hands and knees. Finally we had to crawl forward on our bellies. I pushed the candle ahead. The damp smell was stronger now, and the candle flame curved and flickered.

Then there was a steep pitch, almost a chute, which opened into a roughly triangular stone room. It was large enough so that the candlelight could not penetrate to its limits. I heard a ticking that was like the steady drip from a faucet. We slowly circled half of the perimeter. There were large, clear droplets of water on the walls. The ceiling, low at the entrance, slanted upward until it reached twenty feet in height at the juncture of the back wall. The base of the back wall was honeycombed with holes, some large enough to enter. The dark rock was streaked and peppered with lighter-colored minerals that sparkled like rhinestones in the candleglow. On the floor, and on the ceiling—upside down—were rounded formations that resembled giant mushrooms.

I placed the candle on one of the mushrooms, and Maria and I began to greedily lick condensation from the wall. After a while my tongue was sore and I could taste blood, and it occurred to me that so much water—

the floor and walls and ceiling blistered with droplets—
had to collect somewhere.

I picked up the candle and moved out into the room.
There were a few tiny puddles in depressions in the
rock, and some cracks had filled, and near the center
of the chamber I found a pool that was about a yard in
diameter and five or six inches deep. The water was as
smooth and clear as air. The basin was coated by glossy
white minerals that looked like clusters of pearls.

"Maria. Come here."

She came toward me out of the shadows. I placed
the candle on another of the mushrooms, lay prone on
the rock, and began drinking. Maria stretched out on
the other side of the pool. The water was cold and had
a sharp mineral flavor. I was aware that one should not
drink too much or too quickly when suffering from
thirst, but I could stop until my stomach ached and my
throat spasmed with the vomit reflex. I pulled away.

"That's enough for now," I told Maria.

She drank until she was satisfied, then sat up and
looked at me. Her face and the ends of her long hair had
been wetted in the pool.

"God," she said.

The candlewick sputtered briefly, then burned
cleanly again. And now I saw that on the mushroom
were a cigar butt, a burnt match, one of Biki's elaborate calling cards, and a large initial scratched into the
stone—"A." Both Alexander and Biki had been here.
They'd left evidence of their stop for anyone who followed. But why hadn't they returned to the cavern, and
where were they now?

I was exhausted. Perhaps it was normal fatigue, or

the result of more than two days without food, or the effects of drinking so much water, or the tension involved in stalking down the hushed stone corridors.

"We'll rest," I said.

"Yes."

I snuffed out the candle flame between my thumb and index finger, and we were again overwhelmed by the compressant blackness. Now, without light, we became more aware of sound: a hissing, the metallic chime of dripping water, distant echoes, vibrations that seemed to advance and retreat.

"Where did they go?" Maria asked.

"I don't know. Maybe Alexander and Biki individually decided to hunt for an exit."

"They should have returned for us."

"Yes."

"Jay, how can we bring water to Kon and Nico and Gypsy?"

"We'll have to go back and lead them here."

"But what about Nico?"

"We'll think of something."

41

We slept, but I couldn't estimate for how long—twenty minutes or five hours. Neither of us had a watch, and one's subjective sense of time was wildly erratic here in the vast stone underground. And maybe the more than two days spent in darkness had begun to alter our "body clocks."

We awakened thirsty, and drank from the pool until we could drink no more.

Now we had to find our way back to the other cavern, the bloody Minotaur's lair. Kon and Nico and Gypsy were waiting. They were not far in distance, probably no more than 150 yards away, but they seemed separated from us by a huge gulf of time. Time skewed every calculation. Kon and Nico and Gypsy existed in the past. We had to somehow cross over into that other world, other time.

We crossed the cavern and had just entered the crawl space when there was an abrupt percussion. Maria cried out. Another shock, a pause, and then another. The rescue crew up on the ridge had resumed drilling. The noise, the shuddering of the earth, increased our claustrophobia. The chute seemed longer, tighter, and steeper than it had during our entry. Maria, following me, whimpered.

We reached the tunnel and were able to stand and proceed erect. But it soon narrowed and turned at a near right angle. I didn't recall that or some other features of the tunnel. The drill cracked, succeeded by echoes that I imagined I could feel on my skin. Maria had her fingers looped through the back of my belt.

I noticed a broken yellow streak running along the cave's right wall. The tunnels beyond the Minotaur's cavern had contained similar streaks, but white, which in the dim candleglow I'd vaguely assumed was a vein of mineral in the rock. And now I recalled seeing a small tunnel mouth encircled by orange scribbles. No doubt all of those marks had been left by the French explorers many years ago and each color signified something—but what?

Eventually the tunnel forked. I could not recall whether we had emerged from the right or left tube. It was hard to think amid the spaced pounding of the drill and the ricocheting echoes. I chose the left tunnel, orange-marked, but within twenty yards it ended in a pile of rubble, an old cave-in, and we had to return.

But the other tunnel soon narrowed to a jagged opening that reminded me of great jaws. Beyond the jaws the tunnel expanded into a smooth oval tube that snaked through the rock, descending, and then we entered a little room that in size and shape resembled a stone igloo.

"Jay, where are we? We're lost. Let's go back to the water cave and start over."

"Just a little farther," I said.

Beyond there was another length of oval tunnel, a crawl passage that appeared certain to end in a cul-de-sac but which finally opened into a rectangular room about the size of a railroad car. At one end was a round, vertical opening, the mouth of a shaft that extended vertically deep into the island. You could smell and hear water at the bottom.

"Jay, please, we've got to go back."

There were yellow chalk marks on the wall.

"Jay . . ."

"Just a little farther," I said.

The percussion of the drill was muted in this extension of the cave system, a remote hammering.

Beyond, the tunnel described a figure *S*, descending and rising again, and then we reached a fairly large, dripping chamber that was riddled from floor to ceiling with the mouths of other tunnels, most of them hardly large enough to allow passage of a dog. Sounds were funneled into the chamber, humming, a crackling like static, the ringing drip of water, and human voices too, shouts and whispers. We were isolated, but not completely alone.

The bizarre acoustics of the maze played queer tricks with sound. Detached words and phrases floated down the crooked tunnels and emerged here, amplified and distorted. A female voice heard over the thud of the drill—Gypsy. But how could that be? And stunned, we clearly heard Biki calling from an indeterminate distance and direction. "Hello? Hello? Can you hear me? Yes?"

His voice sounded small and metallic, but clear, like a voice on the telephone. "There is someone or something here with me. It may be the Minotaur. Hello?" We shouted, but apparently he could not hear us or distinguish our voices from the general, crepitant din. "Oh, poor Biki does not like this."

Maria gave me another of the candles. I lit it. There were two candles left in her purse now, one burning, and the flattened wax disk that I put in my pocket. We would have to be stingier with our precious light.

I chose the largest of the exit tunnels. There were whimpers in each of Maria's exhalations. She clutched my belt with both hands. We went deeper into the maze. It seemed so simple, one easy choice after another, but when you totaled the many easy choices you were lost.

We stopped to rest several times. We might have dozed. We went on and on, traversing terrain that appeared increasingly familiar, until finally I realized that we had wasted most of a candle and much of our physical resources exploring over and over again the same complex, looping system—crawl passages, shafts that inclined upward or down, stone chambers—over and over, three circuits, four. I knew that ahead were the "jaws" and, farther on, the vertical tube that exhaled the sound and scent of water, and then the chamber that funneled in voices. The figure S, the long, skin-abrading belly crawl . . . On and on, around and around the same crazy obstacle course—rats in a maze.

In my fatigue and despair I became convinced that this was a "closed system," like a Mobius strip, with no real beginning and no end, just the complicated spiraling loops around which we'd crawl and crawl until our strength was exhausted.

Maria was quietly weeping.

I realized that, of course, this could not be a closed system—we had entered it; the entrance was also an exit.

But it was disheartening to have so persistently and stupidly traversed the same tunnels over and over again. That would not have happened twenty hours ago. The loss of sensory stimuli corresponded to a failure of reasoning. It was hard to think at all, let alone think clearly. We had become slow, dull, unable to concentrate, and incapable of making obvious associations. We were like morons. It was the darkness, the sense of being permanently encysted in rock as flies are trapped in amber, the continual touch and smell and taste of stone, the silence that was not actually a silence but a murmur, a static, a spaced thudding, whistling, voices, but all so soft and remote that you could not be sure they actually existed.

I said, "We'll go on a little farther, and then rest."

"No. Rest here."

"Come on."

"So tired," Maria said. "So thirsty."

"I think there may be an open space ahead."

"How do you know?"

"I can feel it."

And that seemed true to me when I spoke; there were air currents in the cave, cool and warm, dry and moist, and vibrations resonated according to the shape and volume of the rock-configured space. I was stupid, but I was able to sense these things, or stupidly imagine that I sensed them.

We belly-writhed down the low, narrow tunnel, and when my breathing sounded amplified I knew that we had entered the little dome. I snuffed out the candle.

"Jay?"

I cautiously stood up. The cupped ceiling was less than an arm's length overhead. I desperately needed to stand, flex my muscles and tendons. I could hear a soft crackling in my spine and joints. It was wonderful to move without being punished with a bruise or cut.

"Jay, can we have the light again, for just a moment?"

"Not now, Maria."

"Please."

"I'm sorry."

I was afraid that she would recognize the igloo and understand that we'd been covering the same few hundred yards of tunnel for hours.

There was more despair in her silence than in all of her pleading.

"Okay," I said.

I cautiously removed the candle from one pocket, the lighter from another, struck a flame, and touched it to the wick. The tiny, wavering blade seemed to possess a nuclear brightness at its core. It was shaped like the vertical pupil of a cat's eye, glowing yellow-white, and a soft light filled the dome as liquid fills a glass.

Maria, sitting huddled near the entrance slot, squinted and blinked. There were rips in her clothes and patches of crusty dried blood on her arms and face and bruises and swellings that I could see even in this poor light and a cut, still bleeding, on her forehead.

"We blunder," I said. "The rock doesn't forgive."

Her smile faded and turned down at the corners.

"We've come a long way," I told her. "We'll rest."

"Thank you."

She was thanking me for the moment of light, which comforted her, while for me it only revealed the confines of our tomb. I had come to prefer darkness.

The fingers of my left hand were raw and speckled with tiny blisters. Maybe carrying the candle in my hand was another example of my stupidity.

"You're terribly bruised and cut," she said.

"So are you."

"This is horrible. Just horrible. God. Nothing, nothing, nothing could be worse than this."

"We're going to get out of here, Maria. Hang on."

"Nothing could be worse than being buried alive. God."

"I'm going to put out the candle now."

"Will you hold me?"

"Of course."

42

I dreamed that I was being entombed in a great pyramid, the Pyramid of Cheops, the Pyramid of the Jaguar in Mexico—some pyramid, somewhere. I was lying supine on a stone catafalque. Directly above I could see a rectangle of the purest, most radiant blue. White birds flew back and forth through this marvelous blue, and beyond them I saw wispy clouds and above them a seething white light that must have been the sun. I was dead, I knew that, but a remnant of consciousness remained. And then the keystone was set in place, the blue sky and the birds and the wispy clouds and the sun vanished, and I was alone in a darkness that congealed into stone.

I awakened to the realization that my nightmare was only a fancy version of the truth. My body ached. My right arm, encircling Maria's shoulders, was numb. Her breath was acid, a result of her fast. My breath probably smelled the same.

I separated from Maria, did a few stretching exercises in the dark, and then lit the candle. Maria, tousled and bruised, looked like a feverish child in sleep. The room was like the upper half of a hollow sphere cut exactly in two. The stone was smooth and had a glazed look. There were yellow chalk marks above the entry and exit tunnels.

I thought I now understood the color code used by the French explorers: orange indicated an impasse or cul-de-sac; white, the main branches of the cave system; and yellow, the subsidiary tunnels and caverns.

Maria had awakened and was watching me. The centers of her eyes were black. Strange, staring eyes; the pupils had dilated to almost the full circumference of the irises.

"We'll go now," I said.

She stared at me without blinking.

"Maria?"

Her voice was slurred. "Stay here," she said. "Wait for them."

"No, Maria, we've got to go now."

She closed her eyes and apparently went back to sleep. Or perhaps she had not really awakened.

I opened her purse and removed the last two candle stubs and a tube of lipstick.

"Maria." I shook her. "Maria, wake up."

She opened her eyes and again stared at me in the same vacant, unblinking way. She lifted her right hand and then let it drop. She acted like someone emerging from deep anesthesia.

"I'm going," I said. "I'll come back for you."

"Don't go. Please."

"We can't quit. I'll find a way back to the others or an exit. And I'll come back for you."

"No, you won't. You know you won't."

"I will; I promise."

"Wait. Stay with me."

She still spoke in that slurred, drawling somnabu-list's voice. "Come with me," I said.

"I can't. Did you leave me a candle?"

I lied. "Yes."

"And my matches?"

"Yes." I hadn't seen any matches in her purse. "Sleep if you can, Maria. It will seem like a very long time, but I'll be back; I promise."

I know you'll come back for me."

She lay on her side, her knees drawn up and her arms folded over her breast. I stroked her hair for a time, then leaned down and kissed her cheek. She turned her head and smiled up at me. The smile was vacant, silly, and haunted me as I belly-crawled out of the stone igloo and down the crooked passage.

Perhaps she could still see the glow of the candle when she softly called, "Farewell . . ."

For a long time I could hear her calling, "Farewell, farewell," in a conversational tone. Sound was clearly transmitted down the narrow, winding stone tubes. Even when I had reached the big cavern I heard her voice faintly, ironically, heartbreakingly calling, "Fare-well . . ."

Every fifteen or twenty feet there was a horizontal yellow chalk mark on the wall; I drew a short vertical line of lipstick over each, forming a cross.

The terrain was familiar from our previous circuits: a length of oval tunnel; a very long crawl passage; the rect-angular room that was spatially like a railroad car and contained the vertical shaft that exhaled the sound and scent of water; the figure 5 that descended and then rose again before debouching into the large, dripping echo chamber where—it seemed like days ago—we had heard voices funneled in from remote tentacles of the labyrinth.

There were no voices now (Maria had become silent), just the hallucinatory buzzing and hissing and tinkling, the static-crackling emptiness. The walls were honeycombed with openings, most of them small, all but one marked with either orange or yellow chalk.

The single white-blazed opening was a vertical slit that I just managed to squeeze through. I crawled down a cool, dripping, zigzag passage, pushing the candle ahead, and gradually the rock closed down to a hole that looked no bigger than the entrance to a fox's burrow. Impossible. But there was a white chalk mark above the hole.

It was very tight, and halfway through I became jammed and could neither advance nor retreat. It seemed that the clammy rock was closing, increasing its pressure, crushing me. Seized by panic, I heard a man shouting and realized that it was my voice, me, and yet it was not me; it was another. Panic like a rage drove me forward, tearing my clothes, lacerating and abrading my skin, and then I was in a rough stone cylinder that in thirty yards opened into a small room that led to a larger room that gave access to a tunnel that was—as Alexander had described it—as big as a subway tunnel.

My panic seeped away. There were deep cuts on my shoulders, back, and buttocks. The horn wound in my thigh had torn open and was bleeding. My ribs ached too; each inhalation was like breathing broken glass.

But I was in a new section of the cave, walking down a tunnel as wide as a city street, splashing through puddles of clear water. It was something like freedom. I crossed the white chalk marks with a vertical slash of lipstick. My candle had burned down to a flat disk. The flame sputtered, turned from yellow-white to bluish, and went out. I lit another.

The tunnel meandered downward. It narrowed, then later widened to almost its original size. Ahead I saw a shadow on the cave floor. From a distance, in the dim candlelight, it looked like a large, irregular puddle. I went on and the shadow acquired dimension and a vaguely human form.

It was Kon. The bull had gored him in the abdomen, a single wound but deep, mortal. He had hemorrhaged from the mouth, and the blood on his lips was frothy. He was still alive. His pulse was faint and fast and arrhythmical. He was wearing the tuxedo jacket that he'd earlier loaned to Nico, jacket, bloody ruffled white dress shirt, cummerbund, black trousers, and black lace shoes. Konstantin was dressed for a party.

"Kon," I said. "Can you hear me?"

Bulls were not natural killers, like members of the cat and weasel families. They were not predators. They didn't kill to eat or kill for the sport of killing. It was not the bull's instinct to seek out and destroy a man. But if, in the darkness, you blundered into one, he would drive a horn into your guts.

"Kon," I said. "It's Jay."

His cigarette lighter lay on the floor a few feet away. I put it in my pocket. His wristwatch had been broken.

I sat down, picked up his slack right hand, and held it. Perhaps on the deepest level Kon would know that he wasn't dying alone. I blew out the candle.

Soon I felt a tension in Kon's hand, and then he sighed as if in impatience, and died.

Coincidentally, his sister began to scream then, as though mourning, but I knew that she had surrendered to madness. At this distance, down these long winding corridors, Maria's screams sounded like a single prolonged note, a thin, high keening. You could not hear the horror in it, the madness.

I went on. Ahead, far down the gallery, I heard a faint clicking sound like the drip of water into a pool or the slow tick-*tick* of a clock winding down. The tempo was erratic; it speeded up, slowed, even stopped for a minute or two, but gradually it grew louder until the clicks and their sharp echoes were nearly simultaneous.

I blew out the candle, crawled across the rock, and pressed into the juncture between floor and wall. The bull heard me, and stopped. He, of course, was blind down here, but he could hear me and smell me. Neither of us moved. I visualized him standing a few yards away, head up, his ears pricked forward and his nostrils flexing as he sniffed the air. His tossing muscle would be swollen. Perhaps he had been standing just that way when Kon had blundered into him.

He slowly moved forward, click . . . click . . . click, and there was a scraping sound, too, as if he might be rubbing a horn along the wall. Click, and he was close now; I could smell him, that faintly sweetish bovine odor. Click, and then he was past me and walking very slowly down the gallery, the clicks receding until once again they sounded like the drip of water or the ticking of a clock.

I proceeded down the tunnel in the dark. I had gone perhaps eighty or a hundred feet when I heard a voice:

"Kon?"

The voice seemed to issue from somewhere below.

"Kon?"

"Alexander? It's Jay."

"Don't move, Jay. Stay right where you are."

"Where are you?"

"I heard a noise and thought it was Kon. He was here a while ago. We talked. Have you seen him?"

"No. Where are you, Alexander?"

"I heard noises, voices. You haven't seen Kon?"

"Where are you?"

"Don't move."

"All right."

"I fell into a sort of crevasse."

"Are you hurt?"

"Not badly. I fell into water. There's a small river down here. Deep, with a fairly strong current."

"Can you hold on?"

"I found a narrow ledge above water level."

"Christ."

"I held on to the flashlight. It's very dim now, almost finished, but I was able to look around."

I lit the candle. A dozen yards away I saw a shadow that, when I moved closer, resolved into a jagged hole that radiated webs of cracks. I crawled the last few feet and looked down. The candlelight did not penetrate very deep; a few yards of the circular wall were illuminated, and then the hole widened into a sort of inverted funnel. I heard the rush of water and saw a few reflected gleams of light, but nothing more.

"I can't see you, Alexander."

"I see your light."

"How far down are you?"

"I don't know. Thirty or thirty-five feet. Maybe you can see that the walls slant inward. I can't climb out."

"Christ, Alexander, what a fucking mess. Can you hang on until the rescue crew arrives?"

"My ledge is roughly the size of the cot in your tent. Not big, but I'll be fine as long as the water doesn't continue to rise."

"It's rising?"

"Not fast, but yes. Maybe eighteen inches in the last twenty-four hours."

"You've been down there that long?"

"The water's surface is just a few inches below my ledge now."

"Shit."

"The bottom here is a sort of long rock tube, something like a culvert, with the river running through. It enters from one small tunnel and exits through another."

"Maybe the water will stop rising."

He laughed. "That's what Kon said."

"If it comes to it, Alexander, maybe not too far downstream the tunnel opens up into a cavern or something."

He laughed again. "That's what Kon said. You both are equally stupid, maybe because you were educated at the same institution. You haven't seen Kon?"

"No."

"You're wasting that candle."

I blew out the flame. Neither Alexander nor I had anything to say for a time. I pictured him lying on a ledge a few inches above the cold, rushing stream. He had been down there for at least a day. He must be very cold now. Wet, cold, fearful.

But his voice was strong. "Kon said that Biki left the Minotaur's lair. Have you seen Biki?"

"No, but I heard him once."

"Kon said that you and Maria were together. Where is she?"

"She's fine, Alexander. I left her in a safe place."

"Can you find your way back to her?"

"Sure," I said. *Maybe,* I thought. And I knew that if I crawled a dozen yards away from the hissing of the water I might hear Maria's desperate keening.

"Kon said that Nico was all right."

"Sure. I haven't heard any drilling for quite a while. The rescue crew might have broken through by now and taken Nico and Gypsy out of here."

"They know that I've often been a fool."

"They" were his children, named after his murdered brothers and sister: Konstantin, Nico, and Maria.

"I've always had a mean streak, Jay. You know that."

"I know it."

"But they understand; you understand. Even Sophia understands. I really tried very hard, but I couldn't get rid of the mean streak."

"It's been my experience, Alexander, that when a man confesses to his faults, it's only a prelude to the listing of his virtues." He laughed. "You always were a sentimental son of a bitch."

"You, too."

"I told Kon; I'll tell you. Before I fell into this god-damned hole, I came across a line of string running along the cave floor. I figure that it was left by the old rescue team years ago, the ones hunting for the lost Frenchmen. You can't see chalk marks on the wall when your light gives out, but string . . . Pinch it hard and follow it to the end. I'm guessing that the string leads to an exit."

"Where is this string?"

"You're probably lying on it."

"All right. Good luck, Alexander."

"Yeah."

"I'll move on, then. Good-bye."

"Right. Go get Maria. You shouldn't have left her. That was stupid. To leave her alone down here . . ."

43

The string ended at about the same time as I became aware of a gentle throbbing, a distant systole and diastole; and the air smelled fresh and salty; and a little later I found a tortoiseshell hair clip that Maria had lost.

Sunlight seared my eyes. I lay with my head and shoulders outside the opening, blinking and squinting against the light, the pain. My eyes streamed tears. My head ached. I lay there for some time, waiting for my eyes to adjust to the holocaust of light. Below me was the little sand beach, and the cove, blue and green, showering the air with bright points of light. Above was the temple ruin. I was free. Escaping the cave was like a resurrection.

Eventually I was able to see well enough to climb the cliff wall to my camp. Far to the west, scattered along the ridge, dozens of diminutive men were moving about. At this distance the drilling rig looked like a kid's parlor toy.

The plateau was muddy, and the tent had half collapsed beneath the force of wind and rain. I sat on a marble slab and drank water from a jerrican and stared at the sea and sky. My eyes were still very sensitive, but I could see well enough. The vast space, the enormous distances, made me dizzy.

I was exhausted. My body was covered with bumps and cuts and crusty patches of dried blood. No, I was done in, finished. No.

Soon, I thought, when I was rested, very soon, I'd walk up the ridge and alert the rescue people. They were strong, alert, experienced. I would tell them about the string, the chalk blazes, and the vertical slashes of lipstick. The string would lead them directly into the heart of the cave system. I could even draw a map indicating the approximate locations of Maria and Alexander.

Some gulls floated past with their heads cocked, round yellow eyes watching.

I couldn't do it. It was too much to ask. I had suffered a great deal. You could not expect a man to turn around and go right back into that horror.

I went into the tent and packed my rucksack: two aluminum water bottles that I filled from the jerrican, a few cans of food and an opener, a flashlight and spare batteries, 100 feet of nylon rope, a sweater, matches, my little first-aid kit, a knife, a spool of string of the type used to delineate an archaeological site, and a cheap compass that surely could not be trusted in the magnetically confused underground. I filled one of my kerosene lanterns with fuel.

I knew that I should walk up the ridge and tell the rescue people of my escape and my intention to return. Two or three of them would accompany me into the cave. But they would naturally ask many questions, and sooner or later one of them would say something like, "And you left her alone down there?"

44

Late one afternoon I drove down to Sophia Krisos's cottage to say good-bye to her. The place had a desolate look, window shutters closed, front and back doors barred, the gardens weedy and neglected. It was only a week since I'd last seen the place. Only Sophia's continual—almost obsessive—care had maintained the little oasis. I did not really expect to find her at home, but even so I was disappointed. She had, of course, gone to Athens to be with Nico and Maria.

I climbed the hill behind the cottage and walked east along the ridge. It was a beautiful day, more like autumn than late summer, cool and dry, so bright that I had to squint even though I wore sunglasses. I could see my tent and the white marble rubble at the far end of the island. The sea beyond was choppy, whitecapped, and mottled with aqua blues and greens. I was enormously grateful to be alive and walking in sunlight and color.

The drilling equipment had been dismantled and stacked for removal. I looked under the tarps: the derrick itself, lengths of pipe, sections of steel shafting, spools of cable, the diesel engine. A winch and spool of quarter-inch cable were still set up near the mouth of the shaft. I dropped a stone and after a couple of seconds heard it crack far down in Echo's Cavern. The rescue crew had winched Nico and Gypsy up that long rock cylinder on the third day, about the time Maria and I were wandering lost in the maze.

I saw movement out of the corner of my eye and turned; a man was staggering up the ridge's southern slope. He stopped and buried his face in his palms. Biki Benematale. It was impossible, but there he was, sun-dazzled and considerably less fat, blindly stumbling up toward the crest of the ridge. I cut diagonally across the slope. Biki had miraculously found another exit.

"Hello, Biki."

Feet set wide apart for balance, swaying, his eyes streaming, he said, "Ah, Mr. Chandler, my very good friend." Then he closed his eyes.

"Sit down, Biki."

He awkwardly obeyed.

I removed my sunglasses and gave them to him. "Here, put these on."

His eyes continued to blink and stream tears behind the dark lenses. "My eyes hurt," he said. "My vision is poor."

"Your eyes will be very sensitive to light for a few days."

"Yes, yes, I suppose."

"You've lost a great mass of avoirdupois, Mr. B."

He wearily smiled.

He was still a fat man, but far less fat than when entering the cave. There were many small cuts and lumps on his face and hands. His filthy, torn trousers and safari jacket bagged loosely.

"I have a car nearby," I said. "When you're feeling a bit stronger and your eyes have adjusted to the light, I'll drive you to the village hospital."

"Hospital, no. No, sir. They'll only rehydrate me intravenously, Mr. Chandler. I much prefer to rehydrate myself with copious amounts of beer."

"You really should let the doctor have a look at you."

"After my rehydration, perhaps."

Biki finished the first bottle of beer in a few gulps. "Ah," he said. "Ambrosia."

"Slow down," I said. "It's cold, and it contains alcohol."

He smiled. "Why don't you bring me three or four bottles, Mr. Chandler? It will save you shuttling back and forth from refrigerator to Biki."

He had removed the sunglasses and now sat on one of the settees, squinting, blinking, drinking one bottle of beer after another.

I told him all I had learned from Walter von Rabenau. Nico and Gypsy had been rescued on the third day and helicoptered to a hospital in Athens. Gypsy had stayed only a day before flying to the States; Nico had suffered a dislocated shoulder, a fractured wrist, and some ligaments in his arms and shoulders had been torn loose from the bone. His weight lifter's muscles had, in spasm, caused a lot of damage, though nothing lasting.

Maria, too—after our escape—had been evacuated to Athens. Her vocal cords were permanently affected, her voice changed. But, more seriously, Maria had become quite deranged while in the cave, was still very ill, but it was hoped that she would eventually recover.

The bodies of Aguilar and Nigel Rye had been removed from the Minotaur's lair. An autopsy had determined that Rye had died of heart failure.

And Kon's body also had been recovered, and transported to Athens for burial.

Apparently the bull was still loose in the cave system; the rescuers had heard him, but so far he had eluded them. One member of each of the rescue teams was armed with a rifle so that the bull, when encountered, might be destroyed. Von Rabenau believed that the rescuers' fear of the bull had slowed and complicated the search; still, on the other hand, they had the mangled corpses of Aguilar and Kon to justify their caution.

Yes, there had been an earthquake, an insignificant one unless you happened to be touring the cave when it hit.

Alexander, dead or alive (almost certainly dead), was still lost somewhere down in the labyrinth. The four three-man teams were persisting in the search.

"And searching for you, too, Biki. I'm surprised that they didn't find you."

"I am not surprised. Biki was lost even to Biki, down there in the earth's nether bowels."

"I'll prepare a light meal for us," I said.

"Oddly enough, my friend, I am not in the slightest hungry. I lost my appetite several days ago, and it has not yet returned. But I will be grateful for another half-dozen of these excellent beers. And perhaps you would permit me to utilize your shower. I am quite filthy, and can no longer endure inhaling my own foul miasma."

While he showered and shaved, I made two ham-and-cheese sandwiches, mixed a bowl of salad, and opened two bottles of beer.

We sat together at the counter.

"Tell me now about your ordeal, Mr. B."

"How long was I entombed?"

"This is the seventh day."

"Really? It seemed so much longer. I had calculated ten days."

"And I thought that Maria and I had been in the cave for six days, but it was only four."

"I was saved by starvation and a thin, bright scarlet thread." He nibbled at a sandwich in a desultory way while we talked, and very quickly his appetite returned, and he ate both sandwiches and most of the salad.

Because of his bulk, he had been forced to stay mostly in the larger tunnels and had proceeded fairly directly to the chamber containing the pool of water. The steep chute was the only difficult passage. Yes, he'd noticed the letter "A" scratched on the rock mushroom and had left his calling card to show that he too had been there. He assumed that Alexander had gone on to look for an exit. It was his own intention to return to the Minotaur's lair and guide the others to the pool. He felt very confident, very good: surely now they would all survive until the rescue crew completed drilling their shaft. He drank his fill of water and, with a sense of well-being, enjoyed the most satisfying smoke of his life—a Monte Cristo.

The candle was consumed during his return. He was terrified. He had a sense that the tunnel was moving, writhing like a snake. He could not breathe. And so he struck a match, then another. He was wasteful of his matches because he knew that Maria had more candles and the others—Konstantin, Gypsy, and Jay—had cigarette lighters. And so he lit match after match

as he walked down the twisting tunnels. Biki saved
one match. He didn't know why; perhaps because the
knowledge that he could, if he wished, strike one more
small flame preserved his sanity. Yes, he might very well
have gone mad like poor Maria if he hadn't saved that
single fragile, miraculous spark.

He slowly, blindly, advanced down the tunnels,
hopelessly lost. He didn't know how long he wandered,
perhaps for days—but you couldn't calculate time down
there. Time was nothing, really, a blank, until a particular event intruded on your consciousness; the sound of a
human voice, the lucky find of a puddle of water when
you were thirsty, pain—a bad cut or bruise—the sound
of hooves and breathing and the animal smell when the
bull ("the Minotaur") walked past you in the dark. One
came to understand very well the ancient Greeks' notion
of time and life—death, rather—in the Underworld.

He slept often, and for long periods. Only thirst
drove him on. Without the thirst he would have will-
ingly submerged himself in time eternal.

Once—of course he didn't know when—once he
smelled water and, following the scent, crawled into a
cubical chamber the size of a bathroom or large closet.
Cracks in the walls and ceiling oozed droplets of water,
and there was a puddle. He drank, and then found that
he could not leave. Something, the striations of the rock,
the way it was layered, the angles, had permitted him
to enter but denied an exit. He removed his clothes and
tried to squirm through naked, but all he got for that
was abraded skin.

There was nothing to mark the passage of time except when he slept and when he was awake, when he

drank and when he was not thirsty, when he was cold and when he was sweaty. Was he there for days? Two days, three, more? It didn't matter. This was life as experienced by lower life-forms, reptiles, insects. But he decided to try to escape one more time before resigning himself to death, and it worked; he managed to squirm through into the outer tunnel. He had lost enough weight, girth, to squeeze through.

And so again he blindly walked and crawled around the fantastic maze. His thirst returned. The situation was hopeless. He decided to strike his last match, watch it burn down, and die. Biki believed that Africans could do that, die easily and painlessly at will. Enough, he had suffered enough. It was no longer a matter of courage. He struck the match and there, a few inches away from his nose, he saw a thin line of scarlet thread that extended up and down the long tunnel. What Theseus had left that trail of thread?

He had no sense of direction, of course; by now there was no north or south, east or west, hardly any up or down. Which way? *Choose,* he commanded himself. And before the match burned out, he pinched the thread between a thumb and forefinger and began crawling.

"And here I am."

"And I'm very glad to see you, Biki. But now I think I should drive you to the hospital. They'll want to check your heart and blood pressure and kidney function and so forth."

"Very well. But first, a final beer."

He asked me if any of the island's Gothic mysteries had been solved. I told him that von Rabenau had visited me in the hospital before returning to Germany.

He was certain that Alexander had killed Jürgen Leuger. The village physician, Dr. Demetrios, had determined that Leuger had been manually strangled before being strung up on the length of cord. I explained to Biki how Leuger had been responsible for the massacre of Saint Spyridon.

"Mr. Krisos was—is, perhaps—a very strange man. I privately thought of him as the Lord of the Dark Lake. Not in Antigone's sense, as Hades, Death. But as a great man, a sort of feudal lord, a little god. And Homer, you know, referred to the Aegean Sea as a dark lake."

I told him that the paparazzo was just that, in Walter's opinion, a tabloid journalist who had carelessly or stupidly somehow stumbled into the corrals.

Biki frowned. He didn't accept that, and perhaps he was right.

"And the Ryes," Biki asked, "the Ryes, skinned and unskinned?"

"Walter learned that they were Australians, from some remote town north of Perth."

"The antipodes."

"God knows how Alexander found them, or why he brought them here. Walter thinks that he probably had some twin deceptions planned. I don't know. But Simon Rye molested a village boy and was murdered by the boy's father. Then later his corpse was taken from the meat freezer and skinned, and the body deposited on my bed."

"Very well. But why *your* bed?"

"Just a mix-up. The skinned corpse of Simon was meant as a warning to Nigel. Nigel's cottage was two doors down from mine, this one, on the other side of the Blacks' place. It was a mistake."

"Strange semicomical semitragedy," he said. "Bizarre doings. Beyond the understanding, my good friend, of this fat nigger cannibal."

"We'll never know it all," I said.

"No. Well. And you, Mr. Chandler, what do you intend to do?"

"I don't know, Biki. I'll stop in Athens for a couple of days to see Sophia, and visit Nico and Maria. After that—maybe I'll return to the States for a while. What about you?"

"Oh, I shall persist in wretched exile, a king without his kingdom."

"You deposed royals have a tough life," I said.

He squeezed his eyes shut, and began to rumble and quake with laughter, but his unrestrained Biki laugh was not as impressive now that he'd lost so much weight.

45

I dropped Biki off at the little hospital, then drove up the cliff road to the temple ruin. The sun was below the horizon now, but the high clouds still glowed crimson and salmon pink and yellow. A brisk wind was blowing out of the east. Some gulls were beating windward toward a rocky, guano-stained islet. Their cries sounded like the mewing of cats. Four- and five-foot-high waves rolled into the little cove below, bursting white, crashing onto the rocks with reverberant cracks. It was almost as rough as the night Alexander and I had dived from the precipice. The blowhole was not yet active, but the great volume of water created a fizzing rip as it escaped back out to sea.

The sun-rotted fabric of the tent had leaked during the rains, and all of my things were soaked. I packed a few personal items in a small duffel. The rest I would leave for the village boys: the tent itself, sleeping bags, stove, lanterns, the old binoculars, odds and ends. There were a few ounces of whiskey in the bottle; I poured them into an empty cup and went back outside.

The light was changing fast; the evening was all

blues now, ultramarine sea and indigo sky, and even the air around me appeared blue-tinted, as if hazed with woodsmoke. It was almost time for the bats to emerge. I sipped the whiskey and smoked a cigarette. Pinpoint glows were appearing out in the blueness, stars and planets, electrical lights on the distant islands, a speckling of phosphorescence at sea.

And then, at the other end of the island, all of the lights at the villa complex came on, the main building, the cottages, the outbuildings, the patio and grounds—the place blazed as it had at night during the party. No doubt the lights were triggered by an automatic switch, since there was no one there now except a few employees.

When I turned back, the bats were spiraling up out of caves on the southern promontory, thousands of them, rising and curving and swirling like a tornado funnel.

And below I saw an object being borne slowly out on the rip. It vanished beneath a foaming wave, sluggishly rose, rolled, sank, and a few seconds later surfaced again. Limbs, a broad back, head—face down. Alexander, perhaps, his corpse flushed out of the cave system, expelled. The body was swept back a few yards, surfaced, and again was carried slowly outward on the rip.

The light was poor. It was a body, certainly; a man, I was sure, a thick-chested, broad-backed, powerful man—who else but Alexander?

I left the binoculars in the tent. I did not descend the cliff face and swim out to retrieve the body. A small doubt seemed appropriate.

And so I watched the body voyage outward until at last it vanished into the seething wine-dark sea.

9 781620 454428